"Pardon me," a deep voice said. "If I may have a word?"

She stopped, shot the gentleman who had appeared beside her a sidewise glance. Hard experience had taught her that there was nothing a tall, dark, elegant gentleman had to say to her that was remotely polite or legal.

"No," she said, marching forward again. "You may not."

"Harsh words," he murmured, keeping pace. "I mean you no harm."

"Of course not," she muttered. "Proper gentlemen always accost females in the street to discuss politics or fashion, or the weather. I work for a living, sir. I do not, will not and cannot work for you in any sense of the word. Now, if you are indeed a gentleman: go away."

"But you haven't heard my proposal," he said. "It could be greatly to your benefit, and is no risk to your virtue or morals."

Other **Avon Romances**

AT THE BRIDE HUNT BALL *by Olivia Parker*
JEWEL *by Beverly Jenkins*
THE KISS *by Sophia Nash*
RETURN OF THE ROGUE *by Donna Fletcher*
SEDUCED BY SIN *by Kimberly Logan*
TEMPTATION OF THE WARRIOR *by Margo Maguire*
THREE NIGHTS OF SIN *by Anne Mallory*

Coming Soon

LESSONS FROM A COURTESAN *by Jenna Petersen*
LET THE NIGHT BEGIN *by Kathryn Smith*

And Don't Miss These
ROMANTIC TREASURES
from Avon Books

NEVER TRUST A SCOUNDREL *by Gayle Callen*
A NOTORIOUS PROPOSITION *by Adele Ashworth*
UNDER YOUR SPELL *by Lois Greiman*

HIS DARK AND DANGEROUS WAYS

EDITH LAYTON

AVON
An Imprint of HarperCollinsPublishers

This is a work of fiction. Names, characters, places, and incidents are drawn from the author's imagination or are used fictitiously and are not to be construed as real. Any resemblance to actual events, locales, organizations, or persons, living or dead, is entirely coincidental.

AVON BOOKS
An Imprint of HarperCollins*Publishers*
10 East 53rd Street
New York, New York 10022-5299

Copyright © 2008 by Edith Felber
ISBN 978-0-06-125363-8
www.avonromance.com

First Avon Books paperback printing: June 2008

Avon Trademark Reg. U.S. Pat. Off. and in Other Countries, Marca Registrada, Hecho en U.S.A.
HarperCollins® is a registered trademark of HarperCollins Publishers.

Printed in the U.S.A.

10 9 8 7 6 5 4 3 2 1

For Jeanne Simpson Felber: Daughter-in-law, dancer, actor, writer, and gem, who taught toddlers ballet, and gave me an invitation to the dance.

HIS DARK AND DANGEROUS WAYS

Chapter 1

"**A**s you were saying?" the lady cooed to her gentleman caller, when he paused for a moment. She was artfully displayed on a settee in her front parlor. She reclined, pleading a slightly turned ankle, and her flowing yellow morning gown was arranged so that it showed a peek of that one slender exceedingly well-turned ankle. Her gown also gave an idea of the generous form beneath. Gold curls and long-lashed blue eyes showed her pretty face off to perfection.

Ordinarily, a lady would not be wearing such casual attire or be seen in such a casual attitude when receiving a morning caller. But Lydia Stanton, Lady Harwood, was no ordinary lady. She was a little on the raffish side and a lot on the willful one, and as a lady and a widow, there was a great deal she could get away with. Especially when she had a caller in her parlor with whom she'd obviously like to get away with a good deal more.

Which was surprising, the gentleman thought. She was already involved with a wealthy young gentleman, or so he'd been told. That was why he was here. Simon Atwood, Lord Granger, was a match for the lady, at least in looks, and he surpassed her in charm. Tall, dark and deliciously sardonic, he was even richer than she was, and his title was inherited. She'd married into hers. And was now obviously contemplating adding a newer one.

It was becoming clear that she'd hit upon the idea of a hurt ankle the moment his name had been announced. He'd had to wait in the hall a few minutes, which was odd, because though he hadn't given advance notice of his visit, it was the proper time for a morning call. When he was finally shown in, she was a little flushed and looked as though she'd only just settled into her poised invalid pose. She wore no bandages, only a knowing smile when he found himself looking at her ankle.

He was a little disconcerted by this unexpectedly warm reception, and sought a distraction so he could have time to think. So he cocked his handsome head to the side as though listening, although it didn't take much concentration to hear what he was paying attention to.

The door to the front parlor where they sat was ajar. Even a lady such as this couldn't entertain a gentleman with it closed, at least not in the morning when another caller might drop in. So the hysterical giggling and high-pitched screaming coming from down the hall was clearly audible, along with the sound of marching, jumping, and clumping feet.

"Your moving men certainly are jolly fellows, my lady," he commented. "I didn't know you were relocating. May one ask where you are going?"

"Nowhere," she snapped. She was ambitious, but no fool; her smile reappeared in seconds. "I have a young daughter," she said. "Today she has a dancing lesson, and we invited some of her little friends to join in."

"Dancing lessons," he said with a great show of surprise. "But, surely, she's an infant."

She smiled again. "So she is. She's but an infant with only two years in her cup. But I love to hear her laughter." She cast down her gaze modestly.

3

"You certainly have opportunity to," he said as great thumping sounds of marching were heard, accompanied by the hammering of a tin drum and much giggling.

"The dear creatures, I should love to see them," she said piteously. "But they are exiled to the ballroom because there are so many things to break in here."

"Like eardrums," he said agreeably.

"Should you like me to ring and ask them to stop?" she asked eagerly, raising an arm to the tasseled cord hanging beside the settee, as another gust of laughter was heard.

"No, not at all," he said. "They seem to be enjoying themselves enormously. I don't want to be the cause of their being told to be still. Children need exercise and dancing can't be taught too early." He rose to his feet. "I came without warning, as it is. May I come another morning when they are out of doors, so we can speak? Or better yet, when your ankle is healed so that we can go for a ride to the park?"

"Oh yes," she said with a sparkling smile. "What a good idea. In a day? Two days, perhaps? I should be vastly improved by then."

He had a fairly good idea that she could hop off

the settee in an instant and leg it down the hall, but her pose on the couch was alluring and the excuse for it had condemned her to remaining with it today.

"In two days then," he said, bowed, and left the room.

But he didn't leave the house. Instead, he stopped in the outer hall, cocked his head to the side again, listening. "They're having such a good time," he told the butler. "I'd love to see them at their play. May I?"

"Certainly, my lord," the butler said, and led him down the hall to the source of the merriment.

The ballroom was shrouded in white drop cloths, but they had been pushed back to clear the polished wood center. An aged governess sat at a pianoforte and pumped out music, but the noise from the children was louder. Simon stood in the doorway and watched as a ragged, giggling parade of them passed by him. An extraordinary young woman led the ragtag procession. She had a lithe body, padded sweetly where it ought to be. But it was her legs he noticed first. He could hardly help it.

She'd hitched her skirts up and swagged them

at her waist, so that they dropped to her knees, leaving the rest of those shapely limbs free and unencumbered. Her straight honey-colored hair had also been pulled up on the top of her head, but now strands of it came coiling down around her oval face, which was pink with exertion. *A passably lovely young woman*, he thought. But at the moment she looked more like a goose than a goose girl. He smiled.

Her long neck bent forward, and her firm derrière pushed back and outward, making her supple form into an S shape. She stepped with her feet turned all the way out as she chanted, "Honk, honk: make way for the geese." Behind her, like so many drunken little goslings, a hilarious assortment of young girls, weaved and honked, tripping over their own feet. They wore a Gypsy kaleidoscope of tulle and scarves, coronets and feathers, and every little foot wore tiny dancing slippers.

"There, that's our little lady, Leticia," the butler murmured fondly, indicating the lass clomping along just behind the dancing instructor. The child was beating a tin drum. She wore a flowing gauze skirt and had a tinsel tiara on her blond head. As Simon had thought, if Lady Harwood's infant was two years of age, he was one hundred and two. The child clearly had at least three or four years to her exalted name.

Simon stood watching, enchanted, and not only by the daughter of the house. The dancing instructor, if that was what she was, looked amusingly gooseish, and yet still quite human, feminine and delicious.

"Now," she said, stopping slowly, and turning to face her followers. "Remember what we learned last week? How to go from a goose to a ballet step? Fifth position everyone, and hands making a lovely circle over your heads."

That caused riotous mirth. The children struggled to keep their balance with hands up, legs straight and feet together, each foot faced opposite the other.

"More geese," pleaded one poppet as she tipped over and fell to the floor. "More, Miss, please."

"All right," their instructress said. "One more round of geese. Then some real steps, and leaps."

There was an excited stir. The children obviously loved leaps.

"Now, necks out, bottoms out, feet apart," the instructress said. "Let's go!" She marched them goose-like, in a circle. That was, she did until she

7

saw the gentleman standing in the doorway, staring at her. Then she stopped abruptly. The girl behind her crashed into her, as did the one behind her, and in a moment the line of mirthful children were sitting or rolling on the ballroom floor, collapsed with laughter.

Simon grinned too. The instructress did not. She glared at the intruders standing in the doorway. She raised her chin and straightened herself as she helped the girls to their feet again. "Why are you here, Simmons?" she asked the butler tartly. "Our hour surely isn't up yet."

"No, Miss," the butler answered. "But Lord Granger wished to see the children because they sounded so merry at play."

"So they did," she snapped. "But we are not putting on an exhibition today. Are you father to one of my pupils?" she asked Simon.

"No—" he began to say.

"Then brother, uncle, or guardian?" she went on angrily. "If not, please leave."

"I just wanted to see Lady Lydia's charming daughter," he said. He bowed. "Sorry to intrude."

She ducked her head in an answering bow, then dropped to her knees and was immediately covered in the flutter of small girls who were howling with laughter at the effort of getting up again.

She may have muttered something, but Simon couldn't hear it. He strolled to the door with the butler.

"The ladies bring their children every week to get dancing instruction from Miss Chatham," the butler explained as they walked to the front door. "It may all seem like nonsense for such young children, but they do leaps and bounds and dance to music as well. It's started quite a rage among the ladies, beginning dance instruction so early. How clever of my lady to think of it! Play turned into lessons with an English dancing instructor and a female at that, instead of some sneaking, sneering Frenchie dancing master as is the general custom. Bad enough," he sniffed, "that it's the fashion to have French chefs and French ladies' maids.

"But this young woman puts the children's mothers quite at ease," the butler went on. "They are clamoring to have their children invited here for a lesson. Why, Lady Haverstraw actually attempted to hire her away the other week! But she remained loyal to my lady. Miss Chatham comes here twice each week."

"She teaches nowhere else?" Simon asked as the footman handed him his hat.

"As to other districts, milord, we cannot say," the butler said loftily as he signaled for the door to be opened. "But we are the only ones she instructs in this area. Good day, my lord."

"The children have all been dressed, delivered, and collected by their nannies, Miss," the butler said to the lingering dance instructor.

But Miss Chatham, also dressed and looking collected, merely stood by the door. "I know, Simmons," she said as she smoothed on her gloves again. "And it is getting late. But I haven't been paid. Much as I dislike bringing up such a sordid subject, my salary is three weeks in arrears now. If your lady doesn't pay me now, I fear I'll be unable to return. I will not and cannot let the debt grow any higher. You understand, I'm sure."

He frowned. "Will you wait here, please?"

Miss Jane Chatham stood by the door and waited. This was a gamble, one she had to take. She needed the money, and hoped she'd interested enough other ladies of fashion to be hired somewhere else if Lady Lydia got on her high horse and refused to come down with the money on demand. The fashionable world was famous for its debts and Lady L was nothing if not fashionable.

Still, it was a risk for Jane as a lady of good birth who had to stay three steps ahead of her landlord or she'd find herself staying in less respectable rooms. She had to keep up appearances. If she didn't have a room in a decent district, being hired to serve the rich would be more difficult. Her idea of teaching dance to girls just out of the nursery had been brilliant, and she'd been paid readily enough when she'd begun. But she knew she probably had competition now, or soon would. As daughter of a deceased baronet she was good *ton*, but what if some clever baron's widow or viscount's daughter hit upon the same scheme? And why shouldn't they? There were few enough occupations for women of good birth and misfortune these days.

"Miss," the butler said when he returned. "Here is your payment. She was mad as fire, but you did your job and she can't say no. But if I was you," he added in an under voice, "I wouldn't threaten her again. She got fairly high up in the boughs."

Jane sighed. "If I were me, I wouldn't threaten

her either. But I can't help it. My landlord, the butcher, and the baker won't tolerate money owed, and so then neither can I. Thank you, Simmons."

She placed the money in her reticule, nodded to him, and left the town house.

If I were me, Jane thought as waited for a carriage to go by so she could cross the street. She tried to avoid the street sweeper's eye at the same time because she couldn't afford the gratuity he'd expect for getting the horse droppings out of her way. *If I were* me, *I wouldn't be teaching dance to infants*. It wasn't that she didn't love the moppets, but she'd rather be back home at Brightwaters: reading, riding, writing, and gardening . . . *Anything*, she thought sadly. But Cousin Harvey had inherited the place, lock, stock and debts, and she wasn't welcome there anymore. And she didn't welcome the idea of charity from anyone.

Shaking her head to clear it from maudlin thoughts, Jane walked with renewed purpose. She'd left Brightwaters for London to find a way to make a living. And she had. She was proud of herself and her accomplishments.

But for any woman alone in London, there were dangers and indignities to bear. The way that high-nosed nobleman had eyed her just today! As though she were prime roast rib of beef. He'd been handsome and elegant, amused *and* aroused, and she'd longed to slam the door in his arrogant face.

Jane continued down the street. Clouds were overtaking the sun, and a damp chilly breeze brushed her cheeks, murmuring false promises of spring coming right around the next corner. *At least*, she thought, pulling up her collar, *the gentleman had only been visiting*. She doubted she'd see him again. One of the advantages of working for a female on the hunt for a new husband was that though there were many male visitors, there were no stray gentlemen lounging about the place, at least not for long. This had been an unusual encounter and probably, when Lady Harwood heard of it, would never be repeated.

"Pardon me," the deep voice said from her side. "If I may have a word?"

She stopped. She shot the gentleman who had appeared beside her a sidewise glance. *Speak of the devil and he appears*, she thought angrily. Her thoughts had surely summoned him. Now she had to be rid of him. Embarrassing experiences here in London had taught her that there was nothing a tall, dark, elegant gentleman had to say to a female who worked for her living that was remotely polite or legal.

"No," she said, marching forward again. "You may not."

"Harsh words," he murmured, keeping pace. "I mean you no harm."

"Of course not," she muttered, her sense of unfairness rising. "Proper gentlemen always accost inferior females in the street to discuss politics or fashion, or the weather. I work for a living, sir. I do not, will not, and cannot work for you in any sense of the word. Now, if you are indeed a gentleman: go away."

"But you haven't heard what I propose," he said as he sauntered beside her.

"I don't have to," she said. She stopped, turned, and confronted him. "I can guess. You saw me dancing, cavorting with the children, with my lower limbs exposed. *Aha*, thought your overheated brain! A dancer! And not clothed properly. A female with no morals. I'll just wait and waylay her in the street, offer her money or fine clothes, and she'll dance for me, privately. No sir, no, and no. I am not that sort of female.

"Now, please go away," she said. "If anyone

from Lady Harwood's house should see us I could lose my position, and I need it. Being an instructor of the dance is a departure for a female, but that is all, I repeat: all that I am. Be a good fellow now, will you? Move along."

"You haven't heard my proposal," he said mildly. "It could be greatly to your benefit, and is no risk to your virtue or morals. But if we stand here fighting someone will surely note it. I suggest you look down the street, to your right. Yes. There's a vendor standing there in that cloud of smoke. He's selling hot chestnuts, meat pies, and the like. Please point in that direction, as though I asked you where a fellow could get something warm to eat. Then go there yourself. Buy something. Stand there and eat it. I'll be there too, and will manage to ask you what I must without compromising you, I promise."

She hesitated. He sounded like he had a great deal of experience in clandestine matters.

"I've done this sort of thing before," he said, catching her unspoken thought. "But in the past I dealt with men of other nations and loyalties. I've never been caught. And never fear, I am a loyal Englishman."

She believed it. He was a gentleman, and there

was something about him that spoke of his being used to command. Besides, she couldn't just stand there and argue, and he was obviously not going to go away. Jane sniffed, turned, and marched down to the vendor who stood amidst the clouds of steam coming up from the various puffing and hissing pots on his corner stand. She ordered a meat pasty. As he lifted the lid, another puff of smoke arose. She relaxed a little. Between the steam and the gray lowering day maybe no one would see her, after all. She took the hot little pie, and stood to the side, moving it from hand to hand, letting it cool.

Then she noticed the gentleman again. He was standing to one side in the shifting vapors; a cloaked shadow. "I need to know," he said in a low, velvety voice, "about Lady Harwood's visitors."

"What?" she asked. "Then why bother me? Simmons knows everything."

"And tells everything to his employer," the gentleman said mildly. "I think you would not, if asked not to do so."

"You want me to spy?"

"Well, yes. In a light and friendly way," he said with amusement. "No one would be hurt.

16

Rather you might do a world of good. I need to know when and how often various people visit my lady."

"I'd hardly know that!" she exclaimed. "I'm only there two days a week. And with the children then, at that."

"But you do go to the kitchens for a cup of tea every time, and you hear everything that happened all week, do you not? Whether you want to or not," he added.

She nodded; it was true. Gossip was the tastiest part of the servants' dull lives in such houses.

"You suspect my lady of treason, or worse?" she asked, trying to sound incredulous. But who knew what the *ton* got up to? The war was over, but Napoleon was alive, and spies were still said to be everywhere. She bit down on the meat pasty as she waited for him to answer. She didn't want it, couldn't afford the luxury, but she couldn't let it get cold.

"You'll be paid very well," the gentleman said. "We'll meet here and there, I always pay my debts. Oh. I am Simon Atwood, Lord Granger."

She stiffened, and stopped chewing.

"Yes," he said, "a colorful reputation precedes me. Most of it isn't true. What is, is highly elaborated. But doubtless, you also know that whatever my sins, I am not said to be a cad or a wastrel."

"Yes," she murmured.

"Then, we have a bargain?"

She considered it. She'd tell him nothing he wouldn't find out from any other servant in the house.

"You wouldn't be the only one I'd speak to," he added. "But I must insist on your never mentioning this to anyone else. *Anyone*. I'd know, believe me. Besides, I've heard you're a young woman with morals and discretion."

More morals and discretion than money, she thought. He'd offered to pay her. And after all, what harm would it do? She shrugged. "If that's all it is, then we do."

"It is. And we do then have a bargain," he said. The vendor lifted the cover off a pan of chestnuts, and between one rising gust of smoke and the next, the gentleman was gone.

Jane finished her meat pasty, sighed, and began to move on.

"Miss!" the vendor cried.

She looked back. He held out a wadded packet to her. "You paid me too much, Miss. Here you go!"

18

She frowned. "I don't think so. Are you sure?"

"As sin," he said, giving her the packet and a wink.

She took it, thanked him, and walked away. She only stopped in her tracks after she'd unfolded the packet and saw how many banknotes there were in it.

Chapter 2

L ater that evening, in a tall town house in the best section of Town, a gentleman paused as he poured cognac into a goblet for his seated friend. "Did you really have to go to such lengths?" he asked, looking at his guest. "It sounds like you're employing half the lady's household."

Simon sighed. "Proctor, you asked me to investigate, didn't you?"

"Yes. I asked you to investigate the comings and goings of one young man. My brother. But now you say you've employed many others in the lady's household. I can see your interest in observant maids, cooks, and footmen. But a dance instructor? One that isn't even a resident there? Did you have to go so far? Too many spies spoil the outcome. They'll talk to each other, and it will all come to nothing."

"No. I've told them that if they talk to anyone but me, they get nothing. And they believe me."

His host handed Simon the goblet of cognac. "It's costly and time-consuming," he said ruefully. "I wouldn't have asked you if I thought it would put you to such trouble."

Simon accepted his glass, stretched out his legs, and smiled at his host. Viscount Delancey was a tall thin gentleman who looked much older than his three and thirty years; both older and unhealthier. It had always been so, even years ago at school when they had met. The viscount wore spectacles and had begun to lose his hair early. He was pale and spindly, and when he coughed, people winced, because it seemed a premonition, and not a good one. But he'd never had a sick day Simon knew of, and he believed his friend would likely outlive him unless there was some accident. Which, in the viscount's line of work, was not impossible.

The men were the same age and height, but it would be difficult to find two men more unalike. The viscount was reedy and walked head thrust out, like a turtle. Simon walked tall, and his lean frame was muscular. Where the viscount was bald, Simon had thick black overlong hair that brushed his high collar. He looked elegant, but slightly dangerous. His cheekbones were high, his nose aquiline, and his mouth firm but shapely.

No one noticed the viscount's mouth, although on close observation it could be seen to be pale and thin-lipped. Simon had arched black brows; his smile had made many a female sigh, and his frown had frightened grown men. The viscount had no eyebrows to speak of, and no one, male or female, sighed over his smile or felt threatened by his frown. And while the viscount had faded blue eyes behind his spectacles, Simon's were dark and alert. But neither man was known to miss much.

They'd both been agents for England before Napoleon had been bottled up at Elba. The viscount had never been so much as suspected of intrigue, and so he still worked in and at secrecy. It was Simon who had been captured and undergone the physical privation and pain, though it was impossible to guess that at a glance or even with a longer look. He'd escaped whole in body.

"No trouble," Simon told his friend. "It's not much money. And I can hardly stand like a lawn ornament on the lady's front step and watch the comings and goings there. So I need informants. I'm curious now. The lady is charming and lovely, intelligent and rich as well. It seems she could land anyone. And you say it's young Richard she's after? It doesn't make sense. She's too clever to let passion rule her now, at least so far as matrimony. Not saying anything against your brother, Proctor, but he doesn't seem the sort to inspire such mindless lust in an experienced lady. So what could it be? As for putting a stick in her wheel, well, if she *is* after such a youth, I don't see the problem. I tend to side with the victim. Richard doesn't seem to be suffering."

He held up his goblet to salute his host. "To tell truth, Proctor, I can't see *any* red-blooded young man in her clutches as a *victim*. And so I wonder . . . I've been bored and at loose ends since I came home. Actually, it's been dismal for me. You knew it. My concern is if you really have a problem, or if you're only making work to give me something to do."

"You wouldn't be concerned if your younger brother was about to be seduced into marriage by an older woman?" the viscount asked, his eyebrows rising.

"I haven't one," Simon admitted. "But I don't think I would be, if she looked and spoke like Lady Harwood."

"And she an experienced female, a widow known for her extravagance?" the viscount said. "Her late husband was twice her age. I don't know if she cared for him but it's easy to see she certainly doesn't care for the single state. She's been out with half the men in Town since the day her official mourning period ended. Now, she concentrates on Richard. It appears she thinks a boy would be as malleable as a doting old man. Except that the boy is my heir and I dislike the thought of all this going to her." He waved a hand to indicate his entire town house.

Simon silently agreed it was a pretty piece of property, but he couldn't see much to covet. True, the viscount's house was in an elite district and on a fashionable row. The rooms were large and airy, but just as spare and no-nonsense as their owner was. Here in his study, there was a desk, chairs, table, lamp, all that was necessary, and nothing more, except for a few aged sporting prints on the walls. Certainly nothing eye-catching or noteworthy. The viscount's estate in the north, so far as Simon could remember from a boyhood visit, was an impressive structure with good land, but the house wasn't memorable either.

"I don't see a terrible problem," Simon mused. "The 'boy' is of age. He's one and twenty. He hasn't funds of his own, or so you said, so where's the problem?"

"He's my heir," the viscount repeated stiffly. "She's likely looking forward to that."

"Even so. She'll have to look forward for a lifetime. Unless you have some complaint I don't know of?"

"I do not," the viscount said.

"So? Where's the difficulty? If his liaisons distress you, you're not too old to have a child."

The viscount waved a thin hand. "I was married for three years and didn't produce an heir. I don't want to go through the whole process again. Not because of a broken heart, Simon, or a dislike of females. They're well enough, in their place, which is not my house. Henrietta was a good woman, but I discovered I like my solitude and disliked catering to anyone. Whatever they say about a man being lord of the house, I found that if he wants peace, a man must cater to his wife. And besides, I happen to like my brother."

"He's your half brother," Simon said. "Or does that make a difference?"

"It makes him better suited to the task of carrying on the name than I am," the viscount said. "He usually has a good head on his shoulders. He's athletic, and charming. I supply him with an adequate allowance so he'll never live in penury, because he'll make a fine master of the property and title one day. I want to leave that to him. He is feckless, true. But he's young. I think he's the youngest fellow his age I've ever seen. He'll grow up—if he marries when he's adult enough to understand his responsibilities and take them on, and *not* let his wife do that."

As Simon wondered just what sort of marriage his friend had experienced, the viscount added, "And you're no one to talk, Simon. You never wed and don't seem to be looking to do so. Though you were never a rake by any means, I hear that you've had little to nothing to do with females since you returned to England. Just look at you. The style is for close-cropped hair, and what do you do but let it grow long as a Gypsy might do."

"The surgeons cropped my hair to heal my fever," Simon said casually. "They said it was draining my energy, when in fact they were doing that. I don't like the idea of shearing it all off again. And you know I never gave a damn about fashion."

His friend sighed. "Yes, and now you're about to set a new fashion because women seem to like the look of you even more now, if that's possible. But you don't do more than look at them now, do you? You used to enjoy a liaison or two, now and then, as I recall. In fact," he said, turning to his decanter of cognac again, "there was talk of you being rather indiscriminate when you first returned from France, which was unusual for you. You were never one to go in for barmaids and opera dancers. Still, that phase soon passed. And so far as I can see . . ."

"Or so far as your associates can," Simon put in sardonically.

"Yes, exactly, we don't frequent the same places do we? Some of my friends do, however. I was surprised at your taking up with such females at the time, and so many of them. Now I'm surprised to hear that you're playing the monk. For the past months you haven't seen any females, of any sort, socially. Nor have you frequented any places except for your clubs and the homes of old friends."

"Shame on me," Simon muttered into his goblet.

"No dances, no balls, no masquerades or house parties. No taverns or houses of fragrant repute, or even any green rooms backstage. Gone off the pursuit of females?" His expression grew serious. "Simon, did anything happen during your captivity in France that I don't know about? You were examined by our physicians when you got out, and declared in fine fettle for a man who'd been imprisoned the best part of a year, but if there is something amiss we do have the best leeches in London at our disposal."

"Good for us," Simon said. He shook his head. "No, the only thing wrong is my mood. I don't want any entanglements just yet, of any kind. I need to sort things out and I have to be alone to do that. Sorry if my monkishness offends you. I didn't know you lived vicariously."

"Now, now," the viscount said. "You know I have an understanding with a lady in Town. I was worried about you."

"Don't," Simon said. "Just tell me: is this pursuit you've assigned me due to fear of your brother being captured in wedlock by Lady Lydia a real worry, or a device for my benefit?"

"It isn't a device for your benefit, it's for mine. My fears are real."

"That surprises me," Simon murmured. "The lady isn't evil, or poor, now. Her parents arranged her previous marriage to save the family from bankruptcy. They did that and then some. But the old man was kind to her, by all accounts. She's got the money in her own right now. I can't see her in the role of predator. Richard is probably just flattered by her attention. And she's probably just amused by him. She needs amusement after such a marriage. Why don't you just have a talk with him?"

"If you had a younger brother, you'd understand," Proctor said, sighing. "If I tell him she's unsuitable, he'll marry her out of hand. I can say nothing."

"I'll indulge you in this for a while, Proctor, because of old times and old favors," Simon said, rising to his feet and stretching. "I'm investigating, and will report to you, as asked. I'll be a frequent visitor to the lady's salon. I'll flirt with her. But if she gets the impression I'm serious about her, I'll leave instantly. I won't mislead her or you. That's one of the reasons I've hired on so many servants at her house. If I can't be there in person, I'll have ears and eyes there anyway." He cocked his head to the side. "You know, you might try calling there yourself."

"Likely I shall. But you first, Simon; because you'll attract others in the *ton* to her side. You may not care or credit it, but you're intensely eligible: wealthy, back on the Town again, handsome and single. The lady wants her salon to be a success. When word gets out that you visit there, other gentlemen will follow. The more competition Richard has, the better. Thus, everyone will be happy."

"Mostly you," Simon said. "I'll do my best, Proctor. But remember: if the lady takes a liking to me, I'm off the case."

"And if you take a liking to her?"

Simon smiled. "I do like her. But there's no way on earth I'll love her. I'm not ready to get entangled with any female just now, in any way, physically or mentally."

Proctor frowned. "Are you sure you don't want to visit with a physician again?"

"I'm certain. What I need is time for reflection. I didn't like imprisonment, but it taught me the value of both freedom and contemplation. I'm weary," he added, closing his eyes for a moment. "But don't feel guilty," he said quickly, looking at his host again. "I admit I need a bit of livening up. When I'm done with this favor to you, which is probably also a favor to me, I'm going home.

I need rest and peace, and no living female can provide that."

Simon paused. That had been a lie. No rest or peace came to him these days from any source. His nights were ruined by memories of being alone in the dark in a dungeon deep in the living earth, wondering if he'd survive to see the light again. He actually slept with a lamp near his bed, like a child, and hated himself for the comfort it gave him.

Now he strolled to the door and went out into the hall. He accepted his hat and cloak from a footman. Then he sketched a bow to his friend. "So thanks and good night, old friend. I'll see you soon, or as soon as need be." He tipped a finger to his hat in salute, and left the house.

Jane's hands shook. So did the banknotes she held. So much money! *This must be an immoral thing to do*, she thought guiltily. In her experience, morality paid little. So this offer of money in exchange for information about Lady Harwood definitely had to be wrong. But how wrong was it to merely watch, listen, and then tell someone who came to one of her employer's houses? It was a puzzle, one she had to solve alone.

She spread the damp, creased bills on her table-top, and left them there as though afraid to touch them again.

Her parents were gone. Her mother, to an illness that ate up their money, and then her father to drinking and gaming, trying to forget that her mother was gone, which ate up the rest. They'd never been rich, merely comfortable and respectable. Being respectable helped use up the last of the family fortune. Her older brother had joined the navy, seen the war, landed on the Continent, and never returned. He hadn't been hurt, only married. He sent his sister a pittance every month, just enough for her to buy a skein of wool to knit something for his ever growing family.

The family estate had gone to the mortgagers, and Jane had gone to cousins for assistance. She soon discovered that their family, like many respectable far-flung English families, already had enough orphans, widows, and spinsters to care for. She'd have to work for her livelihood, she'd known that. But any position they found for her would be menial and demeaning, because poor relatives were a glut on the market. Wedlock was out of the question for her. Marriage for a female with no living parents and no funds was never a matter of personal choice, unless it was a mad or bad one.

So she'd come to London and despite the odds, actually found a respectable way to make her living. She could dance. Even better, she loved to do it. Her parents had given her instruction in all the feminine arts, but she had excelled in the dance. Of course, females who danced could make money only in the theater and ballet, both of which ruined reputations. But luckily for Jane, male dancing masters had also gotten a bad reputation because a few had a penchant for seducing too many of their rich or noble clients. Many of them were French, not the best thing to be in England these days.

So Jane found she could get a few recommendations from relatives grateful not to have to house her, to teach ladies to dance. One day, she'd also taught a lady's young sister, who had begged for the chance. Amazingly, the toddler had done well. Mothers of friends of the little girl, hearing of this, clamored for a chance to educate their darlings, and Jane had a new occupation: giving classes for children. It had become a "rage" and she began to make money.

Jane dreamed of making more so that she could one day hold her head high again and stop worrying about the price of candles. She knew she'd have to make it quickly because "rages" were ephemeral. But now this!

She sat down in the chair in her room again, staring at the rumpled, much counted banknotes. They would rent her room for the month, feed her, buy candles for every night, and allow her to set some aside for the fund she kept so one day she might open her own dance studio. And this was only a first payment! This much money, if it kept coming, could lighten her life even above daydreams. She could have her own dance studio while she was still young. She could live above it in bright, cheerful rooms. She could buy her own pianoforte and hire someone to play while she gave instruction to adults *and* infants. She'd have a profession, be her own employer, and make a good life for herself.

Was it possible to make a good life from bad money? As the candle on the table guttered, Jane sighed, and not just because she'd have to light a new one. No money was ever bad; it was the means to it that could be. Were they?

A secretive gentleman wanted her to tell him

who came to Lady Lydia's salon, and how often. That wasn't much. Unless, of course, the gentleman had evil aims. Jane grew pale thinking of how many there could be. He could be planning a robbery. He might be thinking of abduction. Blackmail was a possibility.

Jane looked around her rented room. She'd been extravagant this evening. She actually bought violets and put them in a glass on the table to lighten the atmosphere. Violets were valiant but it would take buckets of them to cheer this dim third-floor room, with its shabby furnishings, threadbare rug, and small sagging bed. The only window caught the sun at dawn, if it wasn't raining. Then the light left and the room was in shadow the rest of the day. But the room was in a decent part of town, and decency was something she had to be able to afford.

So she had to look at the situation rationally. She couldn't see how knowing who visited a person's house would make robbery any easier. Abduction would require knowing a deal more than that. But blackmail was possible. Jane stood and went to the dim window. She'd have to ask why the information was needed, and try to judge his answer. And if, by some miracle, it was only some silly benign reason, and the gentleman was just a fellow who had too much money, why then, why not?

Jane saw her reflection in the darkened glass, and turned away. She must not deceive herself. She wasn't a criminal. She wasn't going to go into league with one. But all that money!

Tonight, she didn't have to set the table to have dinner; she'd had hers in the street. That meat pasty had been fresh, delicious, and filling. Now there were hours to go before bedtime. So she stood and thought. She'd been tempted before; mainly because even without wanting to, she tempted men. She wouldn't sell herself for any money, though, to be honest, it was nice to know that she was wanted for whatever reason. Still, she was wise enough to know that wouldn't be for long. Women faded faster than violets. That's why so many men thought almost any young woman beautiful.

Jane discounted her large long-lashed hazel eyes, small, even features, and clear complexion. She didn't think her lithe dancer's figure especially attractive, not compared to the young society beauties with their plump bosoms and dimpled arms. Not compared to opera dancers with their magnificently painted faces, either. But though dancing on stage was a lot more lucrative than teaching dance, it was only a step higher than walking the streets. She'd sell her knowledge of the dance, but not the body that performed them. If a respectable young woman lost her respectability, her brain and beauty counted for nothing. She'd be ineligible for marriage or employment. Family, funds, and position in Society might give a fortunate woman freedom, if she wanted it. Jane wasn't in that class. She wasn't in the same class as the elegant beauty she worked for—and had been asked to spy on.

Jane thought long and hard, long past her bedtime. She had to be up early in order to go to Mrs. McIntyre's house to teach her two daughters and their friends. Jane had three employers, and traveled round London visiting their homes. Lady Harwood was the most socially elevated. If her dance instructress became well known in the *ton*, Jane would never be out of work. She'd have to wait for Lady Harwood's permission, of course, because she'd promised not to go to work for any of her acquaintances until given permission. The lady wanted exclusivity. That rankled. By the time she was given permission, Jane was afraid other needy well-born females would take her idea, and eventually, her success.

So this money would be an extra benefit. The gentleman who offered it was astonishingly elegant and ridiculously handsome, in a clean, virile sort of fashion. Jane mightn't have any designs on him but she had eyes, didn't she? So she had to be on her guard against him and herself when she asked him his motives. Still, if she judged his motives to be innocent, she'd be doing no more than telling the truth, and probably doing less of that than any other servant in the house.

When Jane fell asleep at last, it was to sweet dreams of freedom and ease, in a world filled with music and laughter, the way it used to be.

Chapter 3

～～⟡⟢～～

The Honorable Miss Leticia Harwood threw herself into the air. She had waited impatiently while the other girls did their leaps and then, when Miss Chatham called to her to take her turn, she ran down the polished ballroom floor, her little chubby legs working like pistons on the new Puffing Billy locomotive. Then, with perfect form, one leg out and the other used as a spring, she took off into the ether. She actually floated for a fraction of a moment, and then landed, not farther on down the ballroom, as she was supposed to do, but instead, right in her instructress's midsection.

Miss Harwood came to earth in a froth of skirts and giggles. Miss Charlotte Stratton came tumbling down with her, with an audible "Oof!" The other students saw an excellent opportunity for good fun and with cries of glee, piled onto the writhing heap of toddler and dance master where they lay on the floor.

The piano music stopped instantly. The governess rose from her bench. "Come, girls," she cried. "This is most unseemly. Miss Chatham? Are you all right?"

"I think so," Miss Chatham replied. But her voice was strained, hardly audible from under the heap of children. Her body, or at least parts of it, was clearly visible, though. One shapely leg was bared to her thigh, the other was somewhere beneath her. Her skirt was hiked high, her hair had come undone. She couldn't worry about propriety now. She was more concerned with the agonizing pain in her hidden leg. As she'd fallen, she'd twisted so that the child wouldn't be hurt, and had taken the weight of the girl. Her leg was twisted beneath her. The pain was sharp, but nothing to the terror she felt.

If she lost the use of her limb for any amount of time, she'd lose her livelihood, entirely. Jane waited, eyes closed in a silent prayer, as the governess slowly tried to peel the collection of children off her. Suddenly, the girls stopped laughing, and the removal came more swiftly. Jane abruptly found herself free. She opened her eyes and shook her head to get the hair out of her eyes. She saw a shapely masculine hand reaching down to her. She blinked.

A young gentleman smiled at her. "Here," he said, "take my hand, if you can. Otherwise, I'll pick you up."

"No, no," she cried, scrabbling to sit up and switch her skirts down at the same time, seeing where her rescuer was looking, with interest. "I can manage, thank you very much."

"I should think so," her employer said archly. The lady was standing in the doorway with an assortment of staff and guests, all watching Jane scramble to make herself presentable. "Let her be, Richard. She's turning pink. I believe you're embarrassing her."

"Well, I would let her be, but I don't know if she's able to stand," the young man she'd called Richard said. "And I am a gentleman."

"Just your hand for a moment then, sir," Jane told him. "Help me rise and I'll be fine, thank you."

"Your leg?" he asked, as she took his proffered hand and levered herself up from the floor. "It's all right?"

41

"Fine," Jane lied, releasing his hand as though it were scalding her. "I'm just . . . Just give me a moment, please."

She shook out her skirts, put her injured leg down on the floor, and tested it. She concealed a gasp of pain. It hurt, but she could bear it, and it could bear her. Though her ankle ached, it didn't hurt as much as a break or a sprain would. She let out a shuddery in-held breath. Then she managed a smile. "Right as rain. Miss Stratton just got carried away. I won't be able to continue the lesson today, girls," she told the children crowded around her. "But I'm fine."

"I'm thorry, Mith Chatham," Miss Stratton managed to say around the thumb she'd put in her mouth.

"No need," Jane said. "You just have to straighten that leap out a bit, and you'll be perfect. As will I. Don't worry. But, my lady," she added, looking at her employer and seeing the displeasure writ large on her face, "I must stop this lesson now. I should go home and rest so I can come back on my usual day later this week."

"That's that then," her employer said. "Miss Rogers," she told the governess, "please help the girls dress in their proper clothing. Go now, children. And the rest of you," she said to the goggling servants gathered in the doorway. "The raree-show is over, back to your duties. We'll see you Thursday next then, Miss Chatham. Now, friends," she said, turning to her interested guests, "shall we return to the salon?"

The other guests began to amble back to the front salon, but the young gentleman stayed standing where he was. "Surely she can't walk now," he said in surprise. "I was just leaving myself, my lady. I'd be happy to take her safely home."

But the lady of the house obviously wasn't happy. A rare frown showed on her beautiful face as she looked from the young man she'd called Richard to Jane. Jane wouldn't have taken the young gentleman's offer for any reason. But she was puzzled at her employer's expression of displeasure. She herself might look like a trollop, with her hair down to her shoulders, and everyone had certainly got a look at her limbs. But surely the lady knew it wasn't her fault.

And as for her would-be helper? The young man was clearly at least a decade younger than Lady Harwood herself was. He wasn't handsome: he was a tall, thin, ordinary-looking lad, not anyone to make a grown woman's heart beat faster. He was, at best, pleasant-looking. Jane's eyes opened wide. Richard! He had to be the elusive young suitor the strange gentleman had paid her to look for.

"Thank you, sir, but it isn't necessary," Jane said firmly. "In fact, I was looking forward to resting up in the kitchens with a cup of tea before I set out. I'll be perfectly able by then."

"Of course she will be," the lady said. "Now come along, Richard. Have you forgotten? Our own tea awaits."

"All this excitement did make me forget, forgive me," Richard said. He looked lingeringly at Jane. "Fare thee well then," he said to her, and taking his hostess's arm, left the ballroom with her.

Jane let out her breath. Now she was alone and didn't have to stifle her winces as she hobbled over to a chair to get a look at her ankle. She raised her skirt gingerly. Her ankle was swollen. But not dark purple, and she could bend it, with effort and a few unladylike grunts. She sat back for a relieved moment. It would heal. And at least she'd also caught sight of the young suitor and had a glimpse that showed her employer's attitude toward him. Much good that would do her.

Her information was useless now. Although she'd paused and peeked whenever she'd walked through the hall, and looked into the shadows every night, she hadn't gotten another glimpse of the mysterious fellow who had wanted that information. It had been almost two weeks since she'd first met him for the first, and last time, she decided. She'd found out his name by idly asking the servants who had visited their lady that day. He was Simon, Lord Granger. Much good that information did her, as well.

But now Jane was relieved. She was still leery of the harm she'd done to herself, or rather, the harm the overenthusiastic Miss Stratton had done. The little girl was round and firm as a cannonball, and had hit her like one. Next time, she'd brace herself. But she couldn't stand in the ballroom all day, so Jane combed back her hair with her hands and braided it up again, assembled her belongings, and limped down to the kitchens, suppressing groans as she did.

By the time evening shadows were gathering, she felt good enough to make her way home. Cook and some other servants had fussed over her at first, and then, as time went on, the novelty of her accident wore off. By the time the other servants began to come down for their dinners, Jane was forgotten until she stood up again. She refused their kind offer to join them. She knew her place, upstairs and down, in this house. They stood on ceremony here. They'd have been shocked and embarrassed had she accepted their invitation. She was allowed in and out the front door, but she wasn't exalted enough to be a guest of her employer. Nor was she lowly enough to mingle comfortably with the servants and trades people, those who had to use the back door. Even the governess, an educated female of good birth, ate her dinner alone in solitary splendor, in her rooms.

Jane waited, dinnerless, in the front hall.

"I'm sorry, Miss Chatham," the butler said when he finally joined her there. "My lady said that since you didn't give an entire lesson, there'd be only a token payment to you for coming today. It's a hard life, and that's the truth," he added in an under voice, as he handed her a very few coins.

"Thank you," she said, on a sigh, taking them. "I know I displeased her."

"And not just by turning your ankle," he added in a lower voice. "But by turning a head. Be careful of that, my girl. Good night, be well."

Jane thanked him and limped out of the town house and down the short front stair into the growing shadows. Her workday was done, but thankfully, her career wasn't. Her leg wasn't broken or sprained. She'd injured herself before, and knew that she should be back on her feet in two days for her next scheduled lesson. She didn't think she could go to work for Mrs. Smythe and her daughters tomorrow, or to Mrs. McIntyre the day after that. She'd have to send a note to them.

She'd never tell Lady Harwood about those lost opportunities. But her work here alone couldn't support her, and though she'd promised to never work for any other lady, if Lady Harwood never knew about Jane's middle-class employers, it wouldn't harm anyone.

Jane moved slowly down the street, favoring her ankle. It didn't hurt so much anymore, if she kept pressure off it. It needed ice; she'd have to stop at the fishmonger's stall on the way home and buy some. Any new expense pained her more than her leg did now.

She'd had such bright dreams only a few weeks ago. But since Lord Granger, that mysterious gentleman with an ear for gossip, had never contacted her again, she had to work, as ever, where and when she could. She'd looked for the fellow, stopping at every wavering shadow when she walked home every night. He'd vanished, at least from her sight. Subtle inquiries told her that he had visited the house, but she'd never seen him there. Not that she could speak to him if he had, anyhow.

And now at last she had some real gossip for him: not only the things she'd seen, but what she'd heard in her corner of the kitchens as the servants had forgotten her presence there this evening. They'd started to chat about Jane's accident, and then, quite naturally about how their lady's nose had got into a knot when her current favorite young gentleman had offered courtesy to Jane. They approved of her reticence, and were smug to discover that Lady Harwood hadn't quite hooked him completely. They'd forgotten Jane so entirely that the gossip became interesting, and possibly useful to her secret employer.

Of course, none of it could be told until he'd answered her burning question about what he'd do with the information. But she'd likely never see him again. Blast the gentry with their sudden fancies and forgotten promises, she thought bitterly.

Jane paused on the pavement in front of the town house she'd just left because her leg ached and now, suddenly, so did her heart. She'd glanced back in a forlorn half-hearted attempt to see if there was a tall dark man anywhere who wanted to talk to her. She saw nothing but the town house itself. The meanest, most meager home looked enticing from the outside when it was oncoming dusk; the warm glow of lamps and candles contrasted so vividly with the night. The sight of windows lit, even if only at the margins of closed draperies, said that privileged people were within the light, and the wanderer was forever outside that bright circle of home and hearth. The town houses here in this exclusive crescent were by no means either mean or meager. Their many windows blazed with light.

Jane felt lost, heartsick, betrayed by fortune and circumstance.

"You've hurt yourself," a memorably soft masculine voice said from the darkness.

Jane's shoulders jumped, but not so high as her heart did. "No," she answered, speaking into the night, because she still couldn't see him. "Well, yes. But it's temporary. One of my students mistook me for a pillow."

"Did you get extra wages for it?"

She laughed, and then stopped, because if anyone saw her standing alone, laughing, it could ruin her reputation. She walked on, reasoning that he would somehow follow. "Of course not. Does a soldier get paid more if he's wounded?" she asked in a murmur. "Oh, drat. I can't talk to myself. Where can we speak?"

"Here?" he asked.

"Oh yes," she said mockingly. "A nice stroll with a gentleman will do wonders for my standing with my lady, especially now."

"How can walking with me harm you, Miss?" he asked, stepping out of the shadows to stand at her side.

She gaped. She stood looking at a tall, broad-shouldered and weary workman. He wore high, oversized, stained and scuffed boots. His trousers were bagged at the knees, his loose jacket was a few sizes too big for him, and was open enough to show the colorful scarf tied round his throat, instead of a neckcloth. He had on oversized gloves, and a dusty floppy broad-brimmed hat shadowed his face. He carried a bulging sack over one shoulder.

"A rat-catcher?" she asked, surprised, amused, and appalled at his appearance.

"Lord, no. My tools. I'm a successful workman, going home for the night. But I admit rat-catcher was a thought, until I realized I'd have to go trudging through town with a sack of rodents. I'll do only so much for verisimilitude."

She grinned. It was a good disguise. If it weren't for that unmistakable, remarkable velvety voice, she'd have picked up the hem of her skirt and run, injured ankle or not, at the mere sight of him approaching her.

"We can go anywhere," he said. "Although you're usually graceful as a sprite, tonight you're limping like a bear with her paw caught in a trap. Tell me why, and why you don't have a cane. But that can wait. I don't want to keep you standing on the street. Tell me at dinner. Come to dinner with me? I'm famished."

"You may be hungry, but a workman is never 'famished,'" she corrected him. "And to trade compliments, sir, though you may be an accomplished gentleman, you're not a very good working man. We can't go 'anywhere.' There's not a decent restaurant in London that would allow you in."

"Who said anything about 'decent'?" he asked with a smile in his voice. "At least, as regards Society. But there are good places, if not to dine, then to eat. I know of a place with excellent food for the likes of me, that is, if you don't mind the company of lesser folk."

"I am lesser folk," she said, suddenly grave.

"Then take my arm, and we'll hobble over there. I'd call a hackney cab, but I can already hear your objections at getting into one with a strange man."

"I can't take your arm either," she said, standing still.

"Right, right, right," he muttered. "I'm obviously out of practice. Then start hobbling eastward, and I'll follow, minding my own business."

She nodded, and began to limp along the street. She hadn't gone more than a few paces before she stopped and looked up at him. "No," she said sadly. "It won't do. I can't even walk with you on this street or in this district. It would ruin my reputation if my lady or any of her friends saw us."

He was silent for a moment. "Then it's a cab for you," he said. "And I don't have to go with you. You can ride in high style and proper celibate style, by yourself. Hail a hackney. Tell the fellow to take you to Providence Street, to The Phoenix Feather Inn there. Don't look as though you're about to be kidnapped and sold to Eastern traders. The inn has more tables for dinner than it has bedchambers. You won't be compromised. We'll be in public, very public. I expect only to dine tonight. Go there, and I'll be waiting for you. I'll pay the driver and treat you to dinner, and not a person in the place will know you, or me, I promise."

She hesitated. It was unconventional, a very daring thing for her to do. There were so many possible pitfalls. She could get there and find herself alone in a strange part of town. She'd have to pay the driver herself, and more to get home. That, she could ill afford. Worse, she could get there and find he *was* there, and whatever he said, have to fight her way out of the inn by nightfall.

"Oh, please," he said in a disgusted tone of voice. "If I wanted to ravish you, I wouldn't dress like this and take you to a place of ill repute. Credit me with some style, if not morals. If I wanted company in a bed, I'd choose an expensive one, with a willing partner. All I want from you is information. I see you can't walk very well, and I'm hungry, or famished, or whatever you will. And it is nearly dinnertime. You must be hungry too. And so? Take it or I'll leave you alone."

Jane paused, for a heartbeat. She thought about what he said, and what had happened to her today. She remembered how much she needed the money. And she admitted that she was fascinated.

She didn't say a word. She merely nodded, limped to the curb, and raised an arm to flag down an empty hackney that was coming down the street.

Chapter 4

~~~OO~~~

Well, she was a fool and a fool deserved whatever she got—or didn't get: like money, ice for her ankle, and peace of mind. Jane tried to ignore the throbbing in her ankle and her conscience. She counted and recounted the contents of her purse as she was driven through the darkening streets of London into a part of town she didn't know, near the river. She had enough to pay for the ride if the gentleman wasn't there, and the ride home, even if he was, if she had to. But it was a foolish, costly, unnecessary expense. He'd muddled her wits.

It was all her fault, though. Given one chance to distract her from her mundane and insecure life, and she'd jumped at it. Like little Miss Stratton, she'd leapt without looking and would probably land in an ignoble heap somewhere, and not giggling either.

The cab slowed. Jane peered out the window. She was on a street of crooked old buildings. The hackney came to a stop as it approached a tavern on the corner. It looked as old as London town itself. A torch hung over the crooked doorway, illuminating a chipped hanging sign. It showed what looked like a ragged chicken in flames. As the sign swung in the breeze Jane made out the word *Phoenix* and realized that much at least was true. There was such a place.

But she was leery of getting out of the hackney. She didn't want to be deserted in such a place. So she peered out the window for a moment. She didn't see anyone. That meant she'd have to tell the driver to take her home. Would he stop at the fishmonger's so she could get some ice? It would be the most expensive ice she'd ever bought.

She heard someone talking to the driver, and sat up sharply. The door swung open and she sat up even straighter.

"If I'd known you enjoyed riding so much I'd have asked you to ride around town with me," Lord Granger said, looking in at her. "But I'm deucedly hungry. Come," he said, extending a hand.

She grasped the lumpy glove he offered, and stepped down out of the hackney. "Thank you for being here," she said simply. "I've never done such a daring thing in my life, and I was regretting it every minute."

He paused and looked down at her. The torchlight showed his crooked smile. "That's the most honest confession I've ever heard. Are you always so candid?"

"I suppose I am," she said, and almost added that she didn't know, she was so out of practice. She hadn't spoken to anyone that was remotely her equal in a very long time. Then she remembered that however he was dressed, he wasn't her equal. Then she thought that if her family hadn't been so imprudent, she well might be, if not his equal, then near to it.

"What are you thinking about?" he asked. "Never mind. Tell me inside." He hoisted his sack on his back again, waved the hackney on, and led Jane to the door to the tavern.

She didn't hang back, although if she were alone she'd never have entered a place like the one she saw.

An immediate smell of hot candles and cooking, beer, woodsmoke, and pipe smoke, both delicious and comforting, confronted her. The taproom was large, the ceiling was held up by old wooden beams, and laced with them too. There were many wooden tables and each one, it seemed, was full of colorful, noisy people, none of them ladies or gentlemen, all of them eating, drinking and laughing, often all at once.

"Ho! Mr. Phelps!" the barkeep shouted, seeing them. "Your table's ready. Back there, near the window. We'll be with you directly. We've got your favorite: lamb stew tonight."

"And it's a treat, though a lamb or two more wouldn't of hurt!" one of the patrons shouted, to the amusement of the other diners.

Those patrons, Jane saw, were dressed for the weather, not the fashion. There were as many women there as there were men, and they were just as raucous. She was wearing an olive-colored gown, drab and neatly fashioned, as befit an instructress of impressionable children. Her hair was pulled back and tied in the back in a knot, so as not to get in the way of her movement. That in itself set her apart from the other patrons. Still, she didn't feel terribly out of place here. She was with an escort who fit right in with the clientele, but, she thought, it was more because he exuded such a sense of calm self-possession.

Lord Granger led Jane to a table in a corner. She stood, waiting for him to pull out the chair for her. He bent and whispered, "Were I 'Lord Granger,' I'd do the honors, Miss Chatham. But here, I'm Mr. Phelps, and here, it's every man and woman for him and herself."

Jane flushed, dragged out a chair, and sat down quickly. Her host put down his sack and sat himself down opposite her.

"But what do I call you?" she asked in a faint whisper.

"Good question," he said. "You know who I really am. But I'd rather not be that here. So call me Simon. That is my name. Your eyes are on stalks," he said, grinning. "Never been to such a place before? I'll wager you have, if you think about it."

Her head spun around and she stared at him.

"I know you come from the countryside," he said. "Didn't you ever visit the local tavern in your town? Every village has one. London's no different, only every neighborhood here is like a village. This inn caters to the people who live and work hereabouts, which is why they have so few overnight guests, and so many customers for dinner. Don't look so unnerved. They're decent, respectable citizens—although, I'll grant, they're not ones you're likely to meet, except when you shop or hire on a workman.

"Oh, your face," he said with a grin. "No, they're not criminals. Not a cutpurse in the lot, and if you questioned any female's chastity here, you'd buy yourself a deal of trouble. This isn't a thief's den. Those are closer to the river, they get crowded later in the night. These people are the ones who work at the jobs you don't see. They tend the local shops, work on the river; they service the common man, not the gentry. Ordinary hardworking folk can't wait until nine to dine. They eat early and go to bed soon after, so they can be up early too."

"It's an expense to dine out," Jane said. "How can they afford it?"

"How can they not?" he asked. "Cook shops close early. Even if they didn't, this is a regular treat for these folk; their time to sit back and relax, gossip and chat with each other. They come alone if the wife's home with kiddies. If they can they bring their women to enjoy their scarce free time together."

"And you are 'Mr. Phelps'?" she asked.

"Here, I am," he said nonchalantly. "Ah," he exclaimed as the proprietor and a young boy came toward their table dragging a huge wooden bucket by the handles. "Good man!" Lord Granger said. "Just what I wanted."

"Where?" the innkeeper asked.

"Over in the corner, near the lady," Lord Granger said. "Under the table next to her, if you please."

As Jane, dumbfounded, drew up her feet, they pushed the bucket beneath the table.

"And now," her host said, "a few bottles of your best red, and tonight's specialty, whatever it is."

"You've got it, Mr. P.!" the innkeeper said cheerily, and left them.

Jane stared at Simon.

"Put your right foot in the bucket," he said. "Sans your shoe, of course. Don't worry about propriety. No one can see under the table."

She looked at him as though he'd run mad.

"It's filled with ice, Miss Chatham," he said. "Cracked and chopped ice. That's the best thing for your ankle now. I don't say leave your foot in all night, because if you do when you stand up it might crack off. But for a while, at least, immerse your ankle. It will bring down the swelling. I ordered it up before you got here."

"Oh!" Jane said, vastly relieved, and very touched. "Thank you."

She slid her slipper off, and eased her foot in. She gasped from the shock of the cold ice, but then pointed her toes and plunged her foot all the way through the icy blocks until her ankle was submerged. Simon's eyes widened even as hers did at the jolt she felt of the cold, and she sucked in a hard breath. Then she sighed and, finally, sat back.

She noted Simon's expression. "A dancer has to learn to endure pain," she explained. "If I'd gone slower, it would have hurt more."

"Brave girl," he commented. "But you teach infants, so I should have guessed that. How did you come to do that?"

"I had to earn money, and there are few recourses. I'd rather teach children than adults, I've discovered. They have no embarrassment and they throw themselves into it." She gave him a rueful smile. "Literally, in my case. But my ankle is numbing nicely now, thanks to you, and I really do think I'll be back on both feet before long. That relieves my mind."

"Good," he said. "So your parents left you nothing at all?"

She sat up straighter, and then relaxed. "Nothing," she said, sighing. "I see you've done some investigating."

"It's what I do," he said simply. "Or rather what I used to do, and so I still dabble in it."

She nodded. It made sense. "But I'm lucky," she said. "Because they did give me an education, and so, the ability to look after myself."

"No fellow back at home offered to do that for you?" he asked idly.

She shot him a cold look. "There were some. But since I can do it myself, I have done it. Now, to business, Mr. Phelps, if you please."

He shook his head. "My, my. Clothes do make the man, don't they? No bashfulness from you at all tonight."

She blinked, and then laughed. "You know, that's true! I hadn't thought of it. I suppose I was in awe of you as a gentleman . . . No!" she said suddenly. "You still are a gentleman, no matter how you're dressed. That's not all of it. I think I was afraid of your intentions because I was alone, in the night."

"You are now, as well," he commented.

She shook her head. "No, there's a room full of people present. But even so, it is easier to speak with you now. You've stated your intentions and they have noting to do with me personally."

He smiled. "Now, I never said that."

"You did," she said. "And, seeing and speaking to you without fear or reservation gives me more confidence.

"And yes, seeing you in ordinary clothes does make a difference," she mused, "as I'm sure you knew." She cocked her head. "I was also afraid of losing my position last time we met because I didn't know what to expect from you. You had the upper hand from the first. If any servant runs into conflict with her betters, she's assumed to be the one at fault."

"You're not exactly a servant," he said.

"No, not exactly. But to all intents and purposes, I am." She raised her chin.

"Your eyes are hazel, aren't they?" he asked with interest, ignoring her comment about her station in life. "I'd thought they were brown. But I've only seen them at dusk, and now by candle-light. We'll have to meet by day for me to be sure."

She grew still. Even in his commoner's working

garb, he was ferociously attractive. And when his conversation got personal, Jane began to worry. There was no time or way she could afford an infatuation with such a gentleman, whether he was dressed as a commoner or a prince. Nor could she be at ease with him if he had any real desire for her. "As to that," she said quickly, "I'm not at all sure we should meet again, anywhere."

He raised one dark eyebrow.

She leaned forward so she could speak low. "I must find out what your intentions are."

He put on an expression of shock, sat back, and placed a hand on his heart. "Miss Chatham! I am surprised." The wicked mirth in his eyes was hard for her to look back at. "This is so sudden!"

"You know exactly what I mean," she said, refusing to play a game with him. "This is business, but lately I've been worrying about what kind of business it is."

He leaned forward and laced his hands on the table, suddenly serious. "What kind do you think it is?"

"I've thought of abduction, blackmail, and murder," she said before she could think better of it, her voice beginning to rise. "And I tell you I want no part of any of that."

The tavern keeper approached, bearing plates of steaming stew and fresh bread, with bottles of wine under his arm. Instead of smiling, he was straight-faced and quick about his business. There were a few silent moments as the plates were set on the table, and the wine decanted.

When he'd left, Simon sighed. "Oh, my lamentable reputation. Our host looked nervous. Do you really think any of those things were my intention? Certainly he didn't—at least, not until now."

His thin brows tilted down at the corners, and his dark eyes followed suit. It gave him a faintly satanical look. Jane wondered if those eyes were dark brown or black, but they were so watchful she didn't dare look deeply enough to find out. His cheekbones were high and his nose straight; his skin was clear and closely shaven, in spite of the late hour. He was even more appealing up close like this. But still, he had a dangerous look. She wondered if she should have been so forthright. She wondered why she was here at all. She sat still.

"None of your fears have any basis," he said. "Why would I ask about young Richard if I had any evil intentions? I don't know you well enough to be sure you wouldn't tell someone, do I? What kind of absurd criminal would question the innocent in a household if he had evil plans? Please, Miss Chatham, I don't know what you think of me, but credit me at least with some intelligence.

"In brief, then, and in secrecy please: my old friend, Viscount Delancey, is worried about his younger, impressionable brother, Richard. He is especially concerned about your employer's intentions toward him. He feels Richard is too young to be wed and asked me if I'd take a look at the situation to see what I made of it."

"But the young man surely can't be more than two and twenty, and my lady at least . . ." she paused, feeling disloyal.

"The lady is five and thirty on her next birthday, and the young man has but one and twenty years in his cup. Quite a difference."

"But if it were reverse, it would make no matter," Jane said.

"Exactly. But in this situation, it does. A woman of one and twenty has some sense. It is debatable if a man of fifty does. You females surpass us in that, at least. Or should. Unless there's a reason. I doubt your lady is madly infatuated with Richard. So, my friend is right. There must be a reason.

Now, if I come to your lady's salon every time Richard is there, I'll be taken for a suitor too. That, I assure you, I am not. I need someone to tell me which way the wind is blowing. I need to know if she's really fond or is he simply flirting? Is he really smitten? Are there other suitors? Perhaps one she wants to pay attention?

"The lady won't tell me, and the lad certainly won't. You work there, Miss Chatham, and you can hear, if not always see, what's going on in that household. Servants live on gossip. All I asked was that if you could watch and listen in for me. Now, are you comforted?"

She frowned. "You pay a great deal for very little."

He laughed aloud. "And you're a very bad bargainer. No matter, a contract is a contract. I pay for services rendered. My friend considers the information vital. Now, taste your stew before it gets cold, and then tell me what you've learned. That is, if you're convinced I'm not an evildoer. If you are, why then, enjoy your dinner and good-bye, with no hard feelings on my side. Or, I hope, on yours. And," he added conspiratorially, in a whisper, "I suggest you remove your foot from the bucket for a while."

She hastily lifted out her foot. The conversation had been so enthralling she'd forgotten any pain. But her ankle was so nicely numbed now it didn't hurt. It just ached from the cold. Then she applied herself to her dinner. After the first taste, she looked up at him with widened eyes.

"Yes," he said pleasantly. "Delicious, isn't it? The patrons here may not have social status or very much money. But they do know value, and appreciate good food."

"So do I," she said fervently. She hadn't dined so well for a very long time. As she blotted up the last of her gravy with the last of her bread, she found herself regretting the fact that she couldn't return. Because even here, females couldn't dine alone.

"So," he said, sitting back, "before we taste that plum tart we were promised, tell me what you've learned."

"I learned not to ask little girls to leap before they looked," she said ruefully, gingerly putting her foot back into the bucket.

"Good advice for big girls too. I meant, about the young man in question."

"Oh. Well, the interesting thing," she said with more spirit, "is that he's the young man who rescued me. I mean, he saw the accident and immediately offered me his hand." She looked down at the tabletop because she was sure her face was growing pink. "That wasn't so pleasant for me, though, because my skirts had flown up while I was on a huddle on the floor. But I was surrounded by children," she said, daring to look up at him.

He hid his smile, but not very successfully. "Ah. I see, still, Venus, while half-clad, is usually depicted by artists surrounded by cherubs. She's still considered very provocative."

"Well, I wasn't," she said hotly. She lowered her voice again. "I was fully clad, only in . . . disarray. Well, I was sprawled on the floor. I couldn't help it and as soon as I saw what was happening, I corrected matters. He was kind to me, that's all."

"So, you're the new exhibition at Lady Harwood's salon, are you?"

She looked uncomfortable. "I appear to be. But salons are considered the places with the latest, the newest, and most interesting rages in Town. My lessons appear to be such. It won't last," she said sadly. "That's why I have to work hard now, before I have a dozen competitors. Lady Harwood's salon is currently one of the most successful. It's attracting more and more gentry: titled ladies and gentlemen and now artists and poets, and even those high in the government. I've heard many famous names mentioned. So it won't be long before other hostesses copy her, at least so far as dancing lessons for children, and I'll be out of work, or at least, paid much less.

"At any rate," she went on, "that's not interesting to you. The point is that my lady wasn't happy about the young gentleman's interest in helping the dance instructress. As though I would try to make capital on it!" she said indignantly. "He's a very nice young man, but he's *so* young! I'm three and twenty, and he's younger than I. Apart from the fact," she added more hastily, "that I know such a thing would never do.

"What I'm trying to tell you is that while I was down in the kitchens resting my ankle, I heard the servants talking," she said quickly. "They'd forgotten my being there, I suppose. They said they weren't half surprised that the lady was annoyed with me."

"Was she?"

Jane sighed, remembering her pittance of pay

for the day. She nodded. "Yes. They say that she does have a fondness for young Richard. I can't understand it at all. Lady Harwood is very beautiful, and she's witty, and wealthy; it seems to me she could have any gentleman she chooses. And now that her salon is filled every day, she has a great many more to choose from."

Simon didn't say anything for a while. He stared at her, bemused. It both flattered Jane and made her uncomfortable. But then, she thought, reviewing her speech, she hadn't said anything that would be considered libel, or betrayal, or in any way harmful to her employer. That, she'd never do.

He nodded, at last. "I can see Richard's interest in you. You are, in your present condition, very like our dinner tonight. Surprisingly tasty, and growing more so on better acquaintance."

Jane frowned, not knowing whether to stand and march out, as best she could, or stay and be flattered. But her ankle did throb. And it was the first time she'd ever been able to sit at dinner, in public, with a handsome gentleman. She said nothing.

"Yes, I can see your being put in an uncomfortable position, in every way," he said, acknowledg-

72

ing her unease. "But I can't see the attraction your employer has for the young man."

"No one can. You know," Jane said, on sudden inspiration, "perhaps instead of asking you to spy, his brother ought to come to one of Lady Harwood's salons when Richard is there and see for himself."

Simon tilted his head to the side, studying Jane. Then he gave her a sudden wide, open smile. It was Jane's turn to be bemused, because if he was attractive when he looked dangerous, he was twice as much so when he was pleased.

"Of course," he said, as though to himself. "The lady's no fool, and neither are you, Miss Chatham. I'll wager that's her game! Richard is no catch, but his brother is, only he never swims near her net. He's a recluse. What else would draw him out but a mystery, or what he perceives as danger to someone he cares for? And whom does he care for more than his brother? Well done, Miss Chatham!"

"Oh," Jane said, surprised. "Yes. I just suggested it, but I suppose that well may be so. So then I also suppose my job is done." She said it with flat reality in her voice, but her face spoke volumes about disappointment.

"Of course not," her host said. "I'm not half done with your services."

He said it with such conviction in his voice and sly humor in his expression, that Jane was both comforted and terrified, and at that moment, didn't know which she preferred to be.

Chapter 5

"You're still hobbling," Simon said as Jane rose from the table. He held his sack over his arm, and waited, watching her. "It still hurts, doesn't it? Here, lean on my arm."

"No, thank you," she said nervously.

"Oh, don't be a fool," he said with impatience. "No one here knows you. No one here cares. Why should they? Come, the hackney will be back by now. I'm taking you home. But you ought to have that ankle bound," he added, looking at her thoughtfully. "Please, sit. I'll be back in a moment."

Jane sat again, as Simon disappeared into the crowd. Her ankle did still hurt, but she knew it wasn't the blinding pain that a break would be. She waited. It wasn't long before he returned and offered her his hand again. She took a deep breath, and his arm. Trying not to limp, she left the tavern with him. As he'd said, a hackney awaited them.

"The steps will take you time, and pain. Let's have done with that," Simon told Jane, and before she could object, he scooped her up in his arms and carried her into the hackney. She would have been more worried if he hadn't simply placed her on the seat like a parcel, sat himself down opposite her, and told the driver to go on.

"Now, your ankle," he said, as the coach began moving.

The lanterns hung at the side of each window in the hackney were lit, and Jane could make out his movements and expressions, although the flickering light given by the bouncing flames distorted them.

He opened his sack and rummaged in it. "Put your foot on my knee. The landlord had an old sheet. We tore it into strips. So now," he said, sitting up with a handful of the material and leaning forward, "Put it here, in my hand, and we'll wrap it tight."

She sat stone-still and stared at him.

He groaned. "Oh, Miss Chatham. And here I

hadn't taken you for a fool. Your ankle is strained. If you bear weight on it, it won't heal very soon. But yes, I see. Here we are alone in the dark, or worse still, the comforting soft candlelight. And me: a suspicious-looking and mysterious nobleman, and you, a destitute young charmer. I see. You think I'll grab your limbs, tie you up tight, and have my way with you? Sorry to disappoint. I like my females active, but not in trying to escape. I just want to bring your bloo— blasted ankle over here."

"I'm not such a fool as to think that," she said, although she'd had her doubts. "But I suppose I am one anyway. Surely you know that it's very singular for me to hand my foot to you." She heard what she'd said, and her hand flew over her mouth. But she couldn't hide the giggle that emerged. "Oh, bother!" she said. "It's not done. That's the point."

"It is, if it's done with no one the wiser, and if the woman in question is injured. And the gentleman," he added, in bored tones, "is either a physician, or on his best behavior. Now. Do you want to work again this month? If so, I urge you to comply."

She raised her leg, pulling her skirt down over

it as far as she could, and delivered her foot into his waiting hand.

"Right," he said, as he cupped her heel. He took a long strip of material with the other hand, and began to wind it around her ankle. "Now tell me if I make it too tight. We don't want to cut off your blood supply." After he'd wound that one strip, he took another, and covered it over, and then another over that.

"You've done this before," she said, because she hated silence. And because even though she was injured, the feeling of having her foot in his large, competent hands was more thrilling than she'd imagined.

"Yes," he said briefly, concentrating on wrapping her leg to the calf. "Now try to bend your foot, move it up and down. Toes up. Toes down. How's that?"

"A bit tight," she said, "on the up. The down seems fine."

"Right," he said, and bent to undo his bandage, and do it up again. "Yes, I know how to do this. I was in the war. You learn all sort of things . . . how's that?"

She tried moving her foot. "Tight," she said. "But good."

"As so many things are," he said, with a smile in his voice. "Now, don't walk on it unless you have to. And if you have to, use a stick." He released her foot.

"I'm very grateful to you," she said softly, drawing her leg back, and shaking her skirt down over it.

"I'll make you more so," he said.

She sat up straighter.

"Your payment is due," he added, now with laughter in his tone. "Here." He handed her a bundle of banknotes.

She took it, and then held it out to him again. "It's too much," she protested.

"You haven't counted it," he said.

"I can feel it."

"You did your job," he said, sitting back. "And perhaps even solved the reason why I had to hire you. So you did the work, and maybe put yourself out of work by doing so. You deserve the money, Jane."

His saying her name sounded warm, delicious, intimate. Still, she knew a gentleman didn't use a lady's given name unless she gave him permission to. But she was glad he'd done it. It reminded her that she wasn't a lady, but only a servant in his eyes.

"Then I'll take it. So this is the end of the adventure?" she asked.

"I don't know," he said. "Keep your eyes and your ears open until I tell you otherwise. I don't know if my friend will break his seclusion and come to Lady Harwood's salon, no matter what the lure is. I don't know if young Richard will come to his senses and sheer off anyway. I'd like to know the lady's true aims in this. But, thank you. You're an excellent reporter, Jane."

"You have others," she said.

"I have. But you make the most sense. And I can talk to you as an equal. Makes matters so much simpler."

"I see," she said, and pulled back a corner of the curtain on the window. "Stop here," she said.

He looked surprised. "This isn't where your rooms are," he said.

"Of course, you'd know that," she said on a sigh. "No, they're a street away from here. But you can't take me there," she said, struggling to rise from the deep cushions. "I have my reputation to think of."

He smiled, and tapped on the roof. "Here," he said, when the driver pulled the hatch back. "Stop here first."

The hackney slowed. When it stopped, Simon rose, and scooped Jane up in his arms again. He opened the door, and stepped down with her still in his grasp. When he reached the pavement, he smiled down at her quizzical look. She stared at his face, wondering at this pause, and slowly realized it might come to more. She stayed still, watching him. Then he lowered his head and kissed her lips. She gasped. That seemed to please him, because he lengthened the kiss and brushed her tongue with his own. She gasped again, pleasing him even more. When he put her down on solid ground at last, she wavered on her feet. It wasn't because of any pain in her ankle, and they both knew it.

His kiss had been so light, and sweet and so full of promise. Jane put her hand to her mouth and stared at him, trying to recover her senses. "You said you were a gentleman, and on your best behavior," she managed to say.

"So I am," he said. "And so I was. I don't know one man, gentle or not, who wouldn't have taken that opportunity. You could have stopped me at any time," he added. "It was only a kiss, Jane," he said at her suddenly stricken expression. "Don't refine upon it. It makes you no less a good woman, and me no more of a threat to you. That, I promise. No," he said thoughtfully, "I can't promise what I can't foresee. Say rather, it oughtn't to interfere with our business dealings. I'll never do anything to make you sad or endangered. I simply couldn't resist, and if you hated me for it, I'd be very sorry. I meant nothing by it. I give you good night, my virtuous Miss Chatham, though I wish you didn't insist on tottering home alone."

"It's better now that you've wrapped it," Jane said absently, and turned to leave him. She stopped, and turned again. "Lord Granger," she said stiffly. "It occurs to me that I'm at a disadvantage, and not just because of my accident. I can't afford, either financially or morally, to tarry with you as a lady of fortune and family could do. All I ask is that you remember that. I do believe you are a gentleman, you see."

"Lud!" he said, placing a hand over his heart. "A direct hit. You wound me, Jane."

"I don't mean to," she said seriously. "I mean only to protect myself."

"Consider that done," he said, and bowed to her.

He watched her make her way gingerly

down the street. Then he climbed back into the
hackney and directed the driver to follow her,
at a distance. Only when he saw the outline of
her figure go up a stair to a house, open a door,
enter, and then close it after her, did he sit back,
and signal the coachman to drive on.

Chapter 6

"Today," Jane told her eager students, "we will not be leaping."

There was a chorus of disappointed "Ohhhhhhs."

"But you'll enjoy the lessons, because we'll be twirling," she went on with a reassuring smile. "There's a great deal of twirling in social dancing, as well as in ballet. You will be ladies, not ballet dancers, of course. You'll go to balls and routs, though, and dance all night if you wish. Twirling is important in many dances. You have to learn how to do it without getting dizzy, without falling, and while looking graceful. Grace is what we need to work on," she added. "So stepping lightly is important. You really can't twirl properly if you don't."

Twirling, she thought, could let her take the weight off her bad ankle. It was almost back to normal but if she could have afforded to stay home today, she would have. If she could afford to quit this client and never come back, she'd be even happier. She'd had two days to lament her foolishness in letting Lord Granger kiss her. Nobleman or not, she should have slapped his face. Instead she'd looked up at him like a moonling. She didn't want to see him again. But she really needed the money from this job, and the one she did for him. There were a lot of lessons to be learned today, for her pupils and herself. Humility was the thing she had to learn, she told herself bitterly, because she couldn't work if she didn't.

So she'd borrowed a walking stick from her landlady and had come back as promised, to teach the children. And to keep her eyes and ears open to everything happening in this house.

The fact that she'd also worn one of her best gowns, a violet one made for half-mourning, ordered up when she still had a bit of money to do it, meant nothing. Lord Granger mightn't even come to the salon today, or meet her in the streets afterward. But if he did, she'd look well, and proper too. It was a half-mourning gown with the neck so high it ended just below her chin. She'd given herself a satisfied nod in her small looking glass this morning before she'd set out. Not a speck of skin was showing.

She couldn't see that the gown also fit her to perfection, or that the lightweight muslin fabric caressed her body and showed it off to perfection too. What mattered is that it made her feel well dressed, and when she moved it flowed with her as it swirled around her legs. She'd skinned back her hair, coiled it in a knot, put a small cameo at her neck, and left the house. She felt like a lady again.

"Now," she said to her eager audience, "the first thing you must do is step lightly as a fairy child. Watch." Using her left leg, she took a step forward on her toes, stretching out, her arms up and outward. Then, stifling a grimace, she took another step forward on her right foot. "Like tiptoeing," she said, looking at them. "Quiet as a mouse, light as a feather, and graceful as a swan. Now, form a line, as we always do, and walk around the floor that way. Show me how light you can be on your feet." She nodded to the governess at the piano. "Music please. Something bright and light as springtime."

It wasn't easy for the children to tiptoe. They

tried. But after a step or two, they fell, of course. They tumbled down, falling atop each other, laughing merrily.

"Again," Jane said, rapping her cane the way her old dance mistress used to do to restore order. "Up, point and step, and see how far you can go without falling. You can't go to balls when you grow up and dance with a gentleman until you do."

They tried. They failed. They laughed all the while. Jane stood back, watching them, hiding a grin. Might as well ask an elephant to tiptoe, she thought. They just weren't made for it, at least, not yet.

She clapped her hands. "All right. That will be enough light-footed stepping for today. You can practice it at home. Now, I'll show you what you can do when you *do* learn it. Because you can't do a flat-footed twirl."

She had the children sit and form a semicircle around her. Then she raised herself on her left foot, and raised her arms above her head. She turned, and turned, and turned, pivoting on one foot, pushing with her other foot, while the little girls "ohhed" and "ahhed" as she spun. Finally, she stopped and lowered her hands to her sides.

Then she heard applause and a few "bravos!"—masculine "bravos." She closed her eyes, opened them, and looked to the doorway to the ballroom. Her employer and what looked to her like a positive herd of guests stood there, the guests cheering. Her employer wasn't.

"Good show!" one of the gentlemen exclaimed.

"Brilliant!" exclaimed another. He was young Richard.

Jane's employer was standing by the young gentleman's side and frowning at her. So were the other ladies in the crowd. The gentlemen looked at her admiringly. Assessingly. Jane felt cold.

"Well done! I saw your mishap. Are you well enough to dance today?" Richard asked her earnestly.

"I am, I assure you," Jane said, lowering her eyes and ducking a curtsey. "Thank you for asking."

Her employer's expression changed immediately. "Oh, poor Miss Chatham," she said sympathetically. "Here we are interfering with your lessons again. Never fear! We'll leave you now. We just wanted to be sure all was well this time."

"Nay," one of the gentlemen protested, "the music and laughter we all heard was like a siren's call!"

"You were just bored with the chat in the salon," Lady Harwood chided him.

"Never!" he proclaimed, as everyone laughed.

"And titillated by tales of what happened last time my dance instructress was here, perhaps?" the lady teased.

The gentleman grinned.

"Come away now," their hostess said. "Friends, let's leave poor Miss Chatham to her duties. You won't miss a thing. The lesson is over. There'll be no shocking show today. Oh," she added, as her guests began to file out of the doorway into the hall. "Miss Chatham. Do come to see me when you're done. There's something we must discuss before you leave. If we're still in the salon, come there. Not *in there*, of course," she added with a brittle smile. "Just wait outside, send for me, and I'll come to you."

"Yes, my lady," Jane said, bending in a half bow while her heart sank completely. *Well*, she thought, turning back to the girls, *there goes one position*. The governess at the piano gave her a sympathetic look. "Young ladies," Jane said, clapping her hands together, "let's end with a grand march today, in time with the music."

"But, Miss, you said we could twirl," one of the older girls said.

Jane sighed. "So I did. Those of you who think you can, come form a line and let me see."

The lesson lasted another half hour. And there was so much laughter the piano couldn't be heard.

At last, it was done. No one actually completed a full circular twirl, but no one got hurt. That was the most Jane could hope for these days. She waited for the nannies and governesses to come collect the children, watched the governess at the piano leave, and then tried to neaten up her own appearance. It was time to lose her position, she thought sadly. She raised her head high. At least, she'd do it as a lady.

Of course, she now realized, this would make her lose her other job, the newer one, the better paying one, that of an informant. But she'd find some way to continue making her livelihood. Her middle-class clients wouldn't be aware of her downfall, or so she hoped. The important thing was to get this over with and yet retain her dignity.

Jane walked down the long polished hall to the blue salon where Lady Harwood and her guests were. She heard the sound of their conversation and laughter. It was a warm day and there were so many guests that the door to the salon had been left open. Jane knew she should simply find the butler and tell him she was ready to speak to the lady. But she couldn't resist peeking into the room.

She didn't know daylight affairs could be said to glitter. But the guests crowding the salon were as elegant and fascinating as any in a grand ball-room at midnight. More so, perhaps. They were more colorful for one thing. Casual dress meant that the gentlemen wore more than the approved black and white. They had on blue, black, brown, and green jackets, and their tightly fitted unmentionables were in every hue of cream, puce, toast, and even canary yellow. Their waistcoats could be seen to be bright, their neckcloths were startlingly white and intricately tied, and most wore magnificent, shining half boots.

The women were even more magnificent in gauzy gowns of every shade of spring flower, and all in the latest fashion. They were elegant from the tops of their heads to their dainty slippers. They lounged, they languished, they laughed, and of course, they smiled and pouted, flirting with the gentlemen. Jane stared, entranced. She'd seen filled salons before. Her parents had often had company in, and solidly cultured folk they'd been too. But they were countryfolk. These people were the cream of London Society dressed in the latest French fashion, war or no war.

Jane watched them from the doorway. Her eyes opened wider and she started as she caught sight of Lord Granger. He wore traditional black and white and yet he shone out from the crowd. He was talking with a wispy brown-haired female in a rose-colored gown. As though he'd felt Jane's glance like a touch on his arm, he looked up and over the head of the little lady he was speaking to, directly at Jane. She saw the recognition flare in his eyes. And then he turned to his companion again as though he'd seen and felt nothing at all. Which was, Jane thought as she shrank back from the doorway, what she was to him, after all.

She found the butler, gave him the message, and then waited, hands folded, in a corner of the hall, opposite the salon. She refused to think. But nevertheless a thought did cross her mind, that it might be a while until her employer appeared.

And indeed, the lady did not come. The butler returned instead. "My lady says you're to wait until her guests have left," he said. "In the kitchens. I know it's time wasted," he whispered more gently when he saw her expression. "But what can you do? At least, you can have a cup of tea. I'll come for you when she's ready."

"I don't know how you do it," Lady Harwood told Jane a few hours later, groaning as she eased off her slipper and rubbed her toes. "I suppose dancing slippers are more comfortable than elegant ones, but a hostess must stay on her feet, and those feet must be well shod. My toes feel strangled. Oh, sit down, Miss Chatham. I can't stare up at you, my neck's stiff enough from gazing up adoringly at all the gentlemen."

Jane gathered her skirt and sat on the edge of a chair in the lady's chamber, waiting for her speak again.

"Warm water, a basin full," the lady told her maid. "And some sweet-smelling salts. A nice long soak will do wonders for my poor feet. Now," she said, as the maid left and she turned her attention to Jane again, "we have a problem, Miss Chatham."

Jane nodded. There was nothing to say to that. She just hoped she'd get all her wages owed before she left.

The lady tilted her head to the side and looked

at Jane, studying her. "The thing is, Miss Chatham, that you have been noticed," she said without preface. "Not just by one gentleman, but by many. Not your fault, I know. But you looked so provocative lying there on the floor when you fell the other day that I had twice as many gentleman callers today. Word gets around."

The lady waved a hand to silence anything Jane might say. "I said I know it isn't your fault. But it gives me a problem. If I turn you off, the cats will say it's because I was jealous. If I keep you on, the cats *and* the prudes will say that I'm looking for sensation. The gentlemen will tease no matter what I do, but if I let you go I'll bet the number of my afternoon callers will dwindle."

She looked at Jane narrowly. "I had fascinating guests today, Miss Chatham. Gentlemen from government, ladies and gentlemen from the highest boughs of Society *and* our Regent's circle were here today. My salon has become *the* place to be. Credit where it's due, a great deal of it has to do with you. At first the ladies came because they heard how adorable the little ones were at their dance lessons. Then the gentlemen came to see the ladies. And now you've caused a sensation everyone wants to see again. The caricature in the shops isn't enough for them now."

"*Caricature?*" Jane asked, her head going up.

"Yes, in the window of the printshops the very next day. You, head over heels, in all your delightful disarray. It's sold out, I hear. And your legs are all that's on display. Well, those and a flash of bosom and a bit of cheek, if you know what I mean."

Jane's hand flew to her mouth. Her face grew white, then pink.

"That much is fantasy. I saw you, you know," Lady Harwood said. "I bought out a great many prints. They do say: 'Dancing Instruction at Lady H–W's merry salon.' Do you want one?" She reached down to an end table, picked up a crisp sheet of caricature, and held it out to Jane.

Jane looked at it, colored up, and winced. "Does it have my name?" she asked, eyes closed in pain.

"It says: Miss H-. No more than that. Don't worry yourself to flinders. You look charming, but if you look harder, you'll see this dancing female doesn't resemble you in the least. Mr. Rowlandson is a gifted artist, but he didn't see you, after all. This dancing instructress he shows is much more buxom, with more bottom, and looks more like a serving wench."

Jane looked again, and nodded, swallowing hard.

"You aren't that," Lady Harwood said, putting the paper down again. "You're like a sprite. But it's the talk of the town, today, at least. Tomorrow it may be forgotten.

"Now, it's for me to see how to best use it. If I turn you out, there are others that will hire you on, if only for the fame of it. It's not easy for a hostess to get the illustrious and the well-bred to come to one's salon these days. There's fierce competition. And if you are thinking of deserting me because of that, I remind you that though they may pay well, many employers may not be as kind I am. Though, I grant you mightn't think that either."

Lady Harwood paused, and sat in thought. "Still," she eventually said, narrowing her eyes, "if I keep you on I'm open to jealous censure. And while I do like the controversial, there are some gentlemen whose attention I would rather not have stray."

It was a veiled insult, but Jane couldn't say a thing. This whole interview astonished her. The lady was lovely, she thought again, but today, here and now, she was very different. Those round blue eyes were filled with intelligence; she no longer simpered or pouted. This close, Jane could see faint lines at the corners of the lady's eyes and mouth. If she didn't wear powder, Jane thought, they wouldn't show. But then, the lady's complexion mightn't look as unblemished from afar. Even so, Lady Harwood was still remarkably lovely.

Jane had always thought her most elegant employer was a flighty and careless creature. With no men around, the lady looked far less vulnerable and was much less nonsensical. She put her hands on her knees and stared at Jane. "Here's the truth of it: I'm on the catch for a new husband, Miss Chatham. That's no secret. But I don't want to lose one before I land him. You are therefore, a danger to me. I might tolerate my husband having an *affaire* after the marriage vows are spoken, but not before."

Jane shot to her feet. She held her hands together because they were shaking, as she was, with fury. "I am not on the 'catch' for anything but a salary, my lady, and I am not a loose woman, even if I had an accidental spill and made a vulgar display of myself. I work because I must, not because I please to, and I don't please to be dishonored, or tolerated, or used. I'll go now."

"Oh, sit down," her employer said wearily. "I'm only doing you the courtesy of being honest with you. I think the best thing for me to do is to keep you on. I believe you are a 'good girl,' the more fool you, because you could make a fortune for yourself now. I'm no fool either, Jane. I was married to an old man at my parent's command, and he went the way of old men. Now I want a husband of my own choosing. It's not easy for a woman alone, rich or poor, and well I know it. Let us make a pact then. I'll keep you on, and keep you and your reputation safe. I'll even give you a rise in salary. You promise not to stray to anyone who makes you a better offer. You've already said you've no interest in any male I might attach and I believe you. Fame is fleeting. In a few weeks you'll have been forgotten. Make hay while the sun shines. I intend to."

"Does that mean that if I stay you'll have your company peeking in on my lessons every day?"

"It's likely. Wear clean underthings, Miss Chatham, in case of another mishap. The ballroom floor is polished every morning. So, is this agreeable to you?"

"To be frank, my lady," Jane said, shaking her head, "No. It is not." She thought a moment. "But it is achievable," she said on a sigh. "And I suppose, necessary. May I have my back wages today?"

"Of course," her employer said. "Good thinking, Miss Chatham. You know, in other circumstances we could be friends. You're bright and honest; too bad that there's such a gulf between us. It's only money, but money is everything. Even worse," she said, showing a dimple that Jane had never noticed, "is the fact that you're so charming. Not a beauty, I can keep up with any of them. But you're young and appealing. That can't be beat. Keep that charm for your students, and don't try to appeal to any of my guests, and I'll try to be a good employer. I promise. You may go now. I'll send your wages down in a moment."

Jane ducked a curtsey, went to the door, and then turned around on a sudden thought. "You expect me to fall again, my lady? I usually don't. And I assure you that I don't want to again."

"It's not necessary. We can keep them in suspense. It may be even better that way," the lady said absently as she eased off her other slipper.

"Good evening to ye, Miss," the hackney driver said, tipping his hat as Jane passed him on the street.

She was so deep in thought that she merely nodded and walked on.

"Not a word for me this foine evening?" he asked in a suddenly familiar voice.

She looked up and saw Lord Granger sitting in the driver's seat. He swept a battered top hat off his head before he clapped it on again, setting it at a tilt that partially covered his face. That, and the voluminous greatcoat he wore, helped to conceal his identity in the growing evening shadows.

She didn't smile. "Good evening," she murmured.

"Thought ye could do with a drive home, Miss," he said in the same common accents he'd just used. "Seeing as to yer injury and all. 'Tis free. Hop in."

She shook her head. "No, thank you," she said. "There's no need." Then she turned her face up to his. "No need for any of this charade anymore, sir. I saw you today. You have free run of my lady's house, and so I see you have no real need of my services any longer. Good evening to you."

He looked down at her and frowned. "At least, we can talk as we drive," he said, picking up the reins and shaking them so his horse matched Jane's pace as she marched on. "The real driver is in the back of the hackney. We'll change places when we get farther from here."

"As I said," she said, as she walked head down, "no need, thank you."

The cab inched down the street beside her. "I'm going to look like I'm desperate for business," he said. "Wait! I see. You're angry with me, aren't you?"

"What I am, or am not, doesn't matter," she said as she walked, looking doggedly down at the pavement. "Our business is concluded, so you're right, you do look desperate. There's no point to it, or my continuing services. Again, good evening to you, sir. And good-bye."

"Because I didn't acknowledge you today?" he asked in wonderment. "Wouldn't that have looked fine, though. Should I have hailed you instantly and asked you in to the salon? Perhaps introduced you to the lady I was talking with? Wouldn't your employer have loved that. What did you expect me to do?"

She was silent for a moment as she plodded

onward. "You're right, of course," she finally said. "It was nonsense on my part, I see that now. But that doesn't matter. It's just that I don't see the point in my association with you any longer now that I see you run tame at the house."

"I visit at your place of employment, yes," he said patiently, as the horse clopped on in synchronization with her. "I chat. I don't hear more than gossip. I can't see more than anyone else does. You can."

"I'm also being paid more now," she said proudly. "So I'm not in need of funds. I can't work for two masters."

"Really?" he asked. "And here I thought you were a sensible female, who knew the importance of saving for a rainy day. Working for a Society matron means stormy weather, Miss Chatham. For example, you were supposed to be on your way home hours ago. Were you paid extra for those hours? I doubt it."

She remained silent as she marched on. He was right. But so was she.

"Why were you at work so late today?" he asked. "What do I need from you? We have much to discuss, Miss Chatham. Whether or not you agree, I am a gentleman. Please get in the cab and let me give you a ride home. Your ankle can't be all healed yet. If you have questions, I'll answer them, as I hope you'll answer mine. Now, we're coming to a crossroads. Will you get in? Or must I run you over?"

With a great show of reluctance, but with rapidly beating heart, Jane slowed, and waited for the cab to stop. The regular driver, who had been seated in the back, hopped out, bowed, and lowered the stair for her. She gathered her skirts, and holding her breath, climbed in.

Simon had handed the reins to the real driver, and hopping down, went around to the other door and got in the coach. Soon, it moved on at a sprightlier pace.

They didn't speak at first. Then Jane spoke into the darkness. "It's very simple, sir," she said quietly. "Taking your money now feels like charity, or worse." She put up a hand to signal there was more. He could hear her swallow, hard. "And receiving your attention now seems wrong," she went on. "Well, it is wrong. There can't be anything but sorrow for me, at least, in that sort of thing. So please, as I've nothing to tell you, indeed, as I always wondered what there was to tell you that was worth your time or money, I ask that you allow me to stop reporting to you."

The only sound was that of the horse's hooves striking the paving stones as they traveled.

"I needed the money badly when I took on your commission," she said quietly. "Need makes a person accept strange bargains, and extreme want probably eases more consciences than the Church does. I see that now. I did save what I could from the wages you paid, and am earning more now. I don't know what the future holds, but it makes no difference. I've never been comfortable about working for you. I ask to be relieved of duty, sir."

"And of my kisses?" he asked.

He heard her gasp. And then, to his surprise, she laughed. "Yes, sir. There's nothing good that can come of either, at least, for me. I'm sure you'll agree."

"It depends," he said slowly, "on what you mean by 'good.' But yes then, if you feel that strongly, we'll call it done. I'll pay you for services rendered. And ask that you always consider me a friend, and that if you hear anything you think I might make use of that you send to me."

"I will, I do, and thank you," she said.

They rode in silence until they reached the street before her own, and then, on his order, the hackney stopped. Simon handed Jane a small parcel. She took it, said, "Thank you, sir, and good-bye," and left the hackney.

He watched her go down the long street to her rooms, and then sat back, oddly discomforted, strangely annoyed with himself.

Chapter 7

"**W**elcome to the heart of fashionable London," Simon told his friend, raising his glass of wine in a salute.

"Thank you," the viscount said. "And so, your note told all?"

"All there is to know. But you are welcome to find out more. The lady's salon is all the rage now," Simon explained as he turned the glass of wine in his fingers, studying it. "You can go there now, Proctor, and no one will think a thing of it. Your privacy may not even be breached because you may not even be noticed in the crowd. Everyone's there. Half the War Department rubs shoulders with the fops and the beaus; there are poets as well as members of Cabinet, deposed royalty of every country you can imagine and some you can't. The highest sticklers in society squeeze in

106

with social-climbing mushrooms and attention-seekers. Prinny, yes, the Regent himself, will drop in any day. It's a mad scene. And yes, your brother's usually there.

"If you go you'll get a look at the lady and Richard together and see for yourself. I didn't know what to make of it and so, as you know, I hired informants to tell me more. There's no more to tell. They're friends, they're close. But how close, and why, I don't know. I don't understand the attraction on either side, or even know if there really is one. Your turn, my friend."

"You won't go there anymore?" his friend asked.

Simon shrugged. He looked around the study of the viscount's London town house. It was as quiet, elegant, and bare as the one in his country estate. All he could hear was the dry tick of a clock on the mantel. "You're here now, Proctor. I think it's time for you to appear in public again."

"Nice way to step aside and let the question go," his friend said dryly.

"I may return. I find the salon interesting. I don't find Richard to be so. Sorry, old friend, but whatever youthful folly he's about to commit bores me. The lady in question is lovely and much smarter than she appears to be. She isn't an evil crib-robber. When you come right down to it, she could do much better. Richard, so far as I can see, can't. In fact, he hasn't changed at all from when I first met him."

"He was all of five when you met him."

"Exactly," Simon said, saluting him with his wineglass.

"That may be so," the viscount admitted. "And yet you say you may continue to go there anyway. I'm glad my asking a favor of you got you out of your seclusion, my friend."

"Aha," Simon said, nodding. "So I was right. That was your goal."

"Only partially. I'm still convinced something is going forth beneath your nose, and mine. No matter, time will tell. If you found nothing to be alarmed about at Lady Harwood's house, I am comforted. But I wonder, has this new sociability of yours had anything to do with the crowd of sparkling conversationalists, or is it the delightful young thing who in the guise of teaching infants the dance shows her delightful young bum to the immediate world?"

Simon froze.

"One doesn't have to have been in London to know what's happening," the viscount remarked.

"She doesn't show her bum to anyone, at least anyone I know of," his friend said curtly. "She was knocked down, and when she fell there was a shapely leg showing from under a heap of giggling little girls. That was it. Your brother, by the way, offered her his help to stand up. He earned the hatred of every gentleman there by doing it. But it wasn't a wile on her part, or intentional, I'd swear to that. She's a well-born female down on her luck. And an innocent."

"Indeed? You know her that well?"

"I made it my business to know everything about everyone in that household," Simon said in bored tones. "It's what you asked of me. At least I can tell you that she has no designs on Richard." He slapped his hands on his knees and stood up. "So, my friend, will I see you at Lady Harwood's salon? She receives callers on Wednesdays and Fridays."

"I think I may be there," the viscount said.

"I thought you might," Simon said, smiling.

His friend raised an eyebrow. "Why?"

"Because you came to London."

"I was on the track of an old book I've long sought."

"And a new caricature, no doubt. Good evening, Proctor. I'd ask you to come out with me for a night on the town, but no doubt you'd rather be by your fireside, with another old book or three."

"And you?"

"Me? I'm off to my house, with a new book."

"So your sociability was really only for my sake?"

"Do you doubt it?"

"But now you've found an interest?"

Simon shrugged. "Who knows? That's what makes it interesting."

Jane knew the exact moment that people arrived and began watching her dance class. She'd been waiting for it. The butler had gleefully reported that the salon was filled to the brim with Quality. He even named famous names. Jane wanted to turn around and go home. But if this made her more valuable to her employer, she simply couldn't afford to. Instead, she vowed to give them a show, all right—she'd show them how a dance instructress managed to train even tiny children. She'd consider it as being an advertisement for herself.

She didn't have to look to the doorway to know there was a crowd there now. She saw it in the eyes of the little girls as they moved around the ballroom. Their expressions showed sudden excitement and a new determination. The governess missed a note on the piano. Although the onlookers didn't make a sound, Jane swore she could hear them in the doorway, breathing.

She knew that if she lifted her gaze they'd be watching her avidly, hoping for a spectacular stumble. But she had a living to earn, and it wouldn't be by imitating what she heard those scandalous females in France did at *their* exhibitions. Not if she could help it. She was an instructress of the dance. She was also heartily sick of the whole thing. It had been going on for two weeks now, and it seemed to her that the crowds only increased. She vowed to ignore them.

But the girls might well fall and hurt themselves in their excitement, so she had to keep order. "All right, now children," she said. "We've been ducklings, we've been geese. Today we learn to be swans, graceful and supple. That means easily bent." She heard a titter, quickly muffled. It didn't come from the children.

"I mean," she went on, "we are flexible, we move

with ease. Now, we step forward, like this, and then we swirl around back until we're facing in the direction where we started. Then we step forward again. Remember; be sure to have your balance before you take your next step. Miss Rogers," she told the governess, "some peaceful music for a flock of swans, if you please. Now, girls, form a line, watch, and then follow me."

She took a step forward, arms above her, her slender form in her light blue gown making her look like a nymph rising from the water. Then she gracefully spun around, paused, and stepped forward again. She looked over her shoulder. The girls were doing a creditable job of it; the crowd at the door was silent. They'd soon grow bored with such tame goings-on, she hoped. So she smiled and stepped forward again, swirled, paused, went forward and swirled. Suddenly something hard and cold snatched at her ankle, holding her, tripping her. She stumbled and couldn't stop herself in time to prevent falling.

She fell forward in a crouch, on her knees. She was shocked but retained sense enough to grab her skirt to keep it from flying. She knelt on the ballroom floor, head down, trying to hold sudden tears back as the girls crowded in around her. Her knees hurt, but her feelings hurt more. Someone from the crowd of onlookers had actually tripped her for sport.

There was a rising excited hubbub from the guests; the little girls were shouting and some began crying. Jane discovered that she couldn't get up right away. She placed her hands flat on the floor but couldn't rise. Her wind as well as her wits had flown along with her dignity.

A hand reached out to her, she took it and let herself be pulled to a stand. She looked up into Lord Granger's eyes. His expression was all concern. "Are you hurt?" he asked. "Jane, can you walk?"

"I don't know," she said truthfully. "Who did that?"

"A fool," he said. "He ran the moment you fell, leaving his damned walking stick behind with you."

She looked down at the shiny curved ebony-handled walking stick on the ballroom floor. "Why?" was all she could ask.

"Because George Maxwell *is* a great fool," Lady Harwood snapped, as she stepped up to them. "Richard is even now pursuing him, as are some of my other guests. Maxwell will pay for this

outrage. My lord, can you take her down to the
kitchens? I'll ask Nurse to see to her. Ladies and
gentlemen," she said, turning to her fascinated
guests. "Let us please leave the poor woman to be
tended to. Return with me to the salon and we'll
try to piece events together. Children, wait here
with Miss Green, and we'll have your nannies
and nurses with you as soon as may be."

Before Jane could say anything, or try to bear
weight, Simon put his arm under her knees and
swept her up. "Damn," he muttered, looking
down at her knees as her skirt rose over her legs.
"Blood. You did hurt yourself. Send for a physician," he called to Lady Harwood before she left.
"She's been hurt."

Jane protested that she could walk, and kept
doing so all the way down to the kitchens. But she
didn't want to leave his arms when she got there,
even though by then she was sure she was only
bruised. She wanted to stay where she was so he
wouldn't have a chance to bruise her spirit again.

The staff made a huge fuss over her. They made
sure she had a comfortable chair to sit in, and
hauled another one over for her to put her feet up
on. Cook made her tea. The butler came and went
several times to report her progress to his mis-

tress, so she could inform her guests. He told Jane that a flock of young gentlemen had gone after the unfortunate Mr. Maxwell as he fled, chasing him through the streets, some of them shouting "Tally ho!" Nurse put cold compresses on Jane's knees until the physician came and tested her legs, her reflexes, and then carefully bandaged up her aching knees. And Lord Granger stayed at her side through every moment of it, holding her hand through the bad bits.

Eventually Jane noticed the staff noticing that. They dropped their gazes and went about their duties as they saw Lord Granger looking at them too. "It's done, my lord," she whispered to him then. "I'm fine. Thank you for your help. But you don't have to stay with me any longer."

"I never had to," he said, a smile finally touching his lips. "I choose to."

She nodded, and looked down at the lump her bandaged knees made under her thin gown. "Thank you. But as I said, I can do for myself now."

"Can you?" he asked quietly. "You didn't want anything to do with me when you decided I had no need of you any longer. Now you need me as much as I still require your services."

"But the world is here now," she said, looking him straight in the eyes. "Everyone comes to my lady's salon. Surely you don't need anything from me that you can't get for yourself." She felt her cheeks grow warm, and hastily added, "I mean, I was told that young Richard's older brother, the viscount himself, is here today! That's quite a coup for my lady. Between the two of you gentlemen there's surely no need for me, or any other informant, is what I meant to say."

"Look at you, blushing peony pink," he commented. "I'd love to know what you think you said. What an interesting imagination you must have, Jane."

It was wonderfully attractive, she thought, the way his eyes crinkled at the corners when he was amused. She had to smile too.

"At any rate," he said, "I'll wait until you feel entirely recovered, and then I'll take you home."

"Oh no!" she gasped. Then, seeing some of the staff turn and look in her direction, she lowered her voice and whispered, "That will make the gossip even worse."

"What gossip? Aside from that about oaf Maxwell's stupidity?"

"My lord," she said, in grieved tones, "surely you know what people will say if they see or hear of you paying too much attention to me, a mere servant? Especially a servant who got herself into the broadsheets for what some are saying was a deliberate, vulgar, shocking display of herself."

"No. What sort of people do you know, Jane? I never found gory knees provocative, myself."

"I mean, last time. And this time. I'm becoming famous for all the wrong reasons. And your attentions will make me even more so."

"Do you think so?" he asked with interest. "Well, that will make your Lady Harwood even more pleased, I should think."

As though the mention of her name had conjured the lady up, the butler entered the kitchens and came to Jane's side. "My lord," he said, clearing his throat, "if Miss Chatham is able to walk, my lady wishes to speak with her. If Miss Chatham is unable to walk by herself, I am instructed to tell her that there is a pair of footmen waiting to convey her. The other guests have all left, my lord," he added pointedly.

"And so clearly I overstayed my call," Simon said, rising to his feet. He smiled down at Jane.

"You'll do. And don't worry. I have a feeling that the lady knows that full well too. Then, until we meet again, Jane, I bid you good evening, and better luck in future."

Jane watched his tall slender form as he left the kitchens. She bit her lip. "It isn't what you think," she told the butler absently.

"It isn't my job to think, Miss," he said. "Just to get you to my lady. She's waiting, and one thing I can tell you, she doesn't like to wait."

"Miss Chatham," Lady Harwood said, as Jane ducked a small bow to her. The lady lounged on a settee in her salon. She was relaxing after her stint as hostess. She'd pulled a bright ribbon from her hair and was idly swinging it in her fingers as she watched Jane. "I see you can walk. But I'll wager you'll be stiff tomorrow. Such a dangerous occupation you've chosen, Miss Chatham."

Jane's body stiffened. "Today's misadventure wasn't my fault, my lady. But I'm sorry for it anyway."

"Of course it was your fault. The dolt felt cheated because he hadn't gotten a flash of female flesh for his time and effort. We go from notoriety to infamy."

Jane's stomach felt cold.

"I'll have to give numbers out to my guests if they want to get into my salon next time," the lady murmured with satisfaction.

"You aren't going to turn me out?" Jane asked in confusion.

"Good lord, no! You are the making of me. In time the novelty will wear off, of course, and you can go naked for all they'll care. For now, I've gotten them here. I'll fete them and flatter them and let them take care of the rest. London Society likes to flock, Miss Chatham. I'm trying to provide them with this season's roost. The more people who come now, the more invitations I'll receive now and all year, and soon I'll never have to spend another lonely hour. And if I find a gentleman to while away the rest of my time for the rest of my life by doing so, I'll be pleased. The marriage mart is like a fishing expedition. And I'll have got me the biggest pool in London town." She laughed.

Jane felt both flattered and hurt. It was unusual for any employer to confide in her. It wasn't done, unless they'd known each other for years. She felt flattered. And then, thinking about it, she was hurt. The lady was talking to her without reservation because she wasn't an equal. It was as if she were confiding in a dog, or a horse. She knew Jane was so far beneath her that it would go no further.

And then Jane changed her opinion, quickly.

The lady looked hard at her. "I hear you've gotten yourself a beau, too. Oh, sit down. I have to talk with you, and my knees ache just looking at you and thinking of what you must feel. I'm not heartless, you know. Just single-minded." She laughed again. "How apt. We're both single, hoping to be double. Don't protest your innocence. I saw how you looked at Granger, but give it no thought because it's how most females look at him. It's how he looked at you that made me decide to give you advice."

"I didn't, that is to say . . ."

"It doesn't make any difference if you threw out lures. I'm not blaming you. I'm telling you this for your own sake. Really. I like Granger, but he's not a candidate for my hand no matter how attractive he is, or how wealthy, and he is both. And he's intelligent. Which makes it even more of a pity."

Jane looked at her, uncomprehending.

"Lord Granger was in the light cavalry during the war," the lady said patiently. "Then he left them, and word was that he was running secret missions into France. And then, someone informed on him, they say, and he was caught. He was captured, convicted, and spent a year, a full year, in the deepest dungeons somewhere in Paris."

Jane caught her breath. The lady saw it, and nodded.

"Yes, a terrible experience from all accounts. He won't discuss it, but others do. He was, they say, defiant with his captors. They were, all know, cruel. He was lucky to get out alive, if not precisely whole." She sighed. "You see, one of the strangest rumors has turned out to be true. Granger was a lady's man before he was captured. That is, he was a favorite with all females, of every class, and what's more, was a man who never had to pay for his pleasures. With wit, charm, and fascinating looks, he was sighed after everywhere he went, even though there are surely more handsome men in the world. But he liked females, and they understood that, and liked him in return. A great many good men were maimed or killed in the war, but everyone was devastated when they heard he was captured and being tormented. But all say he never divulged anything to his captors.

"Lord Granger was eventually spirited out of

the prison by His Majesty's own secret agents, and from all accounts, he was in desperate condition. Still, he recovered, and in time returned to England. But since he's been back, he's been celibate. No flirts, no mistresses. He courts no lady. He patronizes no convenients. In fact, he became a recluse. Now he's returned to London, and still avoids intimacy with females. He was, they say," she added in a dramatic whisper, "emasculated, when he was in prison."

Jane's expression was puzzled.

The lady's was impatient as she shook her head. "There's not much to be said for innocence. I've no idea why some men prefer it in a female, although I've a fairly good idea of why Granger does now. They tortured him, beat him, etcetera. But worst of all is that they finally chopped him, my dear. Cut off his vital parts."

Jane still looked bewildered.

"You're a country girl," the lady said in exasperation. "At least you grew up there. What I'm trying to tell you is that he was, they say, *gelded*."

Jane gasped.

"Yes," the lady said, nodding. "Dreadful. That's why he can't be anything but a friend to females now. Which is also likely why he's attracted to you.

You have no experience. And I tell you, Miss Chatham, if you remain with him, you never will. He likely feels as safe with you as you would be with him. I suppose a penniless girl could do worse. You may well be a match for the poor fellow. A worldlier chit might gossip about it. You, well-bred but coming from nowhere with no friends or family, and burdened as you are with morals, would not. All I'm trying to tell you is that I don't disapprove. But let it be said that I was charitable. I warned you."

Jane nodded, too devastated to speak. "Has anyone seen . . . the problem?" she whispered at last.

"He'd hardly show it off!" the lady said. "And at that, there's nothing to show, so why should he? Now, run along, Miss Chatham. I did my bit for charity. You will not speak of this, of course."

"Never!" Jane whispered.

"Then take your money for the day and go home. When you return you will doubtless hear what happened to Maxwell. He eluded capture. But he's lucky if he doesn't end up like poor Granger. The gentlemen are very angry with him. It's one thing for a girl to show her assets; it's another for a man to harm her by trying to do the same thing. At least, it is, while Society is looking on. Good evening, Miss Chatham."

Jane bowed, and backed away. She went into the hallway and accepted her day's wages from the butler.

"There's a hackney waiting for you, Miss," he said. "And a good thing too. You don't want to walk tonight. Good night," he said sympathetically as a footman opened the door for her and helped her down the short front steps. "Better luck next time."

She hardly heard him. Her heart was hurting as well as her knees, and her head was in a whirl. The hackney at the curb had a door open. She accepted the footman's hand and climbed in painfully. Lord Granger was sitting in the backseat, waiting for her, dressed in his laborer disguise.

Jane's eyes were filled with tears. "Too good of you to come for me," she whispered as she sat down.

"You're not angry?" he asked, raising an eyebrow. "You were last time."

"Last time," she said, "I didn't know what I know now. Thank you, my lord, and if I can be of any service to you, please let me know."

He cocked his head to the side. "Well, here's a turnabout. I like it. Will you have dinner with me this evening? The same place? No one will know us, but they will remember our appetite. If I can't heal your knees, at least I can please your palate."

"Thank you," she said softly.

"You're weeping? Good lord, Jane. You *are* hurting!"

She could only shake her head in agreement. She was in pain and nothing he could do or say could help her—or himself.

Chapter 8

The mishaps she'd experienced in the past weeks had changed her, Simon thought as he watched Jane eat her dinner in their usual corner of the tavern with him that night. It was nothing you could see. She wore a simple blue frock that her slender form made appear elegant. She still wore her hair pulled back tightly and tied in a dancer's knot at the back of her shapely head. It was a stark way for a female to dress her hair, but it suited her, showing off her finely made features. She didn't seem to be in any pain, but she was suddenly softer, more docile, and there was sorrow and worry in her eyes. He didn't care for it. He wanted to see the proud tilt of her head and hear the way she shot back at him if he said anything that displeased her.

Damn Maxwell for a fool, he thought again. He hoped that once she knew she wasn't in danger from anyone anymore, he'd see the old Jane Chatham again. And then he frowned, because he knew very well he shouldn't see the old or the new Jane Chatham again. He had nothing to offer her, after all. At least nothing she would be happy about taking, even if she did.

"We can't meet like this again," she suddenly said, breaking into his thoughts.

"What?" he said.

"I mean, this really must be our final meeting. Now that Richard's brother, the viscount, is attending the salon, there's no more need for me to tell you what I hear or see." Her lips quirked in a sad smile. "I hate to give up the wages, but I won't take money out of charity, which would be the only motive for you keeping me in your service."

"Not a word about how reluctant you are to stop seeing me?" he asked before he could think better of it.

"Yes, of course, I am," she said, looking down at her plate. "But there's nothing to be done about it."

"What if I ask you to give me dancing lessons?"

That made her laugh. It gave him time to think. "It's ridiculous that two civilized people can't meet again," he said.

"No, not at all," she answered, looking at him steadily. "Not if they are of two different genders and classes. You'd escape censure. But I wouldn't. I'm not a member of the *ton*. The worst would be thought of me even if we didn't . . ."

He frowned. There was only one question he wanted to ask her. And tonight this new softened look in her eyes when she looked at him gave him the courage to try again. Was he being a slow top? She'd changed toward him. He had to know how much.

"Perhaps you now might consider an alliance with me?" he asked. "No misunderstandings, please. I mean what you think: pleasure for both of us. An association in which I'm responsible for you, and you are obliging to me. I could secure a flat for you, and a maid. I'd pay well and never ask you for more than you're willing to give. It would help you financially and I flatter myself that you don't actually dislike me."

He hoped she wouldn't ask him to explain more. Strangely, he thought it might actually embarrass him. If she did understand, he hoped she wouldn't spring from her chair and storm from the tavern. But given her present sad mood he doubted she would. It was a wild gamble. She might even say yes.

She didn't spring from her chair. And she clearly understood. She put up a hand, as if in defense. "Please," she said in a choked voice. "Don't ask that of me. It's not that I'm a prig, but such an arrangement would be absolutely unthinkable for me. You know my answer, whatever the circumstances."

"I'm sorry. I suppose I did know. But I thought it was worth a try."

The pity of it was that she wasn't wrong, he thought. It was an unthinkable occupation for a woman like her. He knew the way of such things, even with a good, undemanding fellow. Even a charming new mistress grew tiresome after a while. The nature of the relationship itself predicted its uncomfortable ending. Only old men married their mistresses, and Simon imagined that was because once a man was set in his ways it meant all ways.

But Jane? If she accepted such an arrangement it would be delicious. At least, it would be for him, and he'd try to be sure it was for her as well.

Still, an employer and an employee were never equals. Money changed everything. When he inevitably left her she'd have to go to another gentleman and then another, and would either end up a famous courtesan, or a ruined woman, good for little but a position in a bawdy house and then street trade. None of it was what he'd want for her.

She scrabbled in her purse to find a handkerchief. He handed her his. She dabbed at her eyes and nose. Then she held up the handkerchief. "This is snowy white," she said in a thickened voice. "What's a bloke like you doing with a fine bit of linen like this?"

He started, and then remembered his disguise. Tonight, he was a common laborer again. "My old Mam sent it along," he said. "She thinks I should always act the gent even if I'm not one, and it's the best one I have, so hand it back, if you please."

She sniffled, and then cocked her head to the side. "I know that's a joke, but are you close to your mother?"

"I used to be," he said with a shrug. "She died. Father too. And I have no siblings." He smiled. "Sure you don't want to mother me? Take pity on my orphaned state?"

"I never saw anyone less in need of mothering," she said, tried to smile, and failed.

"What the devil has got you so sad tonight?" he asked. "You were sorrowing even before I made my dishonorable offer. Is it the incident with the cane today? You said you were fine. Were you telling the truth?"

"Yes," she said. "I suppose I'm still upset with that and everything else. I spoke to Lady Harwood before I left. She didn't blame me for what happened. In fact, we talked for a while and she was charming to me. Told me all sort of things. One of them upset me."

"And it was?" he asked.

She took a breath, and drew an invisible pattern on the tabletop with her finger. "Nothing I didn't know," she said, evading his eyes. "She was only being kind enough to warn. She was trying to make it clear to me that my services are a novelty and the new rage, and that it won't last. Well, I never thought it would. But hearing it from her made it seem more real, and doubtless, the fact that she told me meant it will come sooner than I'd expected."

She lowered her eyes when she spoke to him. If she were any other female he'd have been sure she regretted her answer to him and was trying to reopen the subject, angling for a position as his companion. But this was Miss Chatham. Pretty and proper Jane Chatham was lamenting her short stay in a lucrative position as dancing instructress. She now knew that watching a young female instructing infants in the dance was a novelty that might have already worn off if someone hadn't tried to make her tumble tonight. This way, the fame of the incident would keep the *ton* coming back. But it wouldn't last.

He reached out and took her hand. Her eyes widened but she didn't pull it from his. "If I could, I'd ask you to marry me," he began to say. Then he shook his head. "No, that's not true. I'm not in the market for a wife of any social status. And marrying you is the only honorable thing I can do with you. But I'm sure you'll agree we don't know each other half enough for something as important as that. So will you at least keep company with me for a while?"

She almost began weeping again. She felt terrible at his having to make up such excuses for his inability to offer her marriage. She'd have had trouble answering him even if he'd been a whole man, but as it was, knowing what she now knew, she hardly knew what to say. She supposed there were things he could do with her as a mistress that he wouldn't think of doing with a wife, poor man.

"Oh my," she said, attempting to joke. "And here I was hoping to have swept you off your feet. I always wanted to have that effect on a man, but never did. I'm not the sweeping sort."

His smile was so tender it made her heart ache. He looked so handsome, so healthy, and was so wildly attractive to her that she kept forgetting his tragedy.

"We can't meet in secret," she said seriously, slowly slipping her hand from his. "I hate secrecy."

"Actually, I enjoy it," he mused. "Hence, I suppose, my work in France before we clapped Napoleon up on Elba. I worked in secrecy for the government. I found it much more exciting than charging, saber held high, into an advancing enemy."

"I heard about that," she said falteringly. "You asked me to listen to gossip and I did. They say that you were captured by the French and imprisoned."

"Then this time gossip has it exactly right," he said on a shrug. "Only the French didn't do it on their own. Someone informed on me. It doesn't matter who now. She's been seen to."

"It was a hideous experience," she said, with no question in her voice.

"So it was," he agreed, and fell still. He refused to speak of it. He'd passed too many long nights since, remembering those dark, cold nights he'd sat alone, wondering if they'd let him live to see another.

They sat quietly a moment. "But nothing is ever without some merit, however small," he finally said. "The one thing I learned from the experience is patience. If you ever change your mind, Miss Chatham, you have only to send to me. I'll come for you. In the meanwhile, would you mind continuing your work with me? I can't see everything."

"Kind of you," she said, sitting up straighter. "But we both know that's unnecessary. Thank you for a lovely dinner. I'll see you again, no doubt, at Lady Harwood's, until she tires of my services. But we both know my work for you is done. However," she said, holding up a finger the way a schoolmistress might, "if I come across anything truly sensational that I think you mightn't know about the lady, or young Richard, be sure I'll let you know."

He looked at her, and in that moment, against all his better judgment, almost offered for her in truth. But he couldn't. It wouldn't be fair to either of them. It wasn't only his recent celibacy. He'd never thought himself susceptible to a pair of lovely eyes and lips; now he knew he was. Still, he was right. She was a stranger. He'd investigated her and taken her to dinner twice, but he knew too well that he didn't know her that well, any more than she really knew him. And she was right; they couldn't keep company, for her sake. Their friendship, or whatever it was growing to be, had to end now.

He beckoned to the innkeeper so he could pay the tally. "Then I'll take you home, Miss Chatham," he said, rising to his feet. "And hope you hold a good thought for me until we meet again."

She smiled, as she rose from her seat. "And I, you, Lord Granger. But it's better said: *if* we meet again."

"So it is," he agreed.

They drove back to her street and said nothing.

Only as Jane left the hackney cab, she paused on the stair and looked back at him. He could see the tears in her eyes in the flickering light of the lanterns set on the side of the hackney cab.

"I wish I could be what I'm not," she said. "But I can only be me."

"Being you should be enough for any man," he said. "I wish I were he."

She nodded, and without another word or backward look stepped down and out of the carriage. She hurried away. He watched until she was entirely gone.

When the cab let Simon down at his town house, he paused a moment on the pavement after paying the driver. He didn't feel like going home yet. In truth, he felt like whistling the hackney back, turning it around, and going straight back to Jane. He felt like pounding on her front door, and when her landlady opened it, marching directly to Jane's room, picking her up, and carrying her off with him. But then reality intruded.

Carry her off where? To the border for a hasty marriage over the anvil? Why not? He had few relatives to shock. His friends would shake their heads, but what of that? He thought of her smile and her laughter, her grace and her wit, her long shapely legs and her warm mouth, and was sorely tempted.

But he stood quietly and let the hackney drive off into the night. Was Jane as warmhearted and kind as she seemed? Could he share his life with her? The war wasn't over; nor was it over for him. He had scores to settle. And when he'd seen to everything, there was the larger omnipresent question: had his imprisonment changed him so irreparably that he could never be a good husband to any woman, let alone a fit one for any female? And specifically, Jane? He didn't know her well enough to decide.

But how could he get to know her, to talk with her, much less make love to her, without harming her? He was a wealthy, titled gentleman. She was well-bred, but she had nothing but her wit, skill, and reputation to earn her livelihood. Still, he'd solved far more difficult problems. This was something he'd have to ponder. First, he'd have to see if his infatuation, for he realized that was what it was now, would last.

Deep in thought, he went slowly up the steps to his house.

"My lord," his man said, opening the door

before Simon had got his key into the lock. "You have a visitor."

"At this hour?" Simon murmured in surprise.

"You once gave me instructions to always allow Viscount Delancey, my lord. I thought you would want to see him now. Or did I presume too much?"

"You didn't," Simon answered as he strode into his house. His pulses picked up their beat. Was there still work for him to do?

"Proctor," he said with pleasure as he went into his study and saw his friend seated by the fireside. "To what do I owe this intrusion?"

The viscount stood, and permitted himself a thin smile. "I can always leave, Simon."

"So you can," Simon said as he took a chair opposite his old friend. "Sit, sit," he told Proctor. Then he leaned forward eagerly. "But not until you tell me why you're here. Work for me, I hope?"

"I thought we had agreed you were out of things now that you're safely home again," his friend answered as he seated himself again.

Simon shrugged. "Time changes some things. So, is there a job of work for me?"

"The war goes on, but my friend, you do not go

on working for us. You've paid enough, we've all agreed. No," the viscount said, looking strangely ill at ease, "I've come for some advice."

"Advice?"

"Yes, if you'd be so kind. You know the Lady Harwood, her salon, and her household. I thought you could counsel me."

Simon sat back, disappointed. He shook his head. "I told you all, Proctor, and what I didn't you surely saw for yourself. If you have any more questions, I'm sure Richard will answer them. He's young and in love for the first time, doubtless he'll want to crow about his lady. Unless," he said, "it's the lady herself you're aiming for? Speaking of jobs of work, that would certainly be one. Not that there's anything wrong with Lady Harwood, but your brother would be beside himself if you courted her now."

The viscount made a dismissive gesture. "He's in calf love, and is bright enough, I think, to begin to realize that soon enough. She's after a husband, and is only interested in him as bait. His constant attendance brings in more gentlemen as company. But no. It's not Lady Harwood, charming and lovely as she may be. The one I speak of is one I encountered at the lady's salon." He held up a hand. "I am not ready to tell her name yet, even to you. It is far too soon for that. But I am certainly ready to hear your opinion."

"Of a nameless female? Proctor, I'm a patriot and a spy, not a fortune-teller. How can I advise you about an unknown lady?"

The viscount squirmed. Simon sat forward, interested.

"I need your opinion—of myself, Simon," the viscount confessed. "There is no one else I would go to for it. I respect your judgment, and further," he added with a steely look, "I refuse to be embarrassed, and I know you would not make mock of me."

"Of course not," Simon answered.

"I believe the difficulty lies in the fact I know I'm not one to fascinate the women," Proctor went on. "My title, my finances, and my holdings do intrigue many of them. That I know, too well. I want a woman to want me for more. I know I'm considered rather dry, in conversation and in appearance. But I'm not ancient. Clearly, that isn't enough. Now I discover I must become more interesting. I ask only that you tell me what I can do to enhance my prospects, as regards women."

"No," Simon breathed, sitting back, looking genuinely surprised. "You?" Then he smiled. "I suppose it makes sense. Even I forget that you're not as old as you appear to be. We're of an age, but you've always acted older. Of course you'd want to consider marriage at your age. Any man would."

Proctor raised an eyebrow.

"Excluding me, of course," Simon quickly said. "I lost a year, and more, in that damned French dungeon, as well as losing the concepts of trust and belief in any female. Well, I'm probably better off without them. I want only to be free now. But you? Proctor," he said, grinning. "I'm honored. Of course I'll be happy to play Pygmalion for you. Together, we can make you an Adonis. By the way, is there any hurry to this? Have you met a lady who interests you?"

Proctor nodded. "Yes. One I should like to see more of."

"In every way?"

"Of course, I am not a monastic, you know. Or if you don't, then you should understand that in all things I am discreet. I do have a liaison of sorts, at home. A female under my wing, so to speak. But she expects nothing but money from me, and that,

I can supply. I want more. I need polish; I need practice in being charming. I have no looks, but I do have a brain. I need you to show me how to use it in order to fascinate a female. That, my friend, you can still do. You were born with the ability and now you radiate it, whether you want to or not."

Simon sat back and studied his friend. "Your clothes are the best quality, you're clean in your habits, and you don't drink or bet huge sums of money on nonsense. You have a good eye for horseflesh, but you don't drive flashy and expensive sporting carriages, and you hunt only the enemies of your country. You're discreet in everything, as a brilliant spy must be. We have to change that. I don't expect you to become a Tulip of the *ton*, or a gamester or a drunkard. But you have to become more interesting."

Simon rose from his chair and stared into the blazing hearth. "No," he said absently. "Forget that. This isn't a comedy, it's your life." He picked up a poker and stabbed a log. Then he put it back and faced his friend. "Any worthwhile woman would want you as you are. You said I was born with the ability to attract women? I wasn't. In truth, the point is that I have always liked women.

They can see that in my eyes, my voice, and my actions. Seeing my interest, they respond to it." He cocked his head to the side. "I know you well, and for years, as you said. But there are still things I don't know. How do you feel about the other half of the population, Proctor? How do you feel about women, in general?"

"They serve a purpose, they provide children and ease. But I find they aren't brilliant conversationalists, at least not until they grow old. I admire them. But I think you're right. I don't think of them often, unless the need is upon me. Though I can speak with them, I find them trivial in mind, and flighty in actions. That, I fear, cannot change."

Simon nodded again. "And there's many a woman who won't find that a bar to marriage with you. Many *are* trivial and flighty. But you'd go mad with a wife like that. You need a woman who is your equal in intelligence."

The viscount coughed.

"It is possible, Proctor. There are women who are even smarter that you are. But the thing is that a clever female hides her wit under her bonnet when she's with a man like you. A man with your attitude doesn't exactly encourage her to show her knowledge. She speaks with you, and then either ignores you, or if she's interested in your title and funds, is as trivial as you expect her to be. If you want a wife like that, you have to change your opinion of her entire sex. Or at least pretend to until you know better."

"I can pretend to anything. Very well, Simon, I will." He walked toward the door. "I'm going to Lady Harwood's grand ball. You can be with me to show me how I must go on."

"I wasn't invited to any ball."

"Yes, you were," the viscount said, rising from his chair. "It is taking place in two weeks time. Your invitation is lying on the front table on that silver dish your man uses to place them in, as all good menservants do, luckily enough for me. I will consider what you said, and see you at the ball, if not sooner, because I intend to visit there often. But wait," he said, turning around. "Now that your errand for me is done, I expect I won't see you there until the ball."

"Then you expect wrongly. I find myself interested in the goings-on at the lady's salon," Simon answered. "Depend on it. I'll be there too."

The viscount frowned. "How so?"

"I can't wait for you to tell me who the lucky lady is," Simon said, laughing. "Care to wager that I'll find her out before you're ready to tell me?"

His friend's expression cleared. "Done," he said with a wry smile. "I doubt you will. But you're welcome to try."

Chapter 9

Jane thought she'd rather be anywhere on earth than where she stood waiting. Even though her work was over for the day, now it seemed it wouldn't be over until late night. This was her employer's grand ball. Jane stood by the balustrade in the upstairs hallway and looked down. It seemed that she was watching the gentry arrive for a night at the opera rather than coming to a ball. She was high above them, but the truth was she seldom witnessed anything that showed her exactly how far beneath them she was.

Even from her viewpoint she could see the guests were gorgeously gowned, impeccably attired. They were smiling, laughing, and chatting as they waited to be announced. When the last guest had crammed into the ballroom, Lady

Harwood's baby daughter, all decked out in a ballerina costume, would be called down to make her bows to the guests. Instead of only her nurse attending her, Jane had been ordered to be there too to give the child confidence so she could dance a few steps for the company.

A chair had been provided for old nurse, and the little Leticia sat in her lap. The child wore long white gauzy skirts and her tiny feet were encased in silver slippers that she kept holding up for her own inspection. They fascinated her more than the arriving company did. But for all her splendor, when she wasn't rubbing her eyes, her thumb slid into her mouth.

Jane wasn't weary even after a day of dancing, but she was deeply distressed. No matter how often she named herself a servant, she'd never really felt so much like one before. She'd named herself as such first so that she wouldn't be shocked if anyone else ever called her that. No one had, but this night, this ball, and her position at it, now screamed the word at her.

She wore a simple lavender gown and pale lavender slippers, hair in her usual knot, as befit a dance instructress, and of course no jewels. She looked, she thought, plain and neat. The women below had peacock, pheasant, and egret feathers bobbing atop elaborate hairstyles. Their gowns were spectacular: colorful, glittering, cut so low at the throat that from where she stood Jane could see clear down their necklines to their breasts. That was, she could when she wasn't blinded by lamp and candlelight reflected off their diamond-encrusted and variously gemmed necklaces and tiaras.

The gentlemen were magnificent in black and white. Even the footmen wore their best livery. A person's costume told their state in life and tonight Jane felt unusually lowly and downtrodden. That was because she was, she thought on a sigh. Not that she'd never attended a ball. Her chin went up as she remembered balls she'd gone to in the days when her family was at least solvent enough to afford to reciprocate. Those balls, however, were in the countryside and even a child's dazzled eyes couldn't mistake one of them for this affair.

This night the ballroom was out of bounds for her too. Ironic, she thought bitterly, because it was the place she used to consider her room in this house, the place where she taught.

She stood patiently until she saw Lord Granger enter. Even from her eagle's eye view, she couldn't mistake him. But then, she'd been watching for him. He came in alone and stood tall after he gave his hat and walking stick to a footman, and his card to the butler. He looked around himself and then, looked up. He saw her in that moment. She was sure of it. Then he casually glanced away. Of course, she told herself angrily. Had she expected him to wave at her? She took in a breath and stood tall herself, and watched the top of his dark head as he gazed at the other guests.

In time, he was announced and she saw him saunter into the ballroom. She waited.

The sounds of waltzes and country dances, minuet and polka tunes wafted through the ballroom doors into the front hall. Jane's feet itched to move. She allowed herself to tap a foot, now and then. And then at last there was a pause in the music. The butler appeared, looked up to Jane, Nurse, and Leticia, and signaled them to come downstairs.

Jane paused at the door to the ballroom. She'd never seen it in such array. Flowers were everywhere. The chandeliers blazed, glittering and flaring with the light of hundreds of candles. The drab covers were gone, what she could see of the dance floor shone like a lake in the sunlight.

Lady Harwood clapped her hands in delight as her daughter came into the ballroom. "Ah, here she is!" she cried. "The premiere dancer we were awaiting. Ladies and gentlemen, my darling Leticia!"

There was applause and laughter as Leticia, as rehearsed, carefully made her curtsey to the crowd, with only a little wobbling. "Will you dance for us, my love?" her mother asked.

Leticia nodded gravely, and stepped forward toward her mama. The guests politely drew back and cleared the floor. With a backward look to Jane, who was trying to blend into the wall, the child struck a pose. Her mother nodded to the leader of the musicians hidden behind a bank of flowers at the head of the ballroom. The music started, and little Leticia began to dance.

It wasn't much of a dance, consisting mostly of a few awkward twirls and small steps that Jane had patiently drummed into her. The girl's plump legs moved as instructed. If she wasn't in time with the music, at least she didn't stumble. Leticia's expression was grim as death. She watched her feet as if she suspected them of trying to trip her, and Jane held her breath until the last step was faithfully taken.

The company applauded, Leticia curtsied again. She stole a triumphant glance toward Jane. Someone must have seen where she was looking. Because then someone in the crowd cried out. "Huzzah! There she is. Now give us the tumbling dance, mistress. Let's have a look at her!" This sally was greeted by masculine hoots and whistles.

Jane froze as quickly as Lady Harwood's smile did.

"Yes, give us the wench in person," another would-be wit shouted into the merriment. "Let's see a bit of the famous legs or a bum. Let's have some of her exotic dancing!"

Jane didn't wait to hear what her employer said. She darted from the ballroom. She made for the hallway and the front door. But she ran into someone, who held her fast. She looked up to see Lord Granger.

"I thought you had courage," he said.

"Courage?" she cried. "There's nothing but shame in that room for me."

"Shame if you run. Pride maintained if you go in as you are, elegant and respectable. Bow to the crowd and accept their praise of the child. If you leave now you may never be let back in.

Don't desert your lady now. Believe it or not, she needs you now as never before."

He looked down into Jane's incredulous eyes, and tightened his hands on her shoulders. "Yes. If you disappear they'll all be convinced that she hired a wench no better than she should be in order to gain notoriety and fame for herself. If they see you return now: modest, calm, polite and better bred than their own daughters and wives, they're the ones who'll feel shame. Courage means facing the worst, accepting it and going on nonetheless. You've done it before. Come, show me you can do it again."

She took a shuddering breath. She remembered that this man knew what he was talking about. He'd had enough courage to survive captivity and the dreadful cruelty inflicted upon him. If he could do that and go on, then she certainly could face the little bit of the world that was in the other room. She nodded.

"I'll go back," she said. "You're right."

"Of course," he said.

"But you don't have to go with me," she said quickly. "No reason to get your reputation involved with mine."

"It can only benefit mine, believe me," he said, taking her hand and placing it on his arm.

This was so sadly true that Jane stopped thinking of the ordeal ahead of her, and thought only of his trials. They walked into the ballroom together.

The room grew still.

"Miss Chatham is Lady Leticia's dance instructress," Simon announced to the company. "And she's shy. Still, she deserves her share of the applause, don't you think? I've persuaded her to take her bows too." He looked at the men in the crowd, stared from one to another, his expression changing, even as theirs went still at the threatening look in his eyes. "And if any of you . . . *any* of you, want to see something more," he continued, "I suggest you leave immediately and take yourselves to the theater or the Devil, and not force me to give you a hand—and a foot—to speed you on your way."

Everyone laughed, some with relief.

"Miss Chatham," Lady Harwood said, "I thank you for Leticia's excellent tuition."

Jane ducked her head as she heard applause and saw smiling faces. She breathed out again, looked up at Simon, whispered a low "thank you" to him before she curtsied, and as sedately as she could, left the room.

She stood outside the ballroom and waited for her heart to stop, or start, beating. She was so flustered she didn't know which it had to do, except that she felt dizzy now that she'd faced her tormentors and got away unmolested. But perhaps not quite safely, she thought, flinching as a tall, thin gentleman approached her. He gave her a small, thin smile.

"Miss Chatham?" he said, bowing. "Bravo. My brother Richard said you were an innocent in the matter that so lately fascinated London, and the moment I saw you I knew it was so. Your behavior in the face of those louts was exemplary. You left in the face of insult or injury, as you rightly should have done. You returned to show your true dignity. I applaud you. I am Delancey. My brother is a frequent visitor to Lady Harwood's salon, and to your dancing lessons as well. I hope he hasn't interfered too much."

"Not at all," Jane said as she curtsied. So this was young Richard's noble brother? The two looked like day and night. The viscount was reedy, balding, and careful in his speech. Richard was a carefree, robust young man. His older brother's manner was also so stilted and correct that it was difficult to imagine the two were related.

She stood and spoke about nothing with the viscount because she had absolutely nothing to say to him, and only yearned to leave and go away from this elegant ball. But she knew her manners too.

"See?" Richard said as he came to join them. "Didn't I tell you? She's sound as a bell. Fuss over nothing."

"But if you two fellows stand with her, out here away from the crowd," Simon said as he appeared beside George, "you'll have her caricature in the shop windows again."

"Indeed?" the viscount said with a thin smile. "And you're being here won't?"

"You're right," Richard said before Simon could answer. "I'm off. Mustn't keep my hostess waiting. She'll have my head. Good luck, Miss Chatham," he added before he headed back into the ballroom.

"And so I must go too," Jane said quickly. "Thank you, gentlemen, for your defense of me. I appreciate it. Good night." She ducked a nod of a bow, left them, and hurried down to the kitchens to get her things.

"She's a lovely creature," the viscount mused once she was out of earshot. "A sweet violet among overblown roses. Bright, well-bred and beautiful in her own quiet fashion. I should have known what kept you on the trail after you found what little there was to find about Richard, Simon."

"She may have," Simon agreed. "But now there are other developments worth noting."

The viscount's gaze sharpened. "Such as . . . ?"

"I see Sloan is here," Simon told him softly. "He was speaking to Price, and then sharing a jest with Sir Randolph."

"You've always suspected Sloan," the viscount said. "We've found no evidence of any wrongdoing. But Randolph is under scrutiny."

"So are we all. They stared at me too. Does that make them traitors? Who can say? This place is the current place to be in London. Poets and politicians rub shoulders every day in the lady's salon. And it's so crowded that no one notices, or seems to care. What an excellent meeting place if you don't want your meetings to be observed. It's hiding in plain sight, much better than plotting during solitary walks by the Thames, or meeting in out-of-the-way taverns. That, my friend, is what's keeping my interest. Miss Chatham is lovely. But it would be unfair for me to engage her interest, wouldn't you say?"

"Perhaps," his friend shrugged. "And so what are you planning to do now?"

"With the delicious dance instructress? Nothing. With those I think may be collaborating with the enemy? Everything I can."

"Be wary, Simon," the viscount warned him. "If you're right they'll stop at nothing to silence you. They've tried before, as you know too well."

"I'm always careful. But knowing a turncoat isn't something you can predict."

"And I remind you that you no longer work for us," his friend cautioned him. "You've given enough already."

"I don't intend to give anything this time. Getting, however, is a different story—and one I find I'd like to someday regale my unfortunate grandchildren with. But shouldn't we be getting back to the ball? Our absence together with Miss Chatham's will cause gossip. She's had enough, I think."

"True. I will speak with you about this again, Simon. I'd rather you didn't investigate anything but my brother's follies, if he commits them. But I know you. Remember, do you discover anything else, I want to be first to know."

"Of course," Simon said. "Dinner will soon be served. Shall we go in now?"

"To different tables when we do, yes," the viscount said. "I don't want to give anyone the wrong idea about you either."

They went back to the ballroom together. But Simon's interest in the night was gone. Proctor arrowed toward some old friends and acquaintances, and Simon followed. He joined them at the punch bowl and made polite, trivial conversation. Soon, he found the conversation too dull, the room too stuffy, and the punch too sweet. Then he discovered he didn't have an appetite for food or inane conversation. It became hard to conceal his yawns. So when the butler struck the silver bell signifying dinner was served, Simon left his friend and sought out his hostess.

She was surrounded by admirers, but was being escorted to the dining room off the ballroom on the arm of Richard Proctor. The young man looked proud and pleased. The lady looked magnificent in silver tissue gauze over satin, her fair hair topped by a crown of white flowers. Her blue eyes sparkled like silver fire. Simon had never seen her looking better, and wondered, for the first time, if her affair with young Richard might actually be real, and moreover, be a love match.

"A brilliant ball, my lady," he told her. "But if your dance card is filled, I confess I've no more reason to stay tonight."

She laughed, and tapped him with her fan. "Bilge, my dear sir, but delightful to hear. I'm sorry to say my dance card is taken, but oh, how I wish you'd asked sooner."

"A lady to your fingertips," he said, bowing over them. "Thank you, and good night then."

She pouted. "If you must go, I suppose I can't stay you. Then be sure to visit me tomorrow so we can discuss all the gossip, will you?"

He put a hand on his heart. "I will, my lady. Be sure, I will."

But as he made his way through the crowd beginning to stream past him into the dining room, he wondered if he'd be able to. He suddenly felt ill. He needed fresh air and cool water. The front hall was deserted now except for a pair of drowsy footmen. Simon asked for his hat and walking stick and stood waiting for them, hoping they'd arrive soon. He'd hate to leave without them. Then he realized he might not be able to leave at all.

The entry hall seemed to be swaying before his eyes; the clearly defined black and white marble squares in the floor were beginning to blur. He put out a hand and leaned against a marble pedestal, anxious now, but trying to maintain his dignity and balance. He cursed the fact that he hadn't brought his own carriage tonight, deciding instead to walk because of the fine night, and the prospect of the swarm of carriages waiting to drop off their passengers in the front of the town house.

He closed his eyes. His ears were buzzing so loudly it was hard for him to hear the soft voice addressing him.

"Lord Granger? My lord? Are you ill? Can I help?"

He opened his eyes to see Jane Chatham standing at his side. Even his defective vision showed her concern. "Yes," he said carefully. "Bad ache in my head. Stomach."

"Shall I call for your friend, the viscount?" she asked.

He shook his head and wished he hadn't. "No need to trouble him," he managed to say. "Will you see a hackney's called for me?"

"Of course," she said. He heard her ordering a footman to bring one around instantly, her voice suddenly as authoritative and regal as any lady guest at the ball. He stood, leaning against the pedestal for what seemed an eternity, trying to stay upright, until she came close and touched his arm.

"May I help you to the carriage, sir?" she asked.

"Aye," he said with difficulty.

With a footman on one side and Jane on the other, he made his way down the front steps to the waiting coach. Jane went in first, and the footman, supporting his weight, helped him up the short stair until he could tumble toward the seat inside. Jane caught him and helped him be seated. Then Simon sat back, blackness closing in at the edges of his vision, his senses fading. But he saw Jane rise, duck her head, and begin to leave the coach.

"Will you stay with me?" he asked. "I need someone to summon my man to come get me."

She paused. With all that was happening to him, still Simon realized what made her hesitate. "It's dark," he said. "Late. Ball's got hours to go. They're all inside now. No one will see you. I'll . . ." he paused, and said with effort, "see that you get home safe too."

He heard her sigh. She sat beside him. "Yes," she said with sudden resolve. "Your address please, my lord. I'll tell the footman to tell the driver, and we'll go immediately."

He managed to choke out his address, heard her repeat it. Then the door was closed, and he felt a jolt as the carriage began to move. And then he felt her small warm hands close tightly over his hand.

"You're so cold," she said. "What can I do to help you now?"

"Stay," he said.

"Oh, my dear sir," she said, "your color, you're so white. And your pulses are racing. What is the matter; have you any idea? Lord Granger? Can you hear me? Please, say you can hear me."

"I can."

"Then talk to me, please. Where does it hurt? What is the matter?"

"Everywhere. Hurts everywhere. And the matter . . . is . . ."

"Is what?" she cried.

"Not to worry," he said, and tried to smile. "I've only been poisoned."

Chapter 10

"**W**ait for me Jane," Simon whispered with difficulty, as his valet and a footman hooked arms around his waist and began to help him up the stair.

"Thomas," the valet told the footman, "when we get my lord to his bedchamber, go down and show her to the front salon. At least until Lord Granger summons her."

Jane's back stiffened. She was being insulted by not being addressed directly, and only as *her*. His valet obviously thought her a common sort of female who had either found his master in the street or had been alone with him when he was taken ill. After all, Simon was dressed for a gala evening and she was dressed plainly and simply. Ordinarily she'd have marched to the door and let herself out. But she had to know what was happening to Simon. "I'll wait until I've word that you'll survive," Jane said. "Then I'll be gone."

Simon turned his head. "Don't worry." He paused. "A purge and I'll do," he told her. "Wait."

The valet condescended to look at her. "I've sent for the physician. You may wait."

It looked as if Simon might say more, but then he clearly faltered, and the two helpers hastened him up the stair, supporting his weight between them.

Jane stood at the bottom of the stair. She glanced around. Lord Simon Granger's London home was gracious and well kept. The house smelled of furniture polish and the furniture that she saw, massive sideboards and chairs, were old and well made. She could see there were several rooms off the front hall to either side of the wide stair that led up to the next floor. The entry hall was marble; the paintings on the walls were dim landscapes framed in gold. Some of them, she thought, might even be by famous artists. There was nothing ostentatious. She could see nothing of Simon's personality in it. It looked like a house he inhabited rather than lived in.

Sooner than she'd thought possible, the footman came hurriedly down the stair and led her to a salon right off the hall, near the front door. Another insult, she thought as she took a chair near the hearth. This was an impersonal room where people unknown to the master of the house were told to wait. It wasn't badly furnished, but was plain and undistinguished, the sort of room one might be told to wait in until the doctor or the solicitor could see you, except that there were no framed pictures on the walls and no certificates of scholarship.

Jane wasn't in need of diversion. She had to think. Had Simon actually been poisoned? He'd said he was investigating Richard and Lady Harwood's strange relationship, but that was such a trivial task, especially in light of the fact that he'd worked at such high-risk spying in France that he'd been imprisoned for it. Imprisoned and mutilated. And now, he said he'd been poisoned. It sounded incredible. But she thought that if anyone knew the difference between a stomach upset and impending death, it would have to be Simon Granger.

Thankfully they'd left the door to the salon where she sat half open, or Jane didn't know if she could have borne the silence. The household seemed to have forgotten her. She knew she had to get home, but nothing could have induced her to leave. She sat and watched servants scurrying up and down the stair, and then saw as the physician was let in the front door. She heard a quick whispered conference with Lord Granger's valet, and then watched the two of them go up the stair.

Then, at last, she heard the doctor clearly as he came down the stair again, and gave last instructions to the valet.

"He'll do. He knew what it was, and he did the right thing even before I arrived. So, liquids now, tomorrow he may eat as he pleases, if he pleases. A sorry situation, this. I'd go to the Runners with it, but he refuses. Ah well, I suppose he knows best. If he develops a fever, send for me. Otherwise, I'll see him tomorrow afternoon. Good evening."

The front door closed, and the house was silent again.

Jane stood up, and stretched. Her vigil was over. She yawned, feeling herself relax again. She wasn't used to such late hours. Now she had to get home, and get some sleep before her day's work began again. She stiffened, remembering that Lady Harwood hadn't paid her for her day's work. She searched her purse, hoping she had the coins necessary for a hackney cab. It would be impossible for her to walk home now. A woman alone on the streets of London at this hour was fair play for whatever foul villains were out there.

She didn't have enough. Her shoulders drooped. Could she swallow her pride and ask the valet to lend her the fare?

"Miss?" he said, appearing at the door to the salon as though she'd summoned him aloud.

She turned to look at him. The note in his voice had been respectful. He bowed. "My master asks that you come up to see him, if you would. He says to tell you it would be quite *comme il faut*, because he is entirely dressed, and in any event, incapable of doing you any harm now."

Poor man, of course not, she thought.

She nodded. "Is he entirely recovered?"

"No," the valet said, as he led her to the stair. "But as much so as possible, and so the doctor said too."

"Was he poisoned?"

The valet hesitated. "That is for my lord to divulge, if he chooses, Miss."

Simon's bedchamber was vast. The many lamps on tables and dresser tops and the blaze from the hearth showed a huge bed, piled with pillows and bedcovers. Heavy crimson draperies covered the windows. It was a luxurious room compared to the parts of the house she'd seen. But Jane had eyes only for the man in the bed. Simon wore a crimson dressing gown, and sat propped up on pillows. He was pale, but calm, as he looked up at her when she came into the room.

"So frightened? Don't be," he said with a wan smile. "I'll do, as I said I would. And you're safe, as I promised."

She took a chair near his bed, and watched him, wondering why he'd asked her to stay. It must have been a momentary lapse; he'd likely only asked because he thought he might be dying and he wasn't responsible for his thoughts. Now she thought he'd probably want to apologize and explain it away. Still, she held a small warm thought close to her heart. When he thought he was dying, he'd wanted her there with him.

"I need you to do a job of work for me," he said.

She blinked.

"Someone did try to kill me tonight," he said. "That, or make me wish I was dead. It was in the punch I drank, and there were too many people around the bowl for me to even guess at how many had access to my cup. But it was the only thing I had there, and there was a bitter aftertaste in my mouth when I finished it. I could feel my heart speeding up. Aconite, or some other pretty poison," he added with a grimace.

He paused, and regarded her. Now she could see the weariness in his face. "Or it may not have been poison. I need to know how many other unfortunates got sick tonight. Or was I the only one? What did people say and do after I got sick. You can find that out for me. When are you due back at Lady Harwood's?"

"Not until day after next," she said unthinkingly.

He shook his head. "No good. Gossip's like trying to warm yourself at a fire; no good stirring up ashes. You get the best of it when it's fresh and raging hot. Have you any excuse for going there tomorrow?"

"I have other work tomorrow," she said, sitting up straighter. It was stupid to be insulted because he hadn't been thinking of her, but only of what he wanted her to do for him. But after this tumultuous evening she was tired of being an object for other people's use or amusement. "I do have a living to earn, you know," she told him.

"And I have to keep on living. Come now, Jane, be reasonable. I'll pay for your time. Can't you go there on some pretext?"

His expression was so weary, his voice so soft and hoarse that she could imagine what he'd just been through. She took pity on him. "She hasn't paid me. I could go and ask for my wages."

"She doesn't pay you quarterly?"

"I'm not a servant in the house, my lord," she said patiently. "My employment is a week-to-week affair. Fashion changes, and my lady and I both know I may be out of work at any time."

He frowned. "Of course. Where's my head?"

"I imagine you were trying to hold it on earlier," she said with a small smile.

He looked at her, his eyes glinting in the firelight. "Too true," he said. "Still am, comes to that. Lord, what time is it?"

"It is two in the morning, my lord," his valet said from the side of the room where he was standing.

Simon frowned again. "Then get you to bed, my

man. I'll do fine now." He looked up at Jane. "Miss Chatham will stay here with me and summon you if I turn green again. You'll stay, Jane? Otherwise, my man won't budge. Surely you're not worried about your reputation. No one knows you're here. My staff won't utter a word. And you certainly can't be worried about improper advances from a man in my condition?"

Tears prickled at the back of Jane's eyes at his casual mention of his horrible misfortune. "No, my lord. But I must get back to my rooms. I can't come straggling in at dawn. My landlady prides herself on the respectability of her house."

"You'll be fine. I'll have a hackney deliver you before first light. It's just that I'd be more comfortable if you stayed a few hours more. I need to . . ." He hesitated, and frowned. "Damned if I know what I need. Sorry for the vulgarity. But I'd rather you stayed."

"Then I will," she said, and sat back. Surely he'd fall asleep soon enough, and he'd said he'd see that she got home safe. There was nothing to worry about now.

The valet bowed himself out. Suddenly Jane's heartbeat picked up and she felt the stirrings of panic. Alone, here in Lord Granger's bedchamber, she suddenly realized that whether he was incapacitated or not, she could lose her reputation if anyone found out she was staying alone here with him tonight.

His smile was sad. "No one will know," he said. "Don't look so amazed at my guess. What else could have got you so upset? You trust me, don't you? Or if you don't, then you certainly should after what I've been through."

She ducked her head to hide her reaction to his words. "I know," she said in a choked voice. "I'm sorry. I don't know what *I* was thinking."

"Come, take my hand. It's been a bad night for both of us."

She let him take her hand, and discovered that his was warm and strong.

"Obviously," he said, as his thumb stroked the back of her hand, "there's more going on at Lady Harwood's than either of us know. I was surprised to see how many notable people were there tonight. Her salon is a beehive. Pleasure seekers and policy makers side by side, and happy to be there. That makes the place perfect for intrigue. People usually think of treason being done in dark streets and empty warehouses. But it's much easier to do in plain sight, in the full public light.

I learned that in the salons of Paris, and then had reason to remember it in its dungeons too." He closed his eyes.

"Does it distress you to talk about it?" she asked softly.

"You've already heard about what happened to me. I suppose everyone has," he said on a sigh. "No. It's done. I wasn't as clever as I thought, they caught me."

She couldn't think of a word to say, or what to do to erase his pained expression.

"This is awkward," he suddenly said. "I'm tired, and so are you, and here we are, our arms stretched out like clotheslines across a long yard. Come sit beside me."

She hesitated. He laughed. "I just passed the last few hours delightfully, ridding myself of anything I ever ate or drank. Why hesitate? You know I'm in no condition to assault you."

She knew, too well. She rose, and using the bed stair, climbed up and then gingerly sat beside him on his bed. It was a soft, deep bed.

"Your back will get tired," he said wearily, watching her trying to perch uncomfortably on the side of the bed. "In for a penny, in for a pound. Take a pillow and stretch out. I'm under the coverlets. You're over them. That's very chaste. Why not talk in comfort?"

And that way he'd fall to sleep sooner, she thought. So she lay down, and put her head on a fat crimson pillow near to him.

"All you need is a lily in your hands and we can plant you," he said, with laughter in his voice. "Relax, my dear. It's good of you to stay with me. I find I need company. I confess, I wondered if my luck had finally run out tonight."

She was glad he couldn't see her face. There were tears on her cheeks. His luck had run out in so many ways and yet he had the courage to go on. It made her feel small and stupid to worry about such a nebulous thing as a reputation, when this man had literally been unmanned by his enemies and yet managed to soldier on.

"Are you weeping?" he asked in surprise.

Was he a mind reader? she wondered.

"It's too late at night and I'm too tired for lies. I can hear your sniffles," he said. "They're ladylike, but audible. Here, rest your head next to mine. I'm fine, I tell you, I will live. I'm grateful for your concern, but there's no need for it now," he said as he gathered her in his arms.

It was all wrong, but it felt so right to be

near to him. Jane sighed and burrowed into his embrace. He'd been persecuted, and tonight he'd almost died. And no one was there but the two of them. A moment longer, she told herself, just one more.

He touched her cheek, and then lowered his head and kissed her lightly on the lips. She moved away.

"Why do you recoil? Do I smell bad? I was ill," he said, drawing back to prop himself on one elbow. "But I swallowed all sorts of minty concoctions and breathed into my poor valet's face until he detected nothing but herbs before I ever let you in."

"It's not that. It's that I oughtn't to be keeping you up. I shouldn't even be here."

"But the kiss suited you?"

She stared into his eyes. "You know it did. But it must be terrible for you."

He smiled. "I ought to ask you what the devil you mean by that. But I don't want to wait for an answer. I don't want to waste another minute." He took her in his arms again, and kissed her. This time she didn't draw away.

Instead, she clung to him, awash in a tide of pity and longing and such pleasure that she couldn't think. She'd never kissed anyone while lying comfortably in a bed before. She'd never felt such a strong, vital, warm body pressed to hers. It had been so long since anyone had held her close that she almost wept. She hadn't understood how much she needed it. Though she knew this was nothing more than the result of the fears of the night, and that nothing could or should come of it, she realized how much she'd missed being held. She found she needed to comfort him as well.

Soon, she found more than comfort in his kisses, and discovered herself wishing there weren't so many covers between them. She wished there were more, though, when his hand found her breast. She stopped wishing, finally, and only clung to him, kissing him and wanting him.

"My lord?" the voice said from the doorway.

Simon sat up.

Jane, in a flurry of confusion, sat up as well, her hands to her hair to tidy it, as though that might erase the fact that she lay burning with desire in Lord Granger's bed.

"Yes?" Simon answered calmly.

"Viscount Delancey is here, and wishes to

speak with you. I told him you were sleeping, but he won't hear of any excuses, he said, unless you are dead. He insists, my lord."

"Aye," Simon said, running a hand through his hair. "And if he insists, he is immovable. Send him up."

Jane's gasp made him turn his head. He closed his eyes. "Damnation. Yes, of course. Jane. Follow Mr. Morris to my dressing room, my dear. There's no hope for it. I have to hear what the viscount has to say. Stay still in there. He'll never know you were here. He won't stay long. I'll see to that."

But he'd forgotten her presence the moment he'd heard his friend had arrived, Jane thought as she went quickly to the door at the side of the room that the valet opened for her. She was not only a fool, but now he must think her a baggage, because what other sort of female would know what a man with his disability wanted from her? Jane sat on a stool in the dressing room, and held her head in her hands. She wished she'd never met him. She wished she could have met him before his trials. She urgently wished to go home and straighten out her head and her heart.

The room was dark and smelled of bay rum

and spices. There was no light, but her eyes became accustomed enough to the darkness for her to see that Lord Granger's clothing was kept in a room as large as the one she lived in. She didn't even dare sigh.

"Proctor," she finally heard Simon say. "What dire circumstance sends you to my bedside at this hour?"

"I heard you were alive," the languid voice answered. "And if you were, then I knew you'd want to know if I had discovered anything."

Simon laughed. "Right you are."

"You are alive, and intend to remain so?" the viscount asked.

A laugh was his answer.

"It was poison," the viscount said. "No one else took ill, though there was a flurry of fainting amongst the fainthearted and a dowager and a fop or two claimed they felt ill. But you were the only one targeted and dosed. Aconite, Mr. Morris said. Good that you knew how to deal with it. What did you see that frightened an enemy? And which one was he, or she? You may have retired from the service, but someone doesn't believe it. And though Bonaparte's snug on Elba, there are those who are obviously still at treachery."

"I didn't see anything," Simon said briefly. "Only old enemies, and they noted me too. But I've been out of their business and yours since I came home, and they must know that. I think someone thought I saw something I shouldn't have. I'd give a good deal to know what that was."

"As would I," the viscount said. "And the girl you left with? The dancing instructress? What part did she play in this?"

"None. I was in difficulties, and I wanted all the help I could get. She was in the hallway; I asked her to come with me."

"I don't blame you, and I am all admiration," the viscount said. "Not many gentlemen would think of such things while in danger of dying." He raised his thin nose in the air. "And you've already had a female visitor, I see—or rather, smell. There are roses in the air, and that's never your scent. You astonish me."

"And you credit me with too much. The scent is that of Mr. Morris's making. My recent bout with aconite made him spray the room 'til it smells like a funeral."

"And the young woman who helped see you home?"

"It's not what you think . . . The devil! You

don't think it, do you?" Simon said, laughing. "I can't astound you that much, though I wish I could. Have a chair, old friend, and tell me who you think it might have been that tried to do me in."

"Thank you, I will sit, and surmise. If you're up to it."

"I wouldn't have asked if I weren't."

"I know," the viscount said. "I've seen you in worse condition. You constantly astound me. I'm not used to such hours, and I haven't been ill. I'm not a carouser."

"Oh, and I am. Out 'til all hours drinking poison."

They laughed, and went on talking.

Jane hung her head, and waited.

The two men spoke the names of old friends and enemies. They conjectured about people and places she'd never heard of. They chatted and she waited as the night flew by. Her heart didn't sink as low as her head was doing until she peered out a tiny window she hadn't noticed in the dressing room, and saw the sky was lightening. The night was passing, and she'd no idea when she could leave.

Viscount Delancey, with many a yawn, finally

left, and when his footsteps had faded, Jane came springing out of Simon's dressing room like a jack in the box unlatched.

"I must get home," she told him. "I must leave at once."

Simon looked at her. "I know," he said, "but there's a problem. If I know my old friend he's having my house watched. Whether it's to protect me from further problems, or because his interest is aroused because of what happened, be sure he's stationed one or two someones at my front and back doors. I'll ask Mr. Morris. He'll know. Don't look at me like that, Jane. I'm safe enough. It's you I'm trying to protect now."

She paced his bedchamber. "If I trail in after dawn, my landlady will have fits. What can I do?"

"You could stay here with me," he suggested, putting his arms behind his head to watch her.

She shot him a glowering look. He laughed. "Speak of poisonous! If looks could kill, that one would. Don't worry. If you refuse my hospitality, we'll be forced to be creative. Ah, Mr. Morris! What's the word? How many does he have on the case outside our door?"

The valet sighed. "One fellow outside, plain

enough. One lurking in the alley out back, and doubtless another up the street."

Simon nodded. He sat up. "As I thought. So then, this is what we must do, and we have to do it fast. Jane, listen sharp, and do as I say. We'll whisk you out clean as a straw through a new baked cake."

Chapter 11

A timid figure came creeping out the front door of Lord Granger's town house as the night sky above was fading from gray to misty white. It was a young female in a hooded cloak. The footman called a hackney that had just set out on the street, and after many a look over her shoulder, the young woman climbed the stair and got in. As the coach pulled away from the curb, a large figure in workingman's clothing that had been standing in the diminishing night detached himself from the shadows. He whistled, and a hackney that had been waiting up the street came and collected him. It followed the first carriage at a distance, and both disappeared around a corner.

At the same time, a young man in oversized clothing stole out of Lord Granger's back door into an alley. His hat was pulled low, his collar was up around his ears, and he hurried out of the alley with timid, mincing steps. He picked up speed when he got to the street and almost collided with a lamplighter's ladder as he did so. The lamplighter appeared from a basement entrance and shouted at the boy for his clumsiness, making him run faster. Another shabby figure detached itself from the shadows and followed the now galloping lad.

There was no activity on the street for a few more moments, and then, as the sky lightened to dazzling gray, suddenly the road became as busy as High Street at noon. Yawning tradesmen appeared, pushing their carts along the road, horse-drawn wagons filled with such essentials as produce, coal, straw, and scissors grinders appeared. Cooks, kitchen maids, and footmen poured out of many of the great houses on their way to their morning errands.

A cook and two kitchen maids strolled out of Lord Granger's back door, carrying huge wicker baskets. Chatting merrily, the three women headed down two streets, and then leisurely went down a crooked lane in the general direction of the fish market. Shortly after, they emerged again, only this time there was only one kitchen maid. The other was lying on the floor of a hackney cab, going in the other direction.

"You can get up now," Simon told Jane after they'd gone a few streets. "No one's following."

Her head popped up to seat level. She looked out the window, then raised herself, and then fell back to sit on the seat with a great sigh. "That was masterful," she said.

"Well, yes. So it was. Thank you," Simon said with a smile.

"But I still think you ought to have stayed in bed," she added.

"What? And miss all the fun? I told you, once the poison was out of my system, I was fine. No one else knows that, though, and so I'm the best person to see you safely home. This way too I can see who's taking an interest in you. And my household was enchanted at the idea of playing games with an invisible threat to their master's well-being. Or," he added with a shrug, "they were just pleased to have a morning out without their usual errands."

She stared at him, dressed in laborer's clothing again, sitting at his ease. "I don't know if you're as fine as you say you are," she said doubtfully. "But

I'm grateful to you for this escape. I can't afford any more gossip. Falling down by accident and looking scandalous is deplorable. Still, anyone who knew me realized it was an unfortunate accident. Being in a caricature was dreadful. But many people didn't know who I was, and that sort of gossip dies as the ink dries, or so Lady Harwood said."

"She's entirely right," her companion said.

"But," Jane said, holding up a finger, "a single female spending the night at a noble gentleman's house is quite another thing, even if that too was an accident. Who would believe it? Even Lady Harwood wouldn't be able to forgive me that."

"Don't bother to think about what might have been," Simon told her. "Nothing is accomplished by it. You'll be home in no time at all."

"I know, but I'm worried because it looks like I really do have no time at all. The sun's rising, and all the cheery assurances in the world won't change that. If my landlady sees me, I'll have to explain where I've been," Jane said, biting her lip.

"I understand that when husbands crawl in at dawn they usually say they've been up with a sick friend," Simon told her. "And here you actually have been. That is, if you regard me as a friend?"

"I do," she said quietly.

The coach slowed. "Ah," Simon said with relief. "Just as ordered. Here we are. Only down the street from your rooms."

"Thank goodness you remembered," Jane said. "Stop here, please. Don't even go near the house. If I meet her, I'll try to explain. If I'm lucky, I won't have to."

"And you'll be back at Lady Harwood's as usual tomorrow?" Simon asked as the coach came to a halt.

"I will, good-bye, stay well," she said, opened the door, and not waiting for the coachman's assistance, she leapt from the hackney and hurried down the street.

Simon sat watching her until she ran up the stairs to her door. He saw the far-off figure go in. Then he tapped on the roof of the carriage. "Move on," he said, and winced. He put a hand on his stomach. It was making itself felt. "Take me back to where you picked me up," he told the driver, and finally allowed himself the luxury of grimacing. He'd live, as he'd said.

But he'd never said it would be pleasant. It was back to bed for him, and nothing but milksops and tea until his stomach returned to normal. But that wasn't what was making him scowl so fiercely.

It was a decision he'd just made. He had to be rid of Jane Chatham, the charming dance instructress. She was not good for his health, in too many ways. For one thing, she'd come into his life too unexpectedly, and had somehow wormed her way into his affections without his realizing it. For another, it now occurred to him that her arrival in his life was too close to an attempt on his life, at least too close for his comfort. It wasn't that he didn't trust her, in particular. It was rather that he didn't trust anyone, in general.

His time in a dungeon had taught him that. And though it looked like Jane Chatham was exactly what she said she was, there were still little things about her that bothered him. If she was so moral, why did she come back to his house with him at midnight? Why was she so conveniently waiting alone in the front hall in the first place? She could have been lying in wait for him.

And even if she knew he was sick, he reasoned, and had been told he'd been poisoned, by the time she had shown up in his room she'd also been clearly told he wasn't dying. So why did she get into bed with him no matter what he said? *That* surpassed innocence, he thought. It rounded the corner of stupidity, and wound up on the doorstep of deceit.

But her eyes were clear, and her position, as she told it, and as he'd discovered after investigating, was tenuous. And she cared for him even though she'd never said it. He knew that much, at least, was true. What else was?

So was she an innocent? Come now, he told himself. A *dancer*, an innocent? She didn't know how seductive that supple body was? She didn't realize how she set a man's pulses pounding? She didn't realize how her soft kisses and clinging body drove a man to want more, no matter how impossible that was for a woman in her position and a man in his? Nor did she know that a woman in her position ought not to be so free with her body with any man? That was more difficult to believe.

He'd always suspected the woman who had eventually betrayed him in France. Why did he so want to believe in Jane Chatham's innocence? That was dangerous. He tried to avoid danger wherever possible. Since he'd neither compromised her nor made her an object of scandal, he could let her go with a clear conscience. But the thing was, he thought, as his stomach growled back at him, that he didn't want to let her go. And wouldn't that be foolish, he realized with rising spirits, to let her go out of his life if he'd any thought that she might not be guilty?

That thought cheered him all the way home.

It didn't last long. Viscount Delancey was waiting for him in his study when he came into his house.

"Ah, returns the wounded warrior," the viscount said as Simon limped into the room. "Shouldn't you be in bed?"

"I will be, as soon as I find out what else you've discovered."

"It seems you've been up to all sorts of hijinks, Simon, my friend," the viscount said, sitting back in his chair. "It was clever of you to send a kitchen maid out and tell her to play act a lady making a daring escape. It was enough to fool the fellow I had positioned at your front door. Still, you could have told me what you planned.

I'm chagrined that I didn't realize your dancing lady was here when I was, although I wondered when you'd started perfuming your rooms with roses." He shook his head. "One must always follow up on intuition, and I should have remembered that.

"The way it did go, however, was that I had another one of my fellows in the alley chasing after your cook and another housemaid. They gave the poor man a piece of their minds when they saw him following. It was clever of you to take the chit home in a hackney. You're positively unrecognizable when dressed as a workingman, or almost so. Had I seen you I would have known. But I didn't. By the by, I don't know who the other fellow lurking at your back door was. He got away before anyone could identify him . . . Who poisoned you, Simon?"

"I thought perhaps that you might have," Simon said, wincing as he sank into a chair.

"Thank you. And the reason?"

"No reason in particular, old friend, it's just that you're the only one I knew at the ball who is in the same business that I am."

"Ah," Proctor said without any evidence of annoyance. "And you didn't suspect old Sloan, or Sir

Randolph, or even Lord Tanager, whom you so circumspectly don't mention?"

"They're traitors with no intent: men who sell secrets to keep out of debtor's prison. They're not murderers," his host said wearily.

"They'd sell a man into prison without blinking," the viscount said.

"And have done, doubtless, but not me. I investigated that. And prison isn't murder, at least not all the time. I think they'd stick at actual slaughter. I'll discover who did it, I promise. But the person who poisoned my punch was someone who neither of us suspected, I think. He didn't know that I was there to find out about your foolish brother, and nothing else."

"Nothing else?" his friend asked with a lifted eyebrow. "And the pretty little dancer didn't interest you?"

"She was someone I knew who could help see me home," Simon said gruffly. "Seeing who was at that ball roused my suspicions, but I had nothing *but* suspicions. The would-be assassin didn't know that; that's where the problem lies, and cheats." He smiled. "There, a pun. I'm not so sick, after all." Then his expression grew serious. "Forgive me for ignoring your young Richard, but now I know there's something far more important than a foolish young man at Lady Harwood's salon."

"Doubtless," the viscount said. "What do you think it is?"

"I've no idea. Someone thinks I do. So I will. And soon."

"I thought you had given up on females," the viscount said idly.

"And so I have. And on men friends too," Simon said. "I only went into Society because you said you needed me. Did you suspect I'd discover anything else at the time?"

The viscount smiled. "You know me better than that, Simon. I wouldn't have sent you into danger. I really did want to find out what had enthralled that fool of a brother of mine, and how far the affair had gone so I'd know whether or not I had to stop it. By the way, do you really believe I have no cause for concern there?"

Simon shook his head. "No, I think not, not there. But cause for concern, yes."

"For you, definitely," his friend said. "I thank you for your efforts on my behalf, but I really think it would be healthier for you to stay away from Lady Harwood's home now."

"Perhaps," Simon said. "But now *my* interest is involved."

"I think it would be folly. You've suffered enough for our country."

"I don't intend to suffer," Simon said. "But I don't like being poisoned and running away to hide like a rat in a hole in the wall."

"I see. So it's not the lovely dancer who lures you on?"

"You know better than that," Simon said as he put his hands on the sides of his chair and slowly pushed himself up to a stand.

"Do I?" the viscount asked mildly. "Have you considered that your friends might be your enemies? Take that lovely dance mistress, for example. Or have you already done so?"

Simon stared at his friend. "Why do you say that?"

"For all the reasons you think I might," the viscount said lazily as he too rose from his chair. "She's new, she's lovely and intelligent. She's obviously engaged your curiosity and your sympathy at the very least. And she's the last person you'd suspect. Be warier, Simon. Be rid of the chit. Unless, of course, you're smitten."

Simon's laugh was bitter. "I'm not your brother.

I've learned that smitten is much too close a word to *smite*."

"Let me give you my arm, Simon. You have to get upstairs and into a bed. If you grow any more pale you'll frighten me."

"Thank you," Simon said, leaning on his old friend. "I could use some rest and quiet. But I'll be back to the scene of the crime, or crimes, and I will find out what's going on there."

"Yes, yes, of course," the viscount said, as he helped his friend up the stair.

"And I'll be sure to be rid of the lovely dancer," Simon muttered.

"Necessary, but a pity, that," his friend said.

"Yes," Simon agreed.

"Aha!" Jane's landlady said as Jane entered her house. She stood waiting for Jane in the narrow front hall, her hands on her hips, blocking Jane's way to the stair. "I thought so! A dancer, you said you was. Bold-faced and bare faced about it you was. Butter wouldn't have melted in your mouth. This is a respectable establishment, said I. It was children you instructed, says you. Ha!" she announced with bitter triumph. "I gave you a room, and here you are, dragging in at all hours of the morning like any common street drab after a night on the tiles, where any of the neighbors can see you and I don't doubt they all did. And what shall they think of me for allowing it? I have a reputation to protect. So out you go, Missy. Collect your things, and leave on the instant! A *dancer*!" she muttered, "I should of knowed better, I should have!"

"I did nothing wrong," Jane protested, her lips quivering. "I've a friend who became sick in the night and I stayed until I was sure she'd see another day." But she didn't say it with conviction. Because it was a lie, and she was sure the landlady knew it. Her conscience was heavy too, because her landlady had never seen the caricatures that had made her employer's salon such a success. If her landlady had seen them, she'd have been evicted days before.

"Go back to your friend, Missy," the landlady said, folding her arms on her ample chest. "Because I won't have you here another day—or night. I run a decent rooming house, I do. And what would happen if I didn't? It would make me a scandal and lower the tone of the neighborhood. We are decent people in indecent times and well we know it. Pack and leave, Miss Chatham."

There was no argument Jane could make that wouldn't make the situation worse. So, head held high, she moved past her landlady and marched up the stair. She didn't let her shoulders droop until she got into her room. There, she sank to the bed. The only lucky thing, she thought, was that she had no work today, so she had an entire day to find new lodgings. One thing she did know. They wouldn't be near here. She'd probably leave under the eyes of every landlady on the street. Gossip, it seemed, followed her to high places and low ones. This district tottered on the fringes of respectability. She didn't blame the local landladies; the neighborhood simply couldn't afford to house her now.

At least she still had her pride, and her reputation, although shredding, wasn't widely known. She could find new lodgings, take on more pupils, and one day, if she were careful, she'd have achieved her dream. Her own establishment, a better existence, freedom of choice, and a life of her own.

She had to be more circumspect in future. She vowed that as she packed. She'd no business consorting with Lord Granger in the first place, or continuing to see him in the second place, no matter how sorry she felt for him. Her pity should be saved for herself for being so fascinated with him, because nothing could come of such a friendship. Thanks to what Lady Harwood had told her, she knew she was safe from his advances. She'd been both relieved and horrified by that, and then the surge of compassion for him that she'd felt had made her feel invulnerable. But she hadn't realized she wasn't safe from the repercussions of being with him. She couldn't even go back to his house to inquire about his health.

She straightened her shoulders. Now she had to find new rooms, get a good night's sleep, and go back to Lady Harwood's house. Once there, she'd surely hear how well he was doing. But she had to rid herself of the thought of him as well as remembrances of their times together, and totally eradicate the memory of his kisses and the feeling of being so safe in his arms. She'd also miss his wit and the way he'd seemed so sympathetic, so capable of protecting her. She'd been afraid of his company at first, and then became suffused with pity for him and his courageous way of continuing to live his life.

She'd even begun to think there might be something else between them. But that was nonsense.

Although she was of his class, she had no funds, no family, nothing to offer him, not even the ease a woman could provide a man. And he, obviously, thought he had nothing to offer her. No, she thought sadly, he didn't want to offer her anything. Nothing could be more futile than to have anything to do with him, in every way.

Jane continued to pack her things. She wished she could assemble her thoughts as easily, and put away her fears and doubts as neatly. It was time to move on.

Chapter 12

"**M**iss Chatham, if I may have a word with you please?"

Jane's shoulders leapt. She spun around. The dry voice had come out of nowhere. She'd been brooding about her problems; feeling worried and frazzled, and was also hurrying to her class. The voice stopped her short. She stood rigidly alert, paused in the long hall leading to Lady Harwood's ballroom where her class awaited her.

The man who'd spoken was a gentleman: tall, pale, very thin, his fair hair almost gone. He wore spectacles. He stood patiently waiting for her reply. She shook herself out of her distraction. *Viscount Delancey*, she remembered, and relaxed. Lord Granger's friend, and brother of the young man she'd been supposed to be watching. Perhaps he'd come to tell her how Lord Granger was.

Terror leapt to her eyes. The word in the kitchens said that he was recovering. But that was gossip. This man knew. Maybe he'd come to tell her something dreadful.

"Don't alarm yourself," the viscount said with a small smile. "Lord Granger fares well. I come to you on my own behalf this afternoon."

The lady's salon was in progress. He must have been waiting for Jane near the door to the salon, and seen her as she passed it. She waited.

"You did a job of work for my friend, did you not?" the viscount asked.

She didn't know what to admit, so Jane stayed silent.

"Very good," the viscount said with approval. "The less said, the less misunderstood. My point is that we both know that our friend came to grief here the other night. I cautioned him to take himself out of the business, whatever it is. It wasn't to do with my brother," he added with a thin smile. "But someone tried to annihilate him. I don't know whom. At least, not yet I don't. I worked with Lord Granger abroad, and though he is retired from his service for His Majesty, I am not. So I'm here to ask you to carry on with the duties you performed with him, for me. At the same wages, of course."

She took in a deep breath. She hoped he hadn't misunderstood her duties the way her old land-lady had done. That could be disastrous. But she did need those generous wages. And the viscount looked as dry as day-old toast. She couldn't imagine him being improper or lecherous. But she didn't dare take chances again.

"And those duties are . . . ?" she finally asked.

"Watching after my brother, of course," he said blandly. "Reporting all interesting gossip to me. And telling no one else—*no one*—what you are doing, and for whom. Do you agree?"

She nodded.

"Brave girl. That is what I'd hoped to hear." He paused and studied her upturned face. "Not afraid of the same fate befalling you as befell our mutual friend the other day?" he asked, watching her closely.

She blinked. She hadn't thought of that. "I can see no reason why anyone would want to do any harm to me," she said truthfully. "Except for insulting me. And that was because of my infamy after my mishap, but since, no one has been rude to me. The truth is no one notices me."

"'. . . Infamy after my mishap,'" the gentleman echoed. "I do see your charm: well-spoken, lovely to look at, and with all the accoutrements of a lady. I shall enjoy our association as much as you will, I hope." He took one of her hands, raised it to his lips, and kissed it.

Jane couldn't have been more surprised than if he'd swept her into his arms and kissed her passionately. She didn't know what to say.

"Until later," he said softly. "Adieu, little one." He bowed, and left her to go back to the salon.

She stood looking after him, astonished. His eyes had actually *glittered* behind his spectacles, she thought. *It was the late afternoon light*, she told herself, *not passion*. But to say that he hoped she'd, 'enjoy her work'? He couldn't have misunderstood what she'd done for Lord Granger. Could he?

She heard a sudden screech, and then loud whoops of childish laughter. The girls were waiting for her, getting bored and into trouble. Her first job, her real job, had to be done. She could think about this new turn of events later. She ran to do her job.

And so, of course, her lessons went horribly. She couldn't banish troubling thoughts from her mind. Her pupils, using the special sense that children had, knew she was distracted, and tried to make her more so.

"No, no, no," she said after an exhausting hour. "Again: the purpose of these lessons is to have fun, no doubt about it. But it is also to learn the dance. You can't learn or dance when you're laughing so much. Or if you're playing tricks. And, Lady Bettina, must I tell you again? You cannot bite Miss Wilson because you think she took your hair ribbon. Miss Wilson, if that new ribbon you have *is* Lady Bettina's, you must give it back, not dance around her waving it and singing 'Mine, mine, mine.' Children, if you don't behave better in future, then no more lessons. At least none from me."

"Oh, badly done, Miss. Let the children have their fun," a masculine voice called out.

"Aye, dancing isn't math or science, let them laugh," called another.

"And math and science masters don't move the way you do," another wag in the crowd of gentlemen shouted from the entrance to the ballroom where they stood with a scattering of tittering ladies.

Her unwanted audience was there again, Jane realized. She'd been so busy with her own thoughts and her wayward students, she hadn't noticed the crowd gathering. She'd done spins and pirouettes, never caring about how her skirts moved with her. And today she'd worn an old gown, thin from many washings, and the late afternoon sunlight had been streaming in through the ballroom's long windows. Doubtless the crowd had ogled her. Color rose to her cheeks. For tuppence, she'd leave her position now and tell them all to go to the devil.

But she needed those two pence.

She turned back at her class. Some looked abashed, some were, as usual, giggling. "That's all for this afternoon, children," she said as calmly as she could. "Practice your steps. And practice your manners, if you want to be real ladies in the future. That's part of these lessons too, you know. I won't teach you unless you are mannerly, nor will anyone want to be friends with you when you grow up if you aren't. A gentleperson is known by their good manners, and those are shown to any or all persons they deal with of any rank, whatever titles or heritage they themselves may possess."

There was a shuffling sort of silence from the previously loud crowd at the door. She looked to them, raising her head defiantly. They had forgotten their manners too. She hoped she'd reminded them.

She looked at the male guests. They didn't look as embarrassed as her students. They looked a bit frightened, she realized. Then she saw Lord Granger, standing, arms crossed, scowling down at the crowd. It was that which had quieted them, not anything she'd said. Viscount Delancey wasn't looking at the other gentleman, though. He was smiling at her, with delight.

She turned, nodded to her class, and stood waiting until the girls went to their nannies, and the crowd at the door had dispersed. And then Jane ran for the kitchens. She'd gather up her things and wait until the crowd left the house. That was when she hoped she might be paid for her lessons. Then she'd wait a bit longer, until dusk. Because she no longer wanted any part of Viscount Delancey's coins for anything, or any reason, and she needed time to rehearse how to reject him.

It was nearly nightfall. Jane walked briskly; a lone female who didn't in any part of London was inviting molestation. There was no one on the street but a lone lamplighter. She paused at the corner to look both ways before she ventured across. She couldn't hear any carts, carriages, or wagons because the road was covered with straw to deaden the noise of horses or transport. Someone in the neighborhood must be sick.

So the softest voice could be heard.

"Good evening, Miss Chatham," the voice said from her right side.

She wheeled around. It was the lamplighter, his ladder hoisted over one shoulder, his heavy canvas bag on the other. She looked closer, peering under the brim of his floppy hat. His face was almost as dark as the coming night, streaked with soot and lampblack. But the eyes were familiar.

"You!" she said.

"I," he agreed.

"You should be in bed!"

"A kindly thought however you meant it," Simon said. "But I'm recovered. I heard that my friend the viscount had a word with you today."

She tilted her head to the side, her eyes narrowing. "How did you hear that? Did he tell you?"

"I meant, I saw the viscount have a word with you. The fact that he didn't tell me led me to you."

She was still. This was getting too convoluted for her. She'd pledged information and silence to both men.

"Come," Simon said. "Dine with me. Our usual spot. No one will see us there. We must talk. I'll walk on now. You continue, and when you get to the corner of the third street you usually pass, there's a small side street. If no one is following you, I'll be in the hackney there. If someone is tracking you, then go on to the next, and the next, and onward, until you either see a waiting cab, or reach your doorstep. If you have to go that far, I'll think of something else. You don't possibly have a balcony I can climb, do you?"

That made her smile, until she remembered her problem. "No balcony," she said quietly.

"A tree?" he asked hopefully.

"No," she said.

"So, you'll do as I ask? Please?"

She nodded, not knowing what else to do. She no longer lived in the direction he spoke of. But no one could know that yet. And she wanted so badly to know what to do.

Simon trudged on across the street, whistling a cheery music hall song. He turned to the right and propped his ladder up against a light on the other side of the road. After she stopped, pretending to shake a pebble from her slipper, Jane followed, reached the opposite curb, and then walked to the left. They didn't meet up again until she had counted past seven streets.

"Good," he said, as she scuttled into the hackney. "You were being watched. But your guard was finally . . . diverted," he added with a smile in his voice.

"Why can't we just talk here?" she asked.

"Because I'm hungry," he said. "Remember, I haven't eaten anything decent for a few days."

"Oh," she said. "True. But . . . I'd decided not to see you again," she said in a rush.

"For what reason?" he asked haughtily, raising an eyebrow, even though he had decided the very same thing.

"Because it can be disastrous for me," she said, and closed her lips on whatever else she might have said.

"*If* discovered," he said.

"Well, yes, of course," she said impatiently.

"Then we won't be," he said simply. "Because it wouldn't be good for me either. But now that I know there's something going on in your place of employment, something more than a wicked lady's fling with a very young fellow, I need to know more. And you, as before, are one of the few with access to Lady Harwood's house who are intelligent enough to discover what I need to know."

She sat still.

"What did Proctor . . . the viscount say to you?" he asked after a moment.

"I don't know what to tell you," she said in aggravated tones. "I don't know who to trust. I haven't taken a penny piece from him, and to be sure, I don't want to, but I am no one. What do I do?"

"Ah," he said. "And the money would be for?"

"I can't say. I said I wouldn't. But if he's your friend why don't you know what he said? I think the best thing to do is to put me down here. I'll take no more money for information," she said a little wildly. "Not for anything but teaching. Not from anyone, not for anything else. That's the best, smartest safest thing to do."

"It turns out it's none of those things," he said. "Let's have dinner. Let's relax, and chat. I'll give you facts and time to think about them and make up your mind. Is that all right? Then you may go home, and if you don't ever want to speak to me again, I'll accept it. But since someone tried to put out my light the other night, and may try again, I really do think it would be kind, if nothing else, of you to talk with me a little now. Don't you?"

She sat quietly.

"And strictly speaking, I do have precedence," he added in a hurt voice. "I hired you first, you know."

She nodded, and then realized what she was doing. "Oh, ridiculous," she said. "I'm not a spy and I don't know the rules of spying, but I'll bet precedence has nothing to do with it."

"There is honor among spies," he said. "But I suppose you're right. The policy is somewhat liberal."

She wanted to trust him. In fact, she already trusted him more than Lady Harwood and the viscount put together. And that worried her. "What's going on?" she asked in a hopeless little voice.

"That," he said, "is exactly what we're going to try to discover."

The low tavern was filled with loud and merry customers, just as it had been the last time Simon had taken Jane to it. The tavern keeper had their corner table ready. As Jane took her seat opposite Simon, she felt a sense of homecoming. Only she was coming home to something she knew could be both dangerous and treacherous. She didn't distrust him so much as she did herself. It was simple to make yourself promises of denial when what you wanted was out of sight.

She shouldn't have come. Only she had to. She sighed, and made excuses to herself. She was hungry too. She had to find out what to do about the viscount's offer. And this, she promised herself, would be absolutely positively the last time she was ever seen with Lord Granger. Fate had put them together. She had to see that her determination kept them apart.

"So," he said, after the tavern keeper had set down their dinners. "What did the viscount offer you, and for what?"

But now Jane had time to recover herself.

"That," she said primly, "is up to you to discover. I shouldn't have said a thing. I gave him my word not to breathe a word, and my word isn't something I break. Anyway, he's your friend. He should own up at once."

She sat back and watched his face with satisfaction, and not a little sorrow. He was so handsome. Or so, at least, she thought. Even with lampblack and soot smeared on his face. And he still exuded such a feeling of solidity and safety, and masculinity. But why wasn't his voice high-pitched? she wondered. And why did he still have the beginnings of a dark beard beginning to show? She decided that it took time for such things to cease to be. And then she felt even worse.

"Don't look so abysmal," he said. "I'll ask the viscount. Whether or not I'm told the truth is another matter. In truth, Miss Chatham, I trust no one now. Not even you, I'm afraid."

She jumped to her feet. "Then I'll leave, right now."

"Oh, sit down," he said wearily. "If you were me, who would you trust?"

She thought about it and sat again.

"Only one more question," he said. "Whatever he offered, whatever he wants, did you agree to do it?"

"Yes. No," she said. "I've thought about it, but all I gave him was a nod, not a handshake, or a verbal agreement. Will he be outraged when I tell him I decided not to do it?"

"No, but I suspect that he'd start suspecting you of terrible things. Don't worry. If you haven't done any of them, you've nothing to fear."

"Well, of course I haven't," she grumbled.

They were quiet as the landlord brought their suppers. Then she looked up, a sudden light in her eyes. *Such pretty eyes*, he thought.

"Then you think you may be in danger from me now?" she asked. "Why, you must, if you don't trust anyone. How brave of you to attempt a dinner in my presence, when I obviously did so well with only a cup of punch." She sat back, looking satisfied and wary all at once.

Lord, but she was adorable, he thought. She was either transparent as water or the best liar he'd ever met, and he'd met some famous ones.

"But if I died here and now, someone would put two and two together and discover it was you all along," he countered, taking a forkful of stew to his lips.

"Someone else knows I'm here with you?" she demanded, starting to get up again.

"The hackney driver," he said after he'd chewed a mouthful. "The landlord here."

"Then I'll leave," she said.

He gestured for her to sit. "The driver works for me, and me alone. The landlord never tells tales about any customer. He'd have no customers if he did. And he doesn't know your name. Who do you have watching over you?"

She sat down, shook her head, and lowered her gaze to her plate. When she looked at him again, her eyes were damp. "No one," she said softly, "and that's the truth." She straightened her shoulders. "But I can watch out for myself, thank you."

"You're welcome," he said softly. "Now eat, please, or both our lives are at risk, from the landlord. He's a proud man."

They ate their dinners, drank some home brew, and then sat back, looking at each other.

"You feel all right?" she asked.

"Yes. You must have used the slow-acting mixture this time."

She smiled, and he realized she had even, white teeth. She was fascinating to be with. At first, she'd looked elegant, if a bit plain; alluring in a subtle way. But like certain great works of art, the more he studied her, the more he saw the beautiful things about her. If she used a bit of paint, he thought, she'd be magnificent. And yet if she did, she'd look entirely artificial. It was the fact that she got a fellow to keep searching her clear hazel eyes, noticing her pure complexion, finely etched lips, and not least, that lovely form; constantly finding new things to admire that made her fascinating, and more and more desirable.

"Now, these are the facts as I know them," he said, leaning closer to her.

She didn't hear all of what he said at first, because he was leaning closer to her. But then he explained everything, and she listened close. As she'd feared, he didn't know any more than she did about what was going on in Lady Harwood's salon.

"So now it's not anything to do with the viscount's brother, or at least, I don't think so," he concluded. "Or can you see him trying to murder me to keep his love affair blooming?"

She smiled. "I can't see it."

He didn't smile. "That's the problem. This is a serious business now, Jane. I hate to involve you in it. Let me tell you that I've met murderers who look so innocent you'd never suspect them. Only anyone who looks that innocent ought to be suspected." He put both hands on the table. They were as clean, she noted, as his face was not.

"I don't want you to be obvious about it," he continued. "I don't want anyone guessing what you're doing. Just listen, and make mental notes of what you see or hear. I don't even like our meeting like this, in public. Not even if that public isn't known to most people we know. So we can't do this again. It might not be safe for you. But I might not be able to always control the time and place of our meetings. Knowing all this, Jane, and accepting the possible danger in it, will you continue to work for me?" he finally asked.

She didn't know if she dared. It was too dangerous. It wasn't murder she feared, or even taking part in a treasonous plot. She thought she knew the right thing to do. But whenever she looked at him, she wanted all the wrong things, and worst of all, knew she could never do them. Or should not.

"Yes," she said. "I will."

"And will you promise not to work for the viscount, or anyone else, or tell anyone, about it?" he asked. "And if you lapse, to tell me?"

"Yes," she said again.

He took her hand in his and held it gently for a moment. "Done," he said. And although he let go of her hand, his gaze remained locked on hers.

Chapter 13

⌒◯◯⌒

"**N**ot here. Go on please," Jane told Simon as the hackney slowed at the top of the street where she was usually let down.

"Why?" he asked.

"I—I don't live here anymore," she said, putting up her chin.

"Really? And I didn't know? This must be a very recent development."

"As of this morning. Please tell the driver to go on for five more streets, then turn left, and continue on for eight more. Then he can go right for . . . let me think, two streets. Yes. He can let me down at that corner and I'll walk to my lodgings," she said. Although she knew her new landlady wouldn't care if she went back up to her rooms with Simon and his driver, and the horses too, probably, she thought bitterly.

Simon sat up straight and stared at her. "That's in Whitechapel! That's where you took new rooms? Are you mad?"

"Not *in* Whitechapel," she said through tight lips. "Nearby, but not in the district."

"Nearby enough to be murdered in your sleep—if you're lucky. It's what will happen to you while you're awake that you should be worried about. Why this sudden change of address? Is someone threatening you?" he asked, leaning toward her to catch every nuance of her expression in the flickering lamp on the wall of the cab.

"Only my last landlady," Jane said with regret. "And she carried through with her threat. I missed the dawn, coming home with you last night. I arrived with first light instead, like a 'draggletail tart,' as she so sweetly put it, among other comparisons. She'd been waiting in the hall for me. There was nothing I could say to change her mind. She wouldn't let me stay, and I can't really blame her. She does have rooms to let, and she works hard to keep up appearances. None of my excuses made much sense, I suppose because even though the truth was innocent enough, it was hard to believe. And she didn't really know me.

"So I left," Jane said. "I went far and wide to find rooms. I walked all day today. It isn't easy for a female alone, no matter how respectable she claims to be. Mind, I'm not mad enough to stay in a vile slum. I'm satisfied. My new room isn't in a bad place."

"No, it's worse than bad. You aren't safe walking those streets on a cloudy day." He held up a hand. "Let me think."

"While you do," she said acidly, "take me home, please."

He stared at her. "Not to that place, no," he said. "Not even to pick up your belongings. I'll send a footman for them."

"No, you won't," she said, flaring up. "You may be a nobleman and I may be your social inferior because I lack family and funds, but I am a free woman and I have the ordering of my own life, thank you."

"You're welcome," he said absently, deep in thought, and added, "but not when it's the ordering of your own death that you're about."

She leaned forward to grab the door handle.

"You will not leave," he said coldly.

The tone of his voice stopped her. "I resent this," she said with muted fury as she sat back, "and I will do as I please when I'm free of you."

"Doubtless," he muttered. "Let me see. You can't go to my house. That would make matters worse. I can't slip you past Proctor's hirelings again. At least, not so soon. Night is on us, and now is not the time for me to find permanent lodgings for a proper female. Ah! I'll take you to a hotel. Not the Pulteney, or the like. But a decent, respectable hotel, although not one frequented by Society, because we don't want you subjected to more such gossip. I have it." He rapped on the ceiling of the hackney, and gave the driver instructions. Then he too sat back.

"Can I afford this respectable hotel?" Jane asked angrily.

"You don't have to. I'm your employer, remember? It's to my benefit to keep you alive and in good condition. My God, Jane, what were you thinking of?"

"Finding a place to put my things, and a place to sleep tonight," she said proudly.

"And you couldn't come to me?"

She stared at him. "And what would you have thought if I had?"

He didn't answer. She was right, although entirely wrong.

They rode back to the heart of London in silence.

"Damn!" he suddenly exclaimed. "Excuse me for the profanity but I just realized I can't go to a hotel with you in this state. I'm dressed like a lamplighter; they won't even let me into the lobby. And I can't go home, not with you." He was still a moment. "I have it," he said. He rapped on the cab's ceiling and gave new directions to the driver.

"Am I to know anything about this?" she asked.

"No," he said. "There's a place I can go even Proctor doesn't know about. From the old days, back in the day when I was a real operative for His Majesty. Everyone had to have several bolt-holes. This is one of mine, or was, at any rate. I have clothing there. Unless I miss my guess, it's still there. We'll go near there, I'll get out of the carriage, and to all intents and purposes, I'll disappear. The driver will take you on a lovely tour of London, and when he picks me up again, I'll be fit to escort you to a decent hotel. Mind, I won't be a *tulip of the ton*. But respectable. Clerkish. Maybe a sales manager for a shipping firm. A neat, clean man of business, with nothing to do with the *ton*. Something like that. I just hope she hasn't moved or left London."

"She?" Jane asked. "If it's a woman, why can't I wait in her parlor?"

"You wouldn't want to chance anyone seeing you there, believe me."

"Oh," Jane said faintly, color coming into her cheeks. "*That* kind of a place?"

"What do you know of *that* kind of place," he asked with amusement.

"I read a great deal," she said primly, and then unable to resist, she laughed, adding, "and you pay me to listen to gossip, remember?"

"So I do," he admitted. "I'd no idea I was corrupting you. The lady of the house is a friend of mine," he said. "I never was a client of hers."

And while he wondered why the devil he had to explain that to her, she sat silently, feeling bad for him because he obviously didn't know the lady's whereabouts now because he couldn't be her client in the future.

When he left the hackney and hurried off into the night, Jane sat back and wondered if she should accept his charity. Because that was what it was. Then she closed her eyes. Because, of course, she had no choice.

She was wakened when the door to the cab was drawn open. Simon climbed in and sat down. She stared. He looked, as promised, entirely respectable. But so different. He wore a dark jacket; his shirt was white, his neckcloth simply tied, and his collar not at all high. His waistcoat was also dark, as were his breeches. He had on dark hose, which she could see because instead of his usual polished half boots, he wore simple dark shoes. His dark hair was slicked back until it shone, and drawn into an old-fashioned queue. He looked, she thought, dead boring. Until, of course, you looked into his eyes.

"*Voila!*" he said. "What do you think? Am I worth waking up to?"

"You look entirely respectable. And very unlike yourself."

"Good," he said, sitting back. "Now on to the hotel."

But the hotel they stopped at was filled up. It was a grand-looking place on the park, where footmen in livery stood guard on either side of the front door. The manager was very sorry, he told them, but there wasn't a room available for love or money.

"If I'd been dressed as usual," Simon grumbled as he climbed back into the hackney, "I wouldn't have needed love or money. The place has gotten pretensions. Oh well, we'll go on."

The second hotel was a simple town house in a quiet street off the park. There was a doorman, and a footman to assist Jane as she stepped out of the hackney. And the manager was pleased to see them. He quoted his rates, and as Jane caught her breath, Simon signed the register.

"I won't be staying with my cousin," he told the manager. "But I will be visiting. We expect no one else. I do hope you can assure me that she will be safe from importunities from any strangers. I'll be with her during the day, or for dinner, but I trust you can keep her safe at night. It's her first trip to London."

"Certainly, sir," the manager said.

Simon had been cool at first, but although he'd changed his clothing, his accent was one of command.

"My cousin's cases are at the posting inn," Simon went on, putting down his pen. "They'll be delivered here as soon as I tell the driver she's staying. But we should like to see the room first," he added, swinging the register back toward the manager.

"But certainly, Mr. Piggott," the manager said. "Miss Piggot? This way if you please."

"Piggott?" Jane whispered to Simon as they climbed the carpeted stair to the third floor behind the manager.

He patted her hand. "My dear Polly," he said sweetly, "don't be worried. I'm sure you'll be safe as houses here."

"Polly Piggott?" she mouthed, aghast.

He smiled. But so did Jane when she saw her room. It was large, with huge windows covered by gauzy white curtains. There was a huge bed—and a dresser, two chairs, and a hearth that the footman, following them quickly, bent to light. It was nicer than any room she'd rented since she'd left home.

"And it faces the park," the manager said proudly. "In fact it wouldn't have been free save for the fact that the gentleman who had reserved it sent word this very afternoon that he had to change plans. Shall I give word to your driver that the lady would like her bags brought here?"

"Oh, yes!" Jane exclaimed as Simon nodded.

"And her maid?" the manager asked.

There was a stilted silence, until Simon spoke. "We intend to hire one here in London. My cousin's servant was too old to make the trip. So what do you think of the room, Cuz?"

"I like it very well," Jane said.

"If it pleases you, dear Polly, so it shall be," Simon said. "I'll stay with my cousin until her bags arrive," he told the manager.

The manager bowed, and with the footman, left them.

Jane was so happy that she swirled around in a circle, her arms out. "And look, I can dance and my arms don't touch the walls!" She hopped to the bed, leapt up on it. "Oh, it's deliciously soft. I can tell you now, my lord, that I had every expectation of sitting up all night in the room I'd rented today. I saw the baseboards were chewed, you see. And I'll bet it wasn't by puppies," she added, laughing.

If his clothing had changed him, Simon thought, then surely the hotel room had transformed Jane. It looked commonplace enough to him, even a little spare, but it was obviously luxurious to her. Simple comfort made her glow. She looked very lovely, and supremely happy.

"Well then," he said, sitting by the hearth. "Here you stay until we can find more permanent digs for you."

She stopped bouncing on the bed. "That is not your problem, my lord."

He sighed. "It is. If I hadn't hired you on as my informant, none of this would have happened. Don't worry. I'll find lodgings you can afford, one that isn't infested by puppies or other wood-gnawing creatures."

He laid his head back and closed his eyes. He looked weary, Jane thought. The poisoning had obviously leeched him of his usual energy. And maybe, a little voice in her head whispered, the idea that here he was, in a lady's bedchamber, and there was nothing he could do. Nothing he could even pretend he might take advantage of, much less her herself. That was, she quickly thought, if a man like Lord Granger, who used to have a second home in a bawdy house and who knew where else, would be so interested in a female like her.

"Are you feeling well, my lord?" she asked quietly.

"I confess, I'm tired," he said. "I must be getting old."

"It will be a while until your driver returns," she said. "Would you care to lie down until he comes?"

"Excellent idea," he said, opening his eyes. He stood and ambled over to the bed, shucked off his jacket, pulled off his shoes, and sat on the edge of the bed with a long audible sigh.

Jane jumped up.

"No, no," he said, with a wave of his hand as he sank back to lay his head on the pillows. He crossed his arms over his abdomen and closed his eyes. "No need to leave. In fact, at this hour, after all this time, with our misunderstandings resolved, it would seem downright unfriendly of you to leave me."

So it would, she thought, and lay down beside him, on her side, hands beneath her cheek, watching him.

"Yes," he said, though he'd his eyes closed and she'd said nothing. "It would be comforting if you lay next to me."

"I am."

"Next to me?"

"Are you ill again?"

"No," he said, a faint smile curling his lips. "But in need of comfort, oh yes."

After a silent moment, she bunched her body together and moved closer to him: rather like a caterpillar moving across a stem, he thought. When she was beside him, and he could feel the warmth of her body, and hear her slightest exhalation, she put a hand on his heart.

"I really do appreciate your efforts on my behalf," she said quietly. "I didn't want to be an obligation, not to anyone. But I—some things I found difficult to do by myself. Still, I *did* find honest employment. I *do* work, and fend for myself. And I do thank you for caring."

He opened his eyes to see her looking into his. "I know," he said softly, running a finger down her exposed cheek. "Are you weeping?"

"No," she said, though it was a near thing. "Only, I must say it feels good to have someone care for you again. I'm touched by it, is all that it is."

Her hair, he saw, had come loose from its pins, and lay in smooth tendrils around her face. *Charming,* he thought, and moved his finger so he could stroke her neck.

"I will pay you back when I can," she told him earnestly.

"Doubtless," he said in a low slumberous voice. "Has anyone told you how lovely you are?"

She shook her head, unable to speak.

"Now why should that dismay you?" he asked.

"You're a good and a brave man," she said, her chin quivering. "And kind beyond belief."

"Why do you say that?" he said, frowning.

"Lady Harwood told me about your time and travails in the dungeons of Paris. Yet you bore it, and here you are, willing to try to protect someone else, a stranger, for no reward but the chance that she might be able to help you in your investigations."

"Oh, I wouldn't say that," he said lazily, moving his finger to trace her lips.

That made her even sadder. She raised her head and slowly lowered it, so she could place a light, sweet kiss on his lips.

"Oh, yes," he said, and rising on one elbow, he caught her in his arms. He turned her and kissed her, lightly, gently, but passionately enough to press her head back into the pillow. "Open to me," he whispered against her closed mouth. "Open your lips."

"But," she said, "are you sure it's the right thing to do, I mean, for you?"

It was a strange thing for her to ask, but he no longer cared how peculiarly she was behaving, not with her so close, so obliging. "It is right for me," he said. "Wonderfully right. I'll make it right for you. I vow it, please, Jane."

She opened her lips, and he touched her tongue with his. She was all sweetness, all passion, and all wet, he realized.

"Why are you weeping?" he asked, raising his head.

"Because—because, you know," she said, shivering as his hand cupped her breast.

"Oh. I see. Don't worry, I'll be careful. You're safe. I won't get you with child."

"I know, I know," she said miserably.

"But I won't go on until you stop crying," he added, drawing back his hand. "You might think it convinces me of your modesty, but I'd rather you didn't. It distresses me."

She dashed the tears from her eyes. "I don't want to distress you, not for the world," she said, and pulled his head down to hers.

He wouldn't have thought it, he had never really imagined it, but prim and proper Miss Chatham kissed him with all her heart, and pressed herself tightly to him. *Well, not so prim after all*, he managed to think. *A dancer, after all. And on her own all this time? I should have known. Will I never learn? I was fooled yet again.* Then, with a clearer conscience, he bent to her again.

It could have been the work of a minute. He made it last for much longer than that, kissing every new inch of smooth white skin that appeared to his eyes. He slowly pulled down the top of her gown, and saluted each tilted breast, exulting at how she responded to him. She arched against his hands, his mouth, and gasped. She stroked his hair until it came undone from its queue. Then she ran her fingers through it, murmuring about how silky it was. But she didn't reach to touch him. He was charmed at her show of modesty, and smiled. What sort of men was she used to? He'd soon show her it didn't matter if he was a nobleman; he was a man who liked participation.

He slid an arm under her so he could strip away the gown.

"Oh, look at you," he said, when he had cast it away. "You are delicious."

And so she was, her body lean and shapely, and her eyes—*the little fabricator*, he thought tenderly—cast down, as though she were a maiden being seen for the very first time.

"A moment," he whispered. "I need to join you." He thought he felt her body stiffen as he moved from her. "Don't worry," he assured her, "it will be only for a moment, I just feel constricted."

He quickly let down the fall on his breeches, and returned to her. He caught her up in his arms again, and wished he'd dared take the time to pull off his shirt, because he could feel the tips of her breasts hard against his chest, through his shirt. So he backed off for a minute more, pulled off his shirt, cast it away, and came to her again. He shivered with pleasure. It had been so long a time since he'd been this close to a woman, or this excited by one.

Now she ventured to run her hands gently over his naked back, almost as though she were searching for something.

"Scars," he murmured, when her questing hands stilled. "From my sojourn in Paris. No pain, not anymore. Just not lovely. Ah, but you are."

"I'm so sorry," she said, her hands moving over his tightly muscled back again.

"Why? You did nothing. I said it doesn't hurt. In fact, your hands there, anywhere, are healing. They feel wonderful on my skin."

She didn't take the hint and lower her caresses. He didn't care. She was warm everywhere. And then she was moist and hot when his fingers sought more. She was tense the first time he nudged her knees apart, but then she relented, and opened to him. But she kept her gaze down as he readied her. He didn't need to see her eyes to know when she was ready for him. An obvious tremor of pleasure made her body grow still. She drew away and closed her legs. Not from modesty, he'd swear it. Her skin everywhere was damp with the same fever he had.

"There's more," he said, smiling with effort, because need was driving him hard. "Much more, in every way."

"But what about you?" she asked, her gaze finally searching his.

"Oh, I'm doing very well, thank you," he said on a breathless laugh. "Can't you tell? Almost too well, in fact. Are you ready?"

She frowned.

A foolish question, he didn't blame her. He pulled away from her so he could balance on his knees and elbows before he came back to her. She looked up at him and then down at him. He was definitely ready.

Her eyes widened. She backed up against the pillow. She crossed her arms over her naked breasts, and drew her knees up to her chin. And then, still staring, she clapped a hand over her mouth. But not before she'd let out a horrified cry, a surprised exclamation of shock and dismay.

Chapter 14

∞

The landlord came rushing into the room, brandishing a fireplace poker. "What's amiss?" he shouted. Two footmen followed him, waving stout sticks. Doors all along the hall popped open, and heads stuck out to see what the screech was for and all the subsequent fuss was about.

"Be at ease," Simon said, facing the manager. "The lady, my cousin, overreacted. She thought she saw a mouse."

"A rat," Jane said, from the corner of the room where she stood.

The manager stared at Simon. His expression said it clearly. When Simon had checked in, he'd been cool and businesslike. Now his overlong black hair was out of its queue and wildly mussed, his collar was askew, his jacket off, his shirt rumpled, and his face was flushed.

"I've looked for it, even crawling under the bed to see," Simon explained when he saw how the manager's gaze was evaluating him. "But I saw nothing."

Jane was standing stock-still. "I'm sorry," she said. "I am from the country but I never could like rodents."

"We have no rodents in our rooms," the manager said stiffly. "The ratcatcher comes every month, and goes home with an empty sack. Many places in London may have mice and rats. *We* don't."

"I think it was perhaps a shadow," Simon said. "My cousin is weary from her travels, and half asleep as it was."

"It may have been so," she agreed. "My apologies for upsetting everyone."

The manager nodded. "If we may be of further service, do not hesitate to call," he said.

"We shall. Only not quite so loudly," Simon added.

The manager bowed, shooed his footmen from the room, and left to tell his other guests that it was much ado about nothing. A hysterical female, after all.

"A *rat*?" Simon said when they'd gone.

She ducked her head.

He ran a hand through his hair. "Sit down. Let's talk about this."

She took a chair and sat warily watching him.

"You got into bed with me," he said, with no preface.

She nodded.

"You willingly came into my arms. You kissed me. You—we did a great deal more. You seemed pleased with my company. And then, suddenly, you leapt away and shrieked as though your hair were on fire. Why?"

She hung her head.

"Did I hurt you?"

She shook her head.

"Were you coerced, drugged, or threatened?"

"No," she whispered.

"Did I promise anything more, or less?"

Again, she shook her head.

He stopped, and stared at her. "Had you never seen a man before?"

"Well," she said with more spirit, "not like that."

"I admit it might be an awesome sight, and while flattered, I suppose, by your reaction, I'm also confused. The sight of a man about to make love terrified you that much?"

"No," she said, lifting her chin, "but I was most cruelly misled and mistaken."

"By me?" he asked, shocked.

"By Lady Harwood." Jane's face turned even pinker, but she took a deep breath and added, choosing her words carefully, "I was told you didn't have . . ." She started over, "I was told, in no uncertain terms, that you . . . the rumor was that while you were in prison you were . . . emasculated. And you certainly were not. So I was surprised, and yes, shocked." She put up her chin and met his stupefied gaze.

He sank to a chair. "Let me consider this," he said. "You went to bed with me thinking I couldn't consummate the act? No, no," he said, rising and pacing, "I think I see. It's beyond that. You went to bed with me out of *pity*? Of course you did!" he said, turning on his heel and facing her. "Hence: the tears when we kissed. And then when you saw I was actually capable, you were shocked. And horrified. That's it, isn't it?"

She nodded, gazing down at her toes.

"Lord!" he said, sitting back. "I thought you were just eager. And," he added, shaking a finger at her, "you certainly were, whatever you're original intentions. Now it seems you were trying to be kind." He glowered at her. "Why the devil did you think a eunuch would want to get you into bed in the first place?"

"I thought you wanted affection," she said.

"Lord!" he said again, and sat back again, as though rendered speechless. "But didn't you think that if I were a eunuch there would be some tell-tale signs. Above my belt, that is. Am I plump? Am I beardless, apart from when I'm freshly shaved? Is my voice higher than yours?"

"I'm not stupid," she said defensively. "How should I know what happens to a man when he's rendered incapable?"

"It's a deal more than incapability," he muttered.

"Well, how many eunuchs have you met?" she asked. "You've traveled widely."

He shrugged, "None."

"None that you noticed, you mean. I'd bet you met some, and didn't know. So how should I know?"

He fell still, remembering the endless dark nights he'd spent beneath the earth, with not even a glimpse of the moon, and in those dark hours wondering if day would bring him death or even the disfigurement she had believed had been inflicted. He hadn't known what would happen. Much had been promised. He'd whiled away the wretched hours wondering about it, and woken each morning whole, if sometimes battered, and resolved anew not to worry anymore.

"So," she said, pressing her momentary advantage, "how was I to know except from what Lady Harwood told me? There aren't any books about it that I know of, and why should I read them if I did?"

He looked up at her militant expression, and started to smile, and then began to laugh. "Oh my God," he managed to say, "what a tale! The country girl who went to bed with a capon, only to discover she'd gotten in with a cock—now there's a farce to thrill playgoers, not to mention a double entendre to end them all. Good lord, Jane, I know you're not stupid. But you will admit it's a remarkably stupid thing to do, when you come right down to it, and we almost did."

He stopped laughing and wiped his eyes. A new look came into them, and he leaned forward. "Jane. Do you expect me to offer for you because I've compromised you? And you, all innocent of my real desires?"

She sat up as though he'd poked her with a

stick. "No! Never! And you didn't compromise me. Not really, and no one knows, or will. You only educated me," she added with an unexpected smile. "It was all due to an utter and complete misunderstanding on both our parts. I'm not a sheltered lady, my lord; no one will come to challenge you to a duel for my honor. So under no circumstances should you consider yourself compromised either. Let's call it a grand disillusion, and end it now."

She rose from her chair. "Because now that I know the true circumstances, I can't stay here with you a moment longer. I may not consider myself dishonored, but I'd be a fool to stay here with you now, and that, I am not. I thank you for your efforts on my behalf . . . No, I don't really know if I should, considering that you clearly thought you were going to be rewarded for your efforts, if not in coin then in kind. At any rate, good night, my lord, I think we've spent enough time together, and that this must end now."

"And so you're going out into the streets of London late at night, to sleep where? You have no lodgings. And you can't go back to the new ones you took, because I won't let you. Are you thinking of taking a nap until dawn in the park? The gates are locked, and if they weren't, I wouldn't allow it. Lest you think me a tyrant, I remind you that tonight I am responsible for you. You're still my cousin, Polly Piggott, and so you will sleep the way an unmarried female cousin of mine should: alone and untouched. Tomorrow, I'll find you lodgings you can afford, in a decent district. I owe you that."

"Why?" she asked.

"Because you work for me. You still do, don't you?"

She looked at him. Standing there, her gown rumpled, her hair half down, he thought she was delectable. Remembering how she'd come to life in his arms, the softness and the sweetness of her, and what they'd been doing a few moments before, he found her even more so. But he didn't dare show it by word or deed. She was after all, an innocent, and whatever he'd done or would do in future, compromising innocents was not going to be among his sins.

She sat. "I suppose I do work for you." She regarded him steadily. "But what is a landlady to think if you or one of your minions go rent a room for me?"

"They will think some gentleman is seeing to

the welfare of a distant relative. And when they have the rent paid in advance, and no one but you living there, they will think no more."

She nodded. It seemed equitable. "But if I continue to work for you," she added anxiously, "you're not going to try anything like this again, now that I know what you're capable of, are you?"

"No," he said. "That I promise, no matter what you know. In the first place because I don't believe in seducing my employees. You were not seduced tonight, Jane, whatever you think. You do know that?"

She nodded.

"And it was, believe it or not, against my better judgment. That better judgment being somewhat unreliable, I grant you," he said ruefully. "You're safe because in the second place, I wouldn't attempt anything again because I don't think my ears could take it. You have formidable lungs, you know."

She gave him a quick nervous grin, and then became serious again. "This also means we ought not meet in secret again. How will I get information to you?"

"I'll think of something," he said. "As for now . . ." He rose from his chair again. "I think

I should wait here with you until your bags arrive safely, and I see that you are the same. Then I'll leave. Is that acceptable to you?"

She nodded, watching him. It would be acceptable if he chose to stay with her every night, if only the world were different. She'd gotten over her shock at his virility and was now even more shocked at how much more she yearned to know of him, mind and body. She found that every minute passed with him was delicious, and the fact that this might be their last private meeting made them even more so.

"Since we have the time," he said after a moment, stretching out his legs, and crossing his arms, "I do have a question for you. Did Lady Harwood give you an explanation for the wonderful rumor about my masculine capabilities?"

She grinned again at how deftly he'd put it. "Yes." But then, thinking of his imprisonment, all thoughts of humor fled. It was a decidedly awkward question. She thought for a moment, if he could speak so openly, so could she. "She said it was because you were so profligate in your associations with females before you went to France, as well as indiscriminate in your choice of them, and then when you came back, you became a monk, so to speak. She said your incapacity was the reason."

His eyes widened. "Well said," he said with true admiration for her tiptoeing through the thicket of improper words. "I suppose I can see how that might have given rise to lurid interpretations. But I think there's more she didn't tell you."

Jane wanted to ask a dozen more questions, but held her tongue.

"Your eyes," he said on a laugh. "I don't know why I hired you on as a spy. Remember to keep your eyes closed whenever you speak with someone you suspect, will you? All right. I was a troubled youth. No, I wasn't, not really. My parents, when I saw them, were kindly. I went to a good, but strict school. When I got out, like so many of my kind, after years of nothing but dull study, I became a young man on the town, with nothing in my mind but pleasure. Granted, I might have overdone it a bit. But I was never indiscriminate. The fact was that I didn't like personal dealings with a woman unless I liked her, body and soul. So I consorted with some women those of my class might consider beneath me. Well, they usually were, if only in posture," he said with a grin.

"Sorry," he said quickly. "You have such a reasonable mind that I forgot you were an innocent female. The point is that I didn't consider the women I consorted with beneath me in any other way. And since I had no desire to marry or be trapped into wedlock, I didn't pass time with what they call 'Ladies of Quality.' I preferred women of character, which is my favorite quality in any being, of whatever gender. That's what must have given rise to my reputation for being indiscriminate. I was actually the opposite."

He fell silent.

"You don't have to tell me if it's painful," Jane said quickly.

"Actually, oddly enough, I feel I must," he said. "If only because discussing something aloud gives clarity to it, and a kind of peace to the narrator. It's been too long since I've done that. I've grown too used to talking to myself. At any rate, when I returned from captivity, I was ill and must have looked like the very devil. I holed up in my house until I was well again. When I got better, I decided not to have much to do with any females. No," he said with a sad smile, *"decided* isn't the right word. It wasn't a conscious

247

decision. But since it was a woman who beguiled me and then betrayed me, I didn't want to have anything to do with anyone of your fair sex. Silly of me to condemn others because of Mademoiselle Martine's treachery, isn't it? But I suppose I did. Even, so, that isn't enough to have started such a rumor."

"Do you think Lady Harwood knew she was telling a lie?" Jane asked.

He shook his head. "No, I know the lady, and if she believed she had half a chance to nab me for husband number two, she'd have tried. Someone obviously told her the rumor. And that's interesting. You might try to discover who it was, if you can introduce the subject without a breath of your interest in it."

Seeing him in this rare, confiding mood, Jane ventured to ask more. "Were you hurt in prison?"

"Oh, yes," he said absently, as though his mind were already at work at something else. "Beatings and threats, mostly. There was this one brute who took delight in threatening me with death at sunrise, every night. As time passed, and I woke up and lived past dawn, you can see the threat lost some of its credulity. So then, he threatened to . . . part me from some of my more valuable parts." His eyes widened. "Now, that is interesting. No one but the guards at the jail knew of it. Or so I thought."

"What happened?" Jane asked breathlessly.

"Oh," he said too casually, "one day, I caught him off guard, literally, and beat him to a pulp. Chains are good for more than holding a prisoner down. They make excellent weapons, if used correctly. And if your opponent's fellow guards don't care for him much themselves, they're even more effective. Brutes have associates, they seldom have friends. After that they left me alone," he said softly. "Strictly alone, mind you, in a dungeon, with not even a rat—a real rat," he added with a wry smile, "to keep my fleas company. They left me there for four months. I think that wounded me most of all, now that I think of it."

"They didn't want you dead," she commented.

"No. Foreign agents are too important, for information or exchange. I was freed by some of our own operatives. Then I was spirited home. I retired from the business, until my friend the viscount Delancey asked me to watch over his brother. Obviously, though, someone from the old days saw me and thought I was still at work for His Majesty. Then they obviously decided they didn't want me around, at least not breathing, above or below ground. I wish I'd recognized who it was."

"That's what I can do for you!" Jane said, clapping her hands together. "I'll watch and listen. They think you're spying on them, while unnoticed, I'll be spying on them."

He smiled. "You take care! It would be just like one of your students to be plotting against me. The little charmers are probably tireless in their efforts."

"Yes," Jane said. "And they'll work all day for the promise of a boiled sweet."

They sat there, grinning at each other, until each realized how very pleasant it was, and that it was late at night and they were alone together again.

"I do wish things were different," Simon said gently.

"As do I," Jane said.

Neither lied, and yet neither told the truth and they both knew it. But now she felt safe again, and so did he. In that moment, Simon, looking at her, remembering her, anticipating her, wished that he could open his lips and ask her to marry him. Her status in life didn't bother him. Her lack of funds was nothing to him. Her lack of family was actually an asset, so far as he could see from his friends' marriages. But he realized he didn't trust her and didn't know if he'd ever trust any woman enough to marry one.

He'd end up, he supposed, a crusty old gent who'd either hastily marry a juvenile and try to get a child on the way to his grave, or be an old man sitting alone in his parlor watching his life ebb, thinking of what might have been.

Jane stole glances at him, and wondered what would happen if she could suddenly throw off all her heavy bonds of respectability. Surely he'd respond to her if she told him it was what she really wanted. And she did, with all her heart, if not her brain. Surely, if the worst happened he was the sort of man who would take care of his child even if he weren't married to its mother. And surely, one day he'd find a wife, and she herself would end up as either a woman with a broken heart and reputation, or worse, one who had to love for money for her own sake as well as for any child she might have.

There was a knock at the door. Simon leapt to his feet, and greeted his footman with gratitude. The man bore two rather shabby bags that belonged to Jane.

"Good, good," Simon said mindlessly. "Thank you, Thomas. Now, Cousin," he told Jane, because the door was open, "you have your things, and you can go to bed peacefully. There won't be a rat or a mouse in the room. All the rodents are accounted for. And so I bid you good night. I'll get word to you in the morning and tell you if I've managed to find you suitable, respectable new digs."

She sketched a curtsy. "Thank you, Cousin," she said. "I know you will. I thank you for saving me from my foolishness, as well as from phantom rodents. I'll sleep well knowing I'm safe here in London."

He bowed, and left her, thinking of her alone in that bed. He frowned.

"My lord?" the footman asked as they took the stair down to the hotel lobby.

"Yes?"

"Are you displeased?"

"Oh. My expression?" Simon asked, running a hand over his face. "It's just the hour," he said.

"I suddenly realized that it's much later than I knew."

And Jane sank to her lonely bed realizing—for the first time and likely not the last—that she found it to be a cold and lonely one.

Chapter 15

⟨ 〰 ⟩

It was more of an attic than a room, but it was spacious, running from the front of the house to the back. The ceiling was high; it was a large, airy space with a rear window that looked down at a little back garden, and a front one that looked over the street. There were spring flowers in bloom at the back, and the street had tall trees coming into light green leaf. Green-tinted spring sunshine poured through the windows. Jane was thrilled.

It was the first lodging she'd had in London that had two windows. The bed was soft, the linens clean, and the room itself big enough to give dancing lessons in. One day, she promised herself as she unpacked her belongings and stowed them in a cedar-scented wardrobe, she'd have just this sort of aerie as a bedroom for herself, and a studio for pupils downstairs.

And it was in a very respectable neighborhood, one where she could walk, not run, at night, if she had to go out. Of course she'd never have gotten such a place by herself. In fact, she shuddered to think of the price of the rent. It was leased for a six-month period. If her work with Lord Granger were done by then she'd likely have to move on.

It had been difficult for her to accept that a male would pay her rent, and one she wasn't related to, at that. Last night she'd reasoned she had no choice in the matter. This morning, she didn't want to think about it. If he said that lodgings were part of her wages, then so be it. She loved her room and would be sorry to leave it when her job was done. Unless, of course, she was successful in finding his foe and there was a reward for capturing an enemy of His Majesty. This lovely morning she let her rosy daydreams run as wild as her dire ones usually did.

Once she'd washed and dressed, she spun around and looked at herself in the mirror. For once, it was no small spotty image that she saw. There was a large looking glass mounted in gilded wood, standing on its own two feet. She could see all of herself now. And what she saw didn't look bad. She hadn't slept too well last night at the hotel, but there were no rings beneath her eyes: they were clear and alert. Her hair was neatly pulled back; her blue gown was perfectly fitting for an instructress, with a high waist, neckline, and puffed sleeves. She was so pleased at the image she vowed to broach a new matter to Lady Harwood. If the girls could see themselves in a full-length mirror, they might better learn how to position their feet.

Today Jane felt privileged, lucky, and full of new ideas. She glanced back at her wonderful room, threw a shawl over her shoulders, and head high, walked out the door to go to work.

"One, two, three," Jane chanted, "One, two, three, and hop! Count to three and hop. Remember, you're bunny rabbits today."

Some of her students counted to one and hopped, some reached two and hopped, some even hopped on three. The lesson was supposed to teach them how to dance in unison. Instead, it was teaching them how to giggle all together.

Jane clapped her hands. "All right. Girls, sit in a circle, please."

They plopped down and gazed up at her, looking for all the world like a ring of panting puppies, she thought. "Now," she said. "How many of you can count?"

Every plump little arm shot up.

"And how many can count to three?"

The arms stayed up.

"Then why can't you do it at the same time?" Jane asked. An idea struck her. "Because when you do it at different times, it just looks silly. But you can't know how pretty and clever you look when you all hop together. This time, I'll lead the line. Watch me. Count as I do, and hop when I do. Now, bend your elbows, dangle your hands up in front of your chests, little rabbits, and we'll try it again."

She lifted her elbows, and let her hands hang like paws. They scrambled to their feet. This time they made it all around the ballroom behind Jane, all jumping when she did, as she called out "three!" She grinned at them when she stopped. Then she looked up, startled. There was sudden riotous applause, calls of "Bravo!" and "Well done, ladies."

Jane sighed, and looked to the doorway of the ballroom. A crowd of Lady Harwood's guests stood there, cheering. The lady herself looked pleased. Evidently, even without her dance instructor falling and making a fool of herself, watching the children dance had become part of the fun of coming to her salon. At least, Jane hoped, they weren't waiting for her to fall. The thought of all those grown men watching her small pupils cavort didn't please her at all. She would wait and speak with the lady alone today. The situation was becoming intolerable on both counts. But she couldn't speak too freely. She needed this employment. Without it she couldn't work for Lord Granger. Without it, there'd be no excuse to see him at all. That might be unendurable. It reminded her of her most pressing job. She studied the assembled crowd.

There was Richard, of course, at Lady Harwood's side. And there was Viscount Delancey, at the edge of the group. Lord Granger, whom she'd noticed first and tried not to keep looking at, stood in the center of the crowd. She didn't know the others. She'd have to get to know them, though, if she were to do any good at all.

"Excellent, Miss Chatham," Lady Harwood said. "And now, the time is up, the children have to go home, and we, my friends, have tea and cakes, sherry for the gentlemen and ratafia for the ladies, awaiting us." She turned to leave. And then turned back. "Oh, Miss Chatham. Would you mind staying on a bit? I have a few things to discuss with you later."

"Of course, my lady," Jane said, and bobbed a curtsey, hating to do it, because it meant Lord Granger saw her being subservient, and exactly what she was: a servant.

When the children were collected by their nurses and nannies, Jane fled to the kitchens, found her corner and waited, listening to the other servants, hoping to pick up a crumb or two of gossip. But she'd other problems to puzzle over. One was why her ladyship wanted to see her. Another was how she could learn to identify the other guests in case she saw them doing anything of interest to Lord Granger. And what the devil did the lady want to tell her in private?

As the servants were busily preparing her ladyship's dinner, a footman was sent to summon Jane. She'd worked herself into a state of high anxiety by then, but had learned at least that Lord Shaw, the plumpish man with the short nose, worked for the War Department. Alfred Banks, the short gentleman in the absurdly fashionable clothing that didn't suit him, was just a fop, although an influential one. And Mr. Oakes, the tall man with the great signet ring, had more money than anyone, but refused to spend it. None of them were suitors for Lady Harwood's hand. But all were eager to be anywhere that was deemed the place to *be*, doubtless each for his own reasons. That made three more gentlemen she could recognize. There were only about thirty or forty more to know, Jane thought bitterly, not counting the ladies, of course.

"Miss Chatham," Lady Harwood said sweetly, as Jane entered her chambers. The lady was relaxing on a long couch of the sort the French had lately made fashionable, her maid brushing out her lovely golden hair. She dismissed her maid, and smiled at Jane. "Do come in. How do the lessons go? They seem wildly successful. Now, don't make them too successful," she said playfully, wagging a finger at Jane, "I don't want all your charges clamoring for a career in the *corps de ballet*! Their mamas will never forgive me!"

Jane didn't know what to say. This wasn't anger, at least. It didn't seem to bode badly. It wasn't the sort of thing you might say to someone you were about to dismiss. All Jane could do was to murmur, "Of course not, my lady. I've told them how much grace, whether in dancing or simply moving about, will mean to their success in the fashionable world when they're older."

"Very good," the lady said. Her lovely blue eyes grew keener. "Sit, my dear, Miss Chatham, do have a seat, will you?"

Jane sat down on a small chair opposite the lady, folded her hands, and looked at her employer expectantly.

"You," the lady said, "in no small part, my dear, have helped to make my salon famous, you know."

"I didn't," Jane murmured, because she knew to do otherwise would offend.

"Well, so it is," the lady said dismissively. "There's always something new in London, and anything new that becomes the talk of the town is somewhere everyone must go. The point is," she said, leaning closer, "I don't want them to leave. I am seeking a worthy man to wed. What better place for me to look than in my own salon? But crazes pass. The children are adorable, and your lessons charming to watch. But I've already heard that both Lady Markover and Mrs. Fanshawe are seeking female dance instructors for their own homes. The French dancing masters will have even more cause to hate you, my dear."

"They hate me?" Jane asked, appalled.

"One would imagine so," the lady answered airily. "So we must try to keep our place as the place to be seen, and to see. I don't suppose . . . there might be another pretty little 'accident' on your part while you're dancing, would there?"

Jane was so angry she threw caution to the winds. "My Lady," she said, standing up. "They *were* accidents, and embarrassing to me. And if the other ladies are hiring on female dance instructors, many will be from the theater or the ballet, trust me; they can arrange even more startling and exciting 'accidents' than I ever could!"

"Oh, sit down," Lady Harwood said peevishly. "It was just a suggestion. Doubtless, you're right. However," she said in a steelier voice, "I gather this employment means something to you?"

"It does," Jane admitted, sitting down.

"And so, would you be interested in another job of work to do here? One that pays very well?"

Jane frowned in confusion.

"Don't make such faces. The gentlemen may find them adorable, but you'll be wrinkled as a prune by thirty if you keep it up. I meant," the lady said softly, "that since you're here now, when my salon is most popular, what would you think of doing a bit of listening and watching for me? You hear the servants gossiping, as I cannot. As their employer I cannot stoop to their level to find out what they're saying. And since they get silent as clams if my maid is nearby, I never find out anything."

"What—what sort of things?" Jane asked.

"Just which gentlemen seem to show a true preference for me, and which simply want to be seen in my salon, and which ones fancy what other females, and who among them may have women in their keeping, that sort of thing. That's all."

Jane blinked.

"It will pay well."

"You mean, being your spy?"

"Faugh!" the lady said, recoiling. "I never proposed such a thing. Come, Miss Jane, I simply want a little more information than I can gather by myself. You're clever and alert, and not connected to anyone that anyone knows, either by family or association. You'd be a perfect set of ears and eyes for me. No one will suspect a thing, and you'll become considerably wealthier. Your dancing lessons won't last forever, you know. Children grow up, fads fade. So. Will you take on this little extra bit of work, if indeed, just being alert and aware can be called work at all? Oh, and if you do not oblige me in this little thing, I'm afraid I won't be able to trust you any longer, and you can't expect me to employ someone I don't trust, can you?"

Jane left her employer a little later that evening, her day's pay for her day's lessons in her pocket and her ears ringing with the sound of many more promised coins. She was still shaking her head as she went out the front door. It was late, twilight was giving way to a deeper dusk, but Jane wasn't afraid to be alone. There wasn't much traffic at this hour. Servants had gone to their master's houses; workingmen and -women, street criers and vendors, had gone to their homes. Those who were going out to dinner were still dressing for it, and the theater had already begun. The bands of drunken young men who sometimes plagued unprotected females hadn't gotten drunk enough yet to roam the city looking for sport. Ladies of the evening were waiting for deeper darkness, because it was their best cosmetic.

These were, for the time being at least, safe streets for Jane to travel. The gaslights had also been lit, and they dotted the streets with comforting pools of light. She'd only walked to the top of the next street, when a tall gentleman joined her.

Her heart leapt up. Until she looked up. It was not Lord Granger, in any guise.

"Good evening, Miss Chatham," Viscount Delancey said in his dry, cool voice as he paced at her side.

She ducked a quick curtsey.

"No, no, my dear," he said quickly. "No need to show such recognition. I just want a few quick words with you, and it would be much better if we weren't remarked by anyone."

Jane paced forward, frowning.

"No need for concern, either," the viscount said, keeping in step with her. "And so, my dear? You've been silent as a clam of late. At least with me. You haven't tried to catch my eye, or send to me. Have you nothing to report? I begin to wonder where your allegiances lie. I asked you to watch the lady's household. Surely you must have heard something that might be of interest to me."

Her head shot up. "I never actually agreed to anything you asked of me," she said.

"You didn't say no," he countered.

"Nor did I say yes, she protested.

"Come now," the viscount said. "You know Lord Granger was placed in grave danger. Surely the household must be talking. I pay well, as I said. I ask nothing of you but gossip. All you have to do is to watch and listen, leave the suspicions to me. I have something to help you." He handed her a folded paper. "Put it away, please."

She held it in her gloved hands, indecisive.

"It's a list of names for you to get to know," the viscount said impatiently. "People that frequent Lady Harwood's salon lately. People I want you to pay especial attention to. So, will you finally oblige me, and by so doing, make yourself considerably wealthier? No nodding; 'yes' or 'no,' please."

She bit her lip.

"It will aid Lord Granger as well, you must know that. I have a care for him," the viscount said. "And I have resources. I cannot believe you'd further endanger him."

"Yes, then," she said, slipping the note into her pocket.

"Good. Oh, and of course, I trust you to keep this discussion secret. This is a devilish complicated business. Anything said of this to *anyone* could jeopardize all I am trying to do. I don't like to make threats and I never make any I can't carry out. If you divulge any of this, I very much fear there will be repercussions. For you."

"That's not fair!" she said. "I didn't ask for this duty or this discussion."

He shrugged. "Life isn't fair. Now let me tell you more. I haven't much time, so I shall have to be brief."

When the viscount finally left her side, walking away as though he'd never spoken to her at all, Jane walked on alone, deep in thought. She was angry and afraid, and puzzled as well. She walked on for several streets before she noticed that a hackney cab was traveling slowly up the road, keeping pace with her. It stopped before a darkened doorway, and the door to the cab swung open.

"Hop in," Lord Granger said in a carrying whisper. "No one's near, no one's watching from afar either. Word of your new rooms hasn't gotten out yet, so no one else knows the route you're taking tonight. They're watching the old one. Hurry, Jane. We haven't got all night."

And because it was his voice, and she was terribly confused, and suddenly he seemed her only friend in the world, she got into the hackney and sat beside him. Then she looked at him in the light from the lantern at the window, and scowled. "A ratcatcher?" she asked, noting his baggy clothing, floppy hat with candle stubs on it, and large sack at his feet.

His smile was crooked. "No screeching, please. I thought you'd be amused. And don't worry, not a rat in sight, and none in the sack either."

"I'm not amused," she said, glad of the dark so he couldn't see her blushing. "I don't know why I even got in here with you. We said we wouldn't see each other again."

"No, we didn't," he said blithely. "I simply said I'd think about it. I have done. There's no other way for us to meet except in secret. I also said I wouldn't try to compromise you. I know I feel safe from you. Am I?" he asked in mock accents of alarm.

She sniffed, and didn't deign to answer him—although she foolishly wondered if he could hear her heart beating faster just at the sight of him.

"Quite right," he said, unconcerned. "The truth is I need to talk with you, and I lack any other means to do it. Can you think of any? I thought not. So, dinner at our favorite tavern, Miss Piggott?"

She smiled; she couldn't help it. And she was hungry. Hungrier still, she realized, for the sight and sound of the man, even dressed as disreputably as he was. Just being near him made her feel both safe and at risk, and most of all, excited and alive.

"I take that for a 'yes,'" he said comfortably. "So," he added, stretching out his long legs and sitting back. "Doubtless you have lots to tell me tonight."

"Doubtless?" she asked.

He sat up and looked at her. "Why, yes, it's been a day since we last met. The lady's salon was packed today. You make a charming rabbit, by the way."

Jane sat still. For all that she'd always spoken to him with absolute truth and a clear conscience, now she felt she had to feel her way in this conversation.

He remained quiet, waiting for her answer. When she didn't speak right away, he spoke again. "Ah, well," he said, settling down again, tipping his hat down over his eyes and folding his hands over his flat stomach. "It has been a long and trying day, hasn't it? We'll talk when we are at dinner."

Jane relaxed. It would give her time to think over what had happened to her today, and put it in perspective. Then she'd ask his opinion. Because for all both Lady Harwood and Viscount Delancey had threatened her, and for all she couldn't afford either of them carrying through on their threats, still she felt safe with this man. It was bizarre, and she knew it. She knew she oughtn't to trust him because he was a gentleman and she a servant, and because he dealt in secrets, and because she was so attracted to him she was afraid she'd do or say something stupid and ruinous for her future. Even so, for all that, still he was the only person in London that she trusted.

It was as well that she couldn't see his face. Because he watched her from under the brim of his hat. And as he did, his mouth quirked in a bitter, sardonic smile, and there was nothing of amusement in it.

Chapter 16

He wasn't surprised; he wasn't disappointed. But a leaden feeling of righteousness threatened to crush Simon's chest. He'd been right. She wasn't any different from any other woman, nor was she any worse. She was just a female, and therefore couldn't be trusted.

His own mother had run off with another man when he was six years old, leaving her husband to curse and rail. She'd returned, of course. Gamblers don't hold on to their funds, and are as fickle in their personal lives as their fortunes are. So his mother eventually left her lover and came home to Simon and his father, and though the cursing and railing stopped, there wasn't a moment of peace in the house after that. It was a silent war that he'd been glad to leave when they sent him off to school.

271

He didn't blame his mother; his father hadn't been a loveable man. But Simon had been distrustful of women after that. He had loved women as he'd grown up, but not from the heart. Unfortunately, he'd loved his French mistress, Martine, from the bottom of his very soul. Even more unfortunately for him, it turned out that she'd been a patriot, and had loved Napoleon even more. So she'd informed on Simon when she'd discovered his reason for being in Paris. And so he'd become personally acquainted with the dungeons of the City. He still didn't blame her. He blamed himself for being foolish enough to fall in love without looking beyond his heart.

And now this, he thought. Jane Chatham. He could have sworn she was what she appeared to be. Honest to a fault, innocent in mind and body, and a victim of circumstance. He'd have sworn to it. And yet he'd seen her in close conference this very evening with his supposed friend, Proctor. He'd seen her surprise meeting with Proctor at a distance. Then they'd walked and talked together. Something had changed hands between them. He'd have thought that would've been the first thing she'd mention when she came into the carriage this evening. Instead, she sat in silence.

Again, he'd forgotten to remember what had made him such a good agent before he'd lost his heart. He'd forgotten that mistrust was necessary for survival. He wondered what it was that the viscount had wanted of her. He wondered if she'd give it to him, or if she'd already done so. He also wondered what kind of faradiddle she'd tell him, if she told him anything about it at all.

The carriage finally slowed in front of the old tavern. At last, Jane spoke. "You've come here as a lamplighter and a workman, and now a ratcatcher. Won't anyone wonder about that?"

"They don't wonder here," he said tersely. "They know everyone has to make a living; they expect everyone has secrets."

He got out of the carriage, and gave her his hand. She wondered why he had a sneer on his face.

"At least, you've left your sack in the carriage," she said, as they ducked their heads and went under the low lintel of the tavern door.

"They may not wonder, but even here, they don't enjoy dining with rats," he said. It wasn't a double entendre, she thought, so she wondered why he wore such a tight, bitter smile.

The innkeeper greeted them, and sat them at

their usual table. The place was busy tonight. It was so loud that they could hardly hear the innkeeper speak to them, and he had a booming voice. Simon shouted their dinner order, and then moved his chair nearer to Jane.

"So," he asked, his eyes on her face, "what have you to tell me today?"

She swallowed hard. Then she inched her chair closer to him too, so that they were almost knee to knee. She stared into his eyes, took a breath and said, all in a rush. "I don't know what to do. I don't know who to trust. You win, I suppose, it has to be you because you've never lied to me, and because you were the first to hire me on. But you'll never guess!

"First, Lady Harwood made me wait until all her guests were gone because she wanted to talk with me, alone. That's why I'm so late this evening. It turns out she wants to hire me on to watch and listen, and tell her any gossip about her guests, the male guests, that is. Then, as I was walking home just now, your friend Viscount Delancey surprised me. He came up to me in the street and asked me to do the very same thing for him. Only he wants to know about everyone. He even gave me a list of names to be on the look out for.

"He said it was to protect you, as well as to find out what's going on with his brother. And *she* said she was looking for a husband and needed to know everything she could about her male admirers. They both promised to pay me well, but she as much as said she'd be rid of me if I didn't agree. And he implied the same, or worse. What am I to do?"

He sat back and stared at her. Then he began to laugh.

"I don't think it's funny," she said in a wounded voice. "Although I suppose you might think so. And maybe it is, but not to me. It worries me. What can I do?"

You can give me a kiss, he thought dizzily *You can forgive me for what I was thinking; you can ask me for anything.*

He stopped laughing. "Jane," he said, holding up his forefinger. "Hush for now. I admit that's a passing strange thing to have happened. But don't be afraid. Nothing will happen to you. So what if you tell the lady what you know about her male guests? As long as you tell me first, there's no problem. As for the viscount, the same thing applies, I think. But I'll have to think more about that. He ought to have told me first. At any rate, I can't see the harm in it, so long as you don't tell him about me, and our bargain, of course.

"Now," he said, smiling, "did you say you have a problem? I can't see it. Except for me, maybe, because you'll soon be earning so much money you'll be able to hire someone to tell you what's going on in that house. So why are you still frowning?"

"What is going on in that house?" she asked. "Someone tried to kill you there. That's certain. Everyone's interested in what everyone else is doing there, that's another. I think it's for more than gossip. There *is* a war on. I think I'm in too deep; this is all over my head."

"You're not in too deep, you're merely dabbling your toes. That's unfortunate, in a way, but you're safe enough. Do as everyone asked. Tell no one else about it, save for me, and nothing will change but the weight of your purse."

"But if I accept I have to promise the others the same thing I promised you," she said unhappily. "I'm not supposed to tell anyone about them either."

"You already have," he said simply, "and no harm will ever come to you from me, I promise that."

"I'm not a good liar," she said in grieved accents. "Well, maybe I am, because I have been for you, so far. But I don't like it; I dislike lies. My father used to say you must have an excellent memory to be a good liar, and I do, but it weighs on my conscience. Still, if I say no to either of them, I'm no use to you, because I'll lose my job there."

He tilted his head to the side. He was sure she'd say she couldn't afford to lose her job, but instead she worried about not being of use to him. If she was telling him the truth, of course. If she wasn't really the best liar he'd ever met.

They stared at each other.

"You were a spy," Jane whispered fiercely. "So was the viscount. My lady said she wants to know about the gentlemen, but why should she tell me the truth? I'm caught in a vise," she said, "squeezed between all of you." Her gaze went to his. "I think the best thing for me to do is to leave London. I could find good accommodations in my home village. I have friends there. I could instruct children in the dance there too.

"It will make my cousin, who inherited my home, wildly angry. But I begin to think that's what I ought to have done in the first place. It was the thought of his anger if I stayed on in my own home that drove me to London. That, and my own sense of pride at having everyone know how far I'd come down in the world from the manor house to a rented room in the village, if I had to do that, and, knowing my cousin, I would have had to do just that. Pride is a sin anyway, and anger is something I can deal with.

"All this," she swept her hand to indicate the room and the world she found herself in, "is more than I bargained for. Someone who is in that house or who visits it is dangerous. I can't forget that. And for whatever reason, interest has been focused on me now. Unless, of course, everyone who works there has been asked to spy on everyone else. And how terrible that would be!"

"I agree with everything you've said," he said blandly. "But surely you're not the sort of person who runs from trouble?"

"Why not?" she asked in surprise. "After all, none of this was my trouble, but it's becoming so."

"I'd like you to stay on," he said. "If I think the situation is getting out of hand, I'll be the first one to tell you to get out of there. I don't like the thought that both the lady and the viscount have settled on you as informer. But if their thinking parallels mine, it makes sense. You are, after all, bright and observant, and a good person to depend on."

"No, I'm not," she countered. "Or at least I won't be if I keep my bargain with you and lie to them." She looked straight into his eyes. Her own eyes were misty. "How can I reconcile spying for you, lying for you, and ignoring my promise to the others?"

"Because you love . . ." he said, and paused. He raised his glass of ale to his lips, as though his throat was too dry for him to keep talking.

Her face grew pale and her breathing shallow. She guessed what he was going to say and wished he wouldn't. It was true, they both knew it now, much good it did her. She loved to talk with him, to be with him, and wished she could make love to him. The fact was that she now knew she'd never meet another man like him, or one she enjoyed being with half so much. She had, she realized, in some corner of her mind, already accepted that. As much as she knew of love, she knew she loved him.

It wasn't just because he was attractive, clever, or well educated, or kind, in his own aloof way. Nor was it because his kisses still burned in her memory and her body reacted whenever she so much as thought of him. It was because she sensed he was, at heart, strangely sad, lonely, and certainly wounded. It was because she believed, in spite of all their differences, that they fit well together. As for herself, now she felt whole only when she was with him. It was indisputable. She loved him.

But she didn't want him to know it. And she didn't want to hear him say it, because then she'd have to lie to him. Worse, she'd have to leave her employment and this city at once, because if he knew her feelings, it was too delicate and potentially disastrous a thing for her to deal with. She'd rather leave London tomorrow morning than actually make love to him this very night, as she wished she could do, because no good would come of it for her. Life was harder for women who dared.

The hardest reality was that whether or not she conceived a child with him, she'd never forget him, though he'd certainly forget her. If they were discovered, she knew she'd be ruined in the eyes of Society, and there was a terrible price to pay for that. Even so, right now, that didn't bother her half as much as the fact that she knew he'd ruin her for any other lover. She sat still, waiting for him to finish what he was saying. Her entire future depended on it, whether he knew it or not.

He put down his ale. "Because you love the truth," he said calmly, as though he hadn't paused for a second, "and you honor your word. But remember, you gave your word to me first. That comes before everything else. If by keeping your word it means you have to mislead others, I wouldn't call that immoral."

She didn't answer at first. She was wondering if that was really what he'd been going to say. It was possible she'd been wrong about what he was going to say, and had panicked only because of her guilty secret. She hoped that was it. His face didn't give the lie to what he'd said. But then, he'd been a spy for much longer than she had. And he'd chosen the work. She hadn't. She wanted to believe she'd panicked for no good reason. And so, she did.

"Now," he said, as the landlord delivered bowls of rich, steaming stew, "we dine. Later, we'll talk some more."

"Can't we do both at once?" she asked.

He put down the fork he'd just picked up. "Fine," he said, looking at her, "about what?"

She thought a moment. There was so much to say and she had to be careful about how she said it. "It smells like a wonderful stew," she said, stirring her bowl with a spoon. "Let's not let it get cold."

But she couldn't keep silent. "Just tell me one thing," she said as her companion broke off another piece of bread from the loaf on the table. "How will I get the news to you before I leave work at Lady Harwood's house? How will I get to speak to you if the viscount intercepts me on my way home again?"

"That's two things," he said, as he sopped up some of the gravy with the bread. He brought it to his lips, chewed, swallowed, and then spoke again. "Good questions, though. I think you'll only have to make things up the first time. After that, you can tell them things you've already told me, if I think you ought."

She sat up straight. "That's ridiculous," she said. "What if something happens, they see for themselves, and I don't tell them? They'll know I'm hiding something."

He sighed. "Yes. True. I had hoped to avoid this, but I see I can't."

"What?" she asked fearfully.

"I'll have to go to every one of my lady's salons, and speak to you sooner than they do. And," he added in cautionary tones, "you will have to promise that there's no way in heaven or on earth that you let either of them think I'm there all the time because I formed a *tendre* for the lady. Or for you, for that matter. I'm not in the marriage mart," he added.

"Little chance of that!" she said, stung.

"Oh no," he said, smiling. "Big chance of that, actually. If the lady gets the idea that I'm not a gelding, she may set her cap for me."

"Don't worry," she said sarcastically. "I'll be specially sure to let her know you're not on the market for dalliance either."

"How?" he asked innocently.

He took her pink cheeks as his answer, and mopped up the residue of his strew with another piece of bread.

They had their sweet for dessert, Simon paid the landlord, and then he escorted Jane back to the carriage, which came around the corner to collect them soon after they emerged from the tavern.

"How does he know to do that?" she asked Simon when they'd settled themselves in the coach.

"He worked with me long, long ago," Simon answered. "So. You haven't said a word about your new lodgings. What do you think of them?"

"I love the place," Jane answered eagerly. "Thank you so much. It's quiet and clean and airy and in a good neighborhood. Perfect for me."

"You're welcome," he said lazily, watching her. He idly took her hand in his. "I'd love to see it. May I come up?"

She stilled. "What has changed since we last met?" she finally asked. "I still have a reputation to maintain, you know."

"Yes," he said, as he stroked her hand. "But Miss Piggott doesn't."

She snatched her hand back. "You took the room in the name of 'Miss Piggott'?"

"Of course. That way it will take longer for anyone who is interested to find where you've moved. I'm sorry to say that your last landlady blackened Miss Chatham's name. The landlady's been paid to say no more on that head, but it was too late to undo the damage she did to your reputation."

"That's why the viscount said that!" Jane said with a gasp.

She felt her companion sit up. "Said what?" he immediately asked.

"Likely I misinterpret it," she said.

"Please let me be the judge of that," he said.

"You're not my father or my guardian," she said.

"I thank heaven for that. I know the man, though. He's not entirely dead, he just seems to be. And he knows you were in my rooms. There was no way you could hide your perfume from him, or yourself from his spies. What did Proctor say to you?"

She told him.

"Damn!" he said. "No question about it. He may look dry as a two-day-old bit of toast, but the man has designs on you, Miss Piggott. Be warned. Unless, of course, you're pleased about it?"

The noise she uttered made him smile. He took her hand again. "Don't worry. I'll disabuse him of the notion. But why not ask me to your room? I'd like to see it."

"Well, you won't!" she said, trying to tug her hand away. He didn't let go, so she did. She refused to wrestle with him. It was only a hand, no matter how much his touch made her tingle. "Just the other day you were saying it would be a bad idea for us to ever be alone again. What happened since to make you change your mind?"

"You," he said softly.

"Oh," she said. "But you know we have no future."

"I was blinded, thinking of the immediate future," he said. "Sorry." But he didn't let go of her hand.

Instead, he drew her closer, and kissed her.

His mouth was warm and enticing, gentle and sweet, asking rather than taking. She knew she ought to push him away, but somehow, her arms went around his neck. He made a small sound of content and tightened his embrace. She was fully dressed; they were traveling through London, what could happen? she thought. She clung to him, caught her breath, kissed him again, and then began to realize exactly what could happen.

Jane pulled back. "Unfair," she said, her hands shaking as she tried to tuck her hair neatly up into its neat bundle again.

"Yes," he breathed, against her neck. "So come back here."

"No," she said, though she longed to say yes. He smelled of ferns and spice, leather and healthy male. She hadn't known how intoxicating that was. "I can't. You know that. And you know it can't come to anything but momentary pleasure and then grief, for me."

He let her go. "Do you want a proposal of marriage?" he asked.

"Oh yes, something you can regret forever," she said angrily. "A marriage for a night's work? How you'd love that! Lord Granger," she added when she had herself under control again. "You told me you don't want to marry. I have come to know that you don't trust women. But I take you for a fair man. Please stop doing this. This kissing and the rest," she said to clarify. "I have limitations I'm only just discovering. I don't want an affaire of the heart, or the body. I do, but I don't. Can you understand? I may never marry, or so I think now. But I might decide differently in time. Please let me be. It's only fair."

He sat quietly for a moment. "Yes," he finally said. "Fair enough. I apologize. I only ask one thing of you. Please don't accept any of the viscount's proposals before you tell me about them."

She laughed. "I'm sure his would only be indecent."

"As mine?" he asked. "Perhaps not."

"And if they weren't? In the remote possibility that he meant something honorable? As though I'd want a husband who only wanted to score one against his friend!" she said scornfully.

"You have a sharp tongue," he said.

"I have to live by my wits," she answered. "In no way are we equal, my lord. I can't forget that. I can only hope you don't either. Oh, but I wonder if I should go on with this," she said earnestly. "There are so many dangers for me, and you not the least of them."

"I'm the least of them, I promise you," he said. "I'm not trying to murder anyone. Stay in my service, please, and forgive me." He took her chin in his hand and tilted her head up to meet his gaze. "I'm sorry, and yet I'm not. Miss Chatham or Miss Piggott, one of you has turned my wits, that's certain."

"Not your wits," she said, looking him full in the eyes.

"Oh, we're back to the rats again, are we?" he asked, and laughed with her.

When the hackney stopped a street away from her lodgings, he spoke again. "So good night, Miss Piggott," he said sadly. "Bid good night to your better angel, Miss Chatham too. I'll see you a day from now. Will you take dinner with me then?"

"I don't know," she said seriously.

"Nor do I blame you," he murmured. "But please. I like to dine with you. And I've another low tavern to offer you. You'll be appalled. But the food is very good. And the company will behave himself."

"Then, yes," she said, although she knew she should say no.

"Done!" he said, and opened the door for her so she could go. He knew, as he watched her hastening to her new address, that he shouldn't have asked her, and that he'd have been crushed if she'd said no.

Chapter 17

— ∽∽ —

S imon was a man of iron control; a man of principles and firm determination. His jailers in France hadn't broken him. Neither beatings nor threats, not even his experience with a deceitful lover had done that. He was a cautious man. Or so he'd thought. But now Simon realized that his sudden longing for a supposedly honest female had made him forget all his resolve, and had made him a stranger to himself. Was it her claim of innocence in all things that had put him off his guard? Or was it the woman herself, whatever her experience? He felt comfortable with her. He enjoyed being with her. He wanted her. He didn't trust her.

Such longings had come to disaster for him before. He'd every evidence that she was what she said. Her shock and amazement at seeing his readiness to make love, staring, and then screeching as though a real rat had leapt at her still made him smile. That, he thought, couldn't have been feigned. Females pretending virginity affected discomfort during the act, not horror before it. But it was possibly a new gambit. Still, that was only a question of physical innocence; it no longer mattered to him whether or not she was experienced in such matters. He still wanted her.

He was more disturbed wondering about her morals in other things. It was true that he'd recruited Jane. Yet he couldn't ignore the possibility that she'd been placed in his path in the first place, or had been seduced away from his cause after that. Was she working for someone else? Either by one of the people she'd said had tried to hire her away, or someone altogether different? There was only one way to find out. And that, of course, was to continue seeing her, and by doing so, possibly putting himself in harm's way. The thought didn't upset him as much as it should have.

He was prepared to discover more today. He was immaculately dressed, and had arrived after Lady Harwood's salon was in full spate. He felt perfectly in control, and so he was calm and confident.

"My dear lady," he said, bowing over Lady Harwood's hand as she greeted him. "And how are you today?"

"I have to speak with you, Granger," she snapped. "At once, and alone."

His eyebrow rose. Her salon was packed with the elite of London, as usual. The lady herself was dressed in coral, her fair hair was crowned with pink roses, and she wore gold at her neck and ears. She'd been smiling when he'd first come into the salon, and altogether had looked like a confection on display in a sweetshop. But now her lovely face was set in a frown. "In the hallway, if you please," she said.

He sketched another bow, walked back to the outer hall, and waited there. The lady joined him a moment later, and beckoned him further down the hall, away from the salon.

"Now," she said angrily, staring up at him, "what's this I hear about you and my dancing instructor?"

His old skills immediately came into play. *Admit nothing, find out more.* "What did you hear?" he asked, looking as surprised as he felt and as morally outraged as he did not.

"Don't pretend. As if you didn't know," she said scornfully.

Ah, he thought, *the lady knew how to play the game too. Why was that?* He allowed himself to look puzzled. "What is it, my lady? If you tell me, perhaps I can enlighten you. How have I offended?"

"As if you didn't know!" she retorted again.

He almost laughed. Now he was enjoying this exchange. "But how can I know? What are you talking about?" he asked innocently.

Now she looked confused. But she drew herself up and faced him squarely. "I was told you've been seeing my dancing instructress, Miss Jane Chatham, in private, and prizing information out of her about myself!"

He blinked in honest surprise. "And who told you such a thing? Why should I ask her about you? She's only a servant, and at that, one who isn't even here all the time."

She frowned.

"Who said such a thing?" he insisted.

"You were seen with her, after hours," she said, her fair forehead creasing with concern.

So she doesn't know much, he thought, and said, "But where?"

"In a low tavern, sharing dinner and heaven knows what else!"

Now he did laugh. "A *low tavern*? My dear lady, why would I go there? If I wanted to seduce a girl into talking to me, surely credit me with the wit to take her to a fine establishment to impress her."

"There is that," she said, frowning.

"And," he added in a softer voice, "as it happens, I do want to know more about you, but I'd hoped to find that out for myself."

She batted him with her fan. "Oh, you're about as interested in me as last night's beans. But," she said, holding up a finger, "if you are truly interested, well then, we shall see what time produces, shan't we?"

Oh my God, he thought, and smiled back at her.

"There you are!" young Richard exclaimed as he came hurrying down the hallway. He looked suspiciously from his lady to Simon, and scowled.

"We were just going to sneak a look at the dance class, Richard," the lady said, taking his hand, and gifting him with a sweet smile.

"I thought you weren't going to do that anymore," Richard said.

"I changed my mind. Now, hush, come along," she said.

Simon followed, cursing Richard's arrival, because he had yet to discover who told her he'd met with Jane. Still, it might be for the best. When he did get a chance to ask her, he'd make sure it wasn't when they were alone. He wanted information, not a wife. They walked softly until they reached the ballroom, and then they stood and looked in at the dance class.

Jane and her young students were there, but Simon could only look at her. She wore a simple light green gown. Her hair was sleeked back as usual, throwing the classic lines of her face into clear detail. She was, he thought, beyond beautiful. If her employer looked like something from a pastry shop today, then Jane looked like wood nymph, untouched as an image in a mountain lake.

The little girls were all looking up at her raptly.

"Now," Jane told them, "as I promised. We'll try pirouettes again today. But we must go carefully. The floor's just been polished." She wore a momentary frown, wishing she had told Lady Harwood not to have the floor polished just before a lesson. "See how it shines?" she told the children. "You can see your face in it."

Immediately all the children looked down, some crouched to get a better look.

"Yes," Jane said. "So go with care. It will be like ice, adding speed to your feet, but requiring all your concentration. Stand up, if you please. Thank you. Now put one foot in front of you, we'll call it the pointer foot. Show me your pointer foot. Very good. No, Miss Morrow, the other one: the one in front. Yes. Now, ladies, get yourselves steady. Ready? Now, up you go on that foot."

A few little girls tumbled over and went down; most of them wavered.

"Now, soon as you feel steady enough," Jane told them, "hold your arms up over your head. Push off with your other leg, crook that leg, and spin around on the pointer foot. Once only, if you please!"

Most of the little girls fell down.

"Here," Jane said with infinite patience, "watch me before you try again. You don't have to stand on your toes to do it even if I do. But watch how I balance, and turn."

She rose up on one foot, picked up her arms,

pushed off with her other foot, and crooking it, began to spin. As she turned toward the ballroom door, she looked up. There was Simon, and her employer, young Richard, and coming up behind them, his brother, the Viscount Delancey. And they were all staring hard, at her.

Jane's eyes widened. Then she realized she'd done just what she'd warned the children not to do. She was spinning too fast. She tried to slow herself, but the floor was too slick. She lost her balance and went sprawling on the floor in front of them. She lay there, feeling hurt, stupid and hunted at the same time.

There was applause, of course, from the crowd of guests who had pushed in behind the others to see what was going on.

"I am a good instructress," Jane said, holding back her tears. "It was an accident, I swear to it. It was suddenly seeing everyone goggling at me when I didn't expect to see anyone. I can understand if you turn me out," she added, trying to keep any quaver out of her voice, "because doubtless there'll be another caricature in the shop windows tomorrow. But if only your guests didn't watch my lessons, my lady, it would all go perfectly, I promise. Can't they be kept away?"

"They could be," Lady Harwood said calmly, as she sat back on her couch. "And then where would I be? And you? It's your 'accidents' that are the making of you, my girl. If you never fell, they might tire of the sport. But I warn you, if you stumble every time they'll get just as bored, so I'd think you'd be wise to not do so again for at least a week or two. The suspense will build, and so will the betting amongst the gentlemen. You're as popular as a boxing match now."

"I don't do it on purpose!" Jane said.

They were alone in the lady's boudoir. The guests had left long since. Jane had hidden herself in the kitchens until she'd a chance to speak with Lady Harwood, as requested. But this time, she had to bear hearing the servants whisper comments to each other as they stole looks at her.

The lady waved her hand. "It hardly matters. Now, what I really wanted to speak to you about is whether you've decided to accept my offer of doing a second job of work for me. Are you going to keep your eyes and ears open and find out about my gentlemen guests?"

"Oh," Jane said casting her mind back. She'd thought she was going to be reprimanded for her accident. "That. Yes, my lady, I will."

"Very good. Did you hear anything today?"

"I couldn't," Jane said. "Most of the talk upstairs and down was about me."

"True," the lady said. "So listen harder next time. Here are your wages. I haven't added anything for your new job, as you haven't told me anything yet."

Jane nodded her head and took her wages. She was relieved rather than disappointed. She still didn't owe her employer anything but lessons. She curtsied, and turned to go.

"Oh, and Miss Chatham?" the lady said.

Jane turned to face her.

"I've heard a rumor myself," her employer said, as she inspected her fingernails. She looked up, her blue gaze sharp as spears. "Someone told me that you were seeing Lord Granger after hours. That's dangerous. Not for him but for you. Just because he is incapable of one thing doesn't mean he's incapable of everything. Or have I been misinformed?"

"You must have been," Jane said. "I'm not seeing him."

"No," the lady said crossly. "I meant just because he mightn't be able to do the usual doesn't mean he can't do anything."

"I wouldn't know about that," Jane said stiffly, sure her face was flaming. "Who said I was meeting him? Why would I? What would he want from me?"

"Information," her employer said.

"About what?" Jane asked, her heart sinking, as she tried to look as honestly puzzled as she could.

"Me," the lady said.

"What?" Jane asked, honestly confused. "What would I know about you that I could tell him?"

"Or," the lady went on, "he might be after physical pleasures, from you."

"Me?" Jane squeaked. "I couldn't provide him that," she answered with sad honesty. Then on sudden inspiration, she said, "I mean to say, whatever his . . . intimate problems, such as you discussed, surely there are many more females used to such things that he could consort with, high or low. And," she added, "what do you mean, it doesn't mean he can't do anything?"

The lady laughed, looking suddenly happier. "Never you mind. You may go now."

"But my lady," Jane said. "May I not know who is blackening my name?"

"I would call it polishing your name," the lady said blandly. "Lord Granger is quite a catch, whatever one may do with him if one catches him. However, you're right. He is not for you. Good evening, Miss Chatham. We shall see you in a few days."

Jane didn't release her breath until she left the lady's bedchamber. She hurried down the stairs. It was late, no one was expected. The footmen had left their posts, so Jane slipped down to the kitchens. She picked up a shawl that she had deliberately left there, but those few there were so busily at work with preparations for dinner that she was sure no one noticed her. Then she slipped out of the house by the back door.

When she'd been hired she'd been proud that she'd been considered a step above a common servant, and so had been told she could use the front entrance. She usually did. But tonight she wanted to change her route so as to avoid Viscount Delancey, should he appear again. So she moved through the kitchen garden, and walking swiftly, stole into a neighbor's garden, and then another's until she could leave the backyards by going through an alley that let out on a side street. Only then, on the pavement, did she slow her pace. Then she headed toward her old room, rather than her new lodgings as she longed to do. But she wanted to avoid being seen.

It was mild and clear. As spring wore on toward summer the darkness came later. And so Jane didn't mind the thought of having to retrace her path to get home. It was a lovely evening for a stroll. The first star hadn't yet appeared.

"My dear Miss Chatham," the viscount said as he fell into step with her. "May one ask whom you were trying to avoid by leaving in such a clandestine manner?"

Her shoulders leapt with surprise but she managed to turn and smile at him. "I didn't hear your footsteps, my lord," she said, putting a hand on her heart to pretend fear in order to cover her guilty surprise.

"I'm not a noisy fellow," he commented. "Did you hurt yourself today? I mean, when you fell down? Or do you *artistes* have a way of falling without harm, like tumblers or clowns?"

"I am neither, my lord," she said, trying to ignore the implicit insult. "But no, I didn't hurt myself."

"Forgive the unfortunate wording," he said mildly. "And have you any of the information I requested?"

"I forgive you," she said, and then using the same excuse she'd used with the lady, added, "but I have nothing to tell you. All the gossip today was about me and what happened to me in my class." Then she stopped walking and faced him squarely. "There is something I must ask you. Do you know who has been spreading vile rumors about me?"

"Come, keep walking," he said. She did. He stayed at her side and added, "What sort of rumors?"

"You mean there's more than one?" she asked, stopping again.

"Miss Chatham," he said with a touch of annoyance, "will you please keep walking? My time with you must be brief; I don't want to start any rumors about *our* meetings. No, I know of no vile gossip about you. What has been said?"

"How did you know they were about meetings?" she asked, too angry to watch her tongue with such a noble gentleman.

"I didn't," he said testily. "What are they saying?"

"My lady said the rumor is that I've been meeting with Lord Granger after work. That is outrageous, and terrible for my reputation."

"Oh," he said, with what sounded like relief. "No, I hadn't heard that. Are you?"

She stopped again and glowered at him.

He bowed. "My apologies," he said. "We'll meet again," he added, and walked on past her.

Jane kept walking, waiting to reach more crowded streets and the coming of real dusk before she changed her direction. As she moved through the London streets, she kept an eye out for any slow-moving hackney carriages.

She saw one coming up behind her, and her heart began to race. It stopped by her side.

"Miss," the driver said, doffing his high hat, "You wants to go somewheres? Ain't good for a female to be by herself when night falls."

"Oh," she said, disappointed. The fellow obviously just wanted to pick up a fare. "No, thank you."

"I'll give you a special rate," he added, flashing her a grin. "If you ain't got the blunt. There's a way to reduce the fare to naught. 'Cause it's early yet for me, but not too early for some fun, if you gets my meaning."

"I do," she said, drawing her shawl tightly around herself. "And I don't want any. Please be gone."

"Suit yourself," he said with a shrug, cracking his whip. The hackney moved quickly on down the street.

Jane waited until he'd gone before she began walking again. But she went faster. When she reached a livelier district where the theaters were beginning to attract crowds, she tried to blend in with the crowds until she could change her direction and then veer eastward, back toward her new lodgings. She felt very proud of herself for her newly discovered gift of subterfuge. And disappointed, because Lord Granger hadn't appeared. Had she fooled him as well as any unwanted trackers? Or could her humiliating fall today have convinced him she wasn't to be trusted because she was just an immoral sort of female out to make a name for herself? She sighed.

The first stars were beginning to poke through the gathering night when she reached the better residential areas again. There she paused, wondering if it was safe for her to go directly home now. There was a liveried footman hurrying up the street, and two maid-servants walking the other way on the other side, carrying baskets and gossiping together. Otherwise the street was empty. No one was following her. She turned and began to walk home.

"Miss," the footman said, slowing his pace as he came abreast of her. "The gent says as to how you're supposed to go on a bit until you come to the corner where there's a big tree, and he'll have a carriage waiting for you there."

"I'm sure he will," she said, holding her head high. "You tell him to go to the devil, because I won't get into any carriage. Now leave before I call the Watch."

"Why, Jane," the footman said, with a gleaming smile, "what did I do to displease you?"

She stared. The fellow was tall and slender, dressed in regal tones of gold and blue. And when he straightened up for a minute, she could see that he was also indisputably Lord Granger.

"Right," he said, nodding at her. "I've got a better job today. Been promoted from being a mere menial. Now I'm a liveried menial. To celebrate I've found a new tavern for us to have dinner at, where the food and the company is a bit more elevated too. See you at the carriage. And oh, it's not a hackney this time. That one wasn't just out for sport, by the way. He was hired to meet you. Not by me!" he added, before he bent his head again and hurried on his way.

Chapter 18

⟨◦◦◦⟩

This time it was a private coach awaiting her. Jane wondered at the crest on the door, and wondered whose it was. She wavered, but got in when that door swung open. Simon awaited her inside.

"Since you're a footman tonight, I take it that the carriage belongs to your employer?" she said as she settled into the comfortable seat opposite him.

"You're a clever girl," he said with approval. "Livery, coach and horses, all used in the service of my master—who is in actuality an old friend who can be relied on to be silent. I needed a new appearance if I wanted to meet you since you've become so popular. You met with both Lady Harwood and Viscount Delancey this evening. Not many young women can claim such eager acquaintances of such high *ton*. What did they ask? What did you tell? I'm all ears."

And smiles, and confidence, and masculine appeal, Jane thought, looking at him. "I told them nothing and no one minded," she answered instead. "I said my fall in class today was an accident. Which it was. Neither believed me. I also said that all the talk above and below stairs was about me, which was also true, and they accepted that. I think both have other informants in that house. As for me, I begin to believe that the lady is really only interested in her suitors, but frankly, I don't know what the viscount is after and it frightens me. Do you believe me?" she asked suddenly. "I really didn't mean to fall."

He stretched out his legs. "I believe you, but I think few others do."

"That means," she said carefully, "that you're not so sure of me either."

He didn't answer that.

She sighed.

"But don't feel bad," he said. "I'm not sure of Lady Harwood or my old friend the viscount either."

"Then you don't trust anyone?" she asked.

He was still for a moment. "I don't. But I want to. Believe that."

"Well, it was a slippery floor," she said stoutly. "And even though I am a good dancer, looking up and seeing you and then Lady Harwood startled me. Seeing your friend the viscount coming up and looking over her shoulder at me did it, I think. I felt exposed and on display and no one was smiling. I didn't watch what I was doing and I fell. Being totally within yourself and utterly concentrated is the trick to dancing and not making a misstep."

"It's the trick to life, actually," he mused. "And so the viscount saw you too? Interesting. He was gone when I looked around again. But then, that's your fault. I was staring at you too. The others weren't so transfixed, that's why someone else got to help you before I could. I forgot your rule of utter concentration too."

"Did I—did I look indecent?" she asked in a small voice.

"You showed less than any dancer at the Opera," he assured her. "But what was seen was worth five times their price. You have lovely legs, Miss Chatham."

"I'm a dancer," she said, refusing to show she

was either flattered or upset by his comment, but she was.

"Need any ice this evening?" he asked casually.

She'd fallen on her rump, and it did ache, but there was a limit. "No, thank you," she said quickly.

"Hard to sit on ice all night," he commented dryly.

She wanted to swat him, but she had no fan, and anyway only a lady could do that and be laughed at.

"I found a new place to take you," he said. "Servants go there when their pockets are full."

"Won't someone from Lady Harwood's house see us?" she asked nervously.

"So far from their own lodgings? I think not. Servants tend to frequent places nearby so they can get more time out, and still amble, or stagger, home quickly. That way they can fall right into bed and be up and about for their duties early. Anyway, I've had it watched. There's no one from that circle there. It's near an area where old Society lives. My old friend whose coach this is, is actually very old. Like most of the people who live there he's done with trying to make liaisons or impressions on others. It's a tavern, but a jolly place with good food and a discreet landlord. I've paid enough to ensure that and dropped a hint or two to frighten him a little too."

"You've been busy," she said.

"Not enough," he answered, frowning. "I didn't know that Proctor had seen your fall. And he's a good friend—if a spy can have one, that is. I begin to wonder."

"It must be terrible to suspect everyone," she said with sympathy.

"Don't you find it so?" he asked, and silenced her.

The tavern was everything he said. It was clean and nicely lighted, and there was no stench of old beer or smoke, not even from the crisply burning fire in the hearth. There were no workmen or costermongers here, and a ratcatcher or an artisan wouldn't have shown his nose in through the door. There were footmen, in and out of uniform, and young women who must be maid servants, Jane was sure, since most of them were in clean frocks, but had reddened hands. They looked delighted to be there. There were some older servants: butlers and housekeepers by the look of them, and just their presence, whether they were from the same houses as the others or not, seemed to work to keep the tavern orderly. But again, Lord Granger was swiftly greeted at the door, and shown to a quiet table in the back of the room.

A fat bright candle in a saucer with a globe over it bloomed light on their tabletop, and there was a clean tablecloth under it. This was indeed a better-class establishment than their last meeting place.

And Lord Granger made a very handsome footman, Jane thought, watching him in the candlelight. His uniform fit his long lean body perfectly, showing off his fitness, and giving him a slightly military air. The stabs of flaring candlelight suited the stern planes of his face.

"This is very different from where we last met, my lord," she said softly. "I like it very well. Do you think I'm getting spoiled?"

"Simon," he said quickly. "In this place, I am Simon. In fact, I'm Simon to you any place we meet outside of Lady Harwood's."

She didn't know how to answer that, so only blurted what had been on her mind. "I only meant that I'm getting too used to such splendor, and I worry because when my job with the lady is over, and it will be sooner than I'd wish, I'm sure, my job for you will be over too. Then I'll go back to affordable rooms, and dining from cookshops."

He cocked an eyebrow. "Trolling for a proposition from me? I've been waiting for this moment."

She sprang to her feet.

"Sit down, please, Jane. Don't flare up. It's only that when a lovely young woman starts complaining about her poverty that is usually what follows."

She sat slowly and glared at him.

"Mind," he said, raising a finger, "I'd like that. I could keep you in comfort for a long time, Jane. What I mean is that I could keep us in comfort and joy for a long time."

She stared at him. "If you're not jesting, Simon," she said through clenched teeth, "I'm leaving on the instant. I wasn't complaining. I was just musing. The fault was in my thinking, for a moment, that you could be a friend, instead of a lecher."

"Stay," he said with an uncomfortable-looking smile. "I was only testing the waters. I am who I am, and since I love to get my way I keep trying. Excuse me for it. It's in my nature, I suppose. Ah, here's our host. What would you like for dinner, Miss Piggott?"

"You may order for me," she said, a thunderous expression still on her face.

"We'll have your best tonight, Landlord," Simon said. "Some beef. Some fish, and a bit of that good-smelling bird that's roasting. With your freshest ale, and whatever else you think we require. We had a spot of luck at the races today," he added, with a smile for the landlord.

"Look here, Jane," Simon said when the man had bustled away. "I didn't mean to insult you."

"But you must have known it would," she said.

"No, actually I didn't," he said. "After all there's a great deal I can offer you and I wasn't sure what you were angling for. If you think this place is splendor, there are restaurants in London that are plusher by far, and serve manna from heaven. And there are lodgings that your sunny little attic room could fit into with room for a stable of horses to spare. And clothing and jewels. Money is nothing to me, and if it is to you, you have only to agree to come to me and you'll never feel the need of it again. As for

the rest . . . You enjoyed my embraces; such as
they were before you were frightened away. You
have no idea of the physical rapture I can bring
to you."

She looked appalled, and put her hands on
the table, preparing to rise again and take flight
from him. Yet while he was listing the delights he
could offer, he'd watched her eyes. In those moments, he'd seen her weighing the possibilities.
She hadn't interrupted him. She'd been thinking
about it, however briefly. But when he was done
she'd already decided against living with him in a
life of sin. Still, she had considered it.

Now she looked daggers at him.

He winced. Then he closed his eyes and gri-
maced painfully.

"Are you all right?" she asked in sudden alarm.
What had he eaten before they'd met, had someone poisoned him again? He looked sick enough.

"Twinges," he gasped. "Lord, they removed it,
and you think it's gone forever, and then you get a
twinge and you know the damned thing is back."

"What is?" she asked in fear.

"My conscience," he said.

She settled back. "I'm surprised to know that
you had one."

His eyes opened and smiled into hers. "I was raised as a gentleman," he added. "Although I suppose that's no commendation. My parents couldn't bear each other, but my mama had borne me, so they had an heir to see to. They hired the best nurses, governesses, and tutors that they could, and sent me to the best schools as soon as they were able. When they died, I didn't miss them. But that didn't harden my heart. A gentleman isn't supposed to possess one of those. What I said to you, Jane, the offer I made, was true and from whatever is left of that heart. I just forgot that I was offering it to you. I am sorry, believe me."

"Well," she said, "I don't, not really. Nor do I believe you believe me." She suddenly smiled brilliantly. She lowered her voice and her head and leaned across the table to whisper to him. "This is really how spies dine together, isn't it? All mistrust and judging, and on guard all the time? Only you needn't worry about me carrying a knife or a pistol or poison."

"True, I just have to beware your rapier wit and sharp tongue," he said with a sigh. He was delighted with her. She looked lovely tonight, but that wasn't the half of it. Women were enhanced by candlelight, but she looked that way in sunlight too. Elegant, reserved, charming and clever, she was a lass with good manners and a graceful way about her in all things. He'd like to see her with all that honey-colored hair down around her shoulders; he'd like to feel how soft, perfumed, and cool it would feel in his hands; how warm and soft the skin beneath it. He burned for her.

"So, any news for me?" he asked.

"Yes and no," she said slowly. "I saw almost every one of the names of the list that Viscount Delancey gave me and . . ."

He held his hand out. *"That,"* he said. "You've so bewitched me I forgot it. A possibly fatal blunder in my trade. I think I know all the names on it, but one can never be too sure. Let's make it a true spies' meeting. Show it to me, please. I know you have it with you; you probably refer to it from time to time. How did you learn to associate the names with the people?"

"He wrote down their physical characteristics next to their names," she said. She looked troubled. "Most of them were at the salon, and all of them were speaking to each other at some time, but there was nothing in particular that might give anyone alarm. Anyhow, if they had dire secrets to pass on, wouldn't they choose a low tavern where no one knows them to do it in?"

"No," he said, "because they are not masters of disguise, and wouldn't dream of going to any fleapits, and also because they know that doing something in public takes the sting from it. Or so they think. The list, pass it on, please."

She hesitated. "But he gave it to me and I promised to keep it safe."

"What a very bad spy you make," he said, smiling. "Remember, I'm your first employer. What if an agent in the service of His Majesty swore fealty to him, and then refused to hand over evidence because the French spy she'd met asked her to keep it safe? You have to throw your lot in with someone, Jane. Will it be my friend the viscount? Your Lady Harwood? Some other gentleman? Or me?"

She bent her head, opened her reticule, and with much stealth, looking to see if anyone was watching her, took out a much used and folded paper. She passed it to him under the table.

He repressed a grin as he took it from her. "Thank you, I'll study it when I'm alone."

"You can't!" she cried. She lowered her voice and glanced around. "What if I meet him tomorrow and he asks to see it, to cross off a name or something?"

"I'll read it in the coach then," he said, as he tucked the note into a pocket. "I'll give it back before you arrive at your lodgings. It that acceptable?"

She nodded.

"Such an admirably honest spy," he said. "Now, if you please, will you tell me more about yourself? I have informants, but they can only give me sketches. Will you fill them in?"

"Will that make you trust me?"

"I doubt it," he said merrily. "I am not so admirable as you are. But I'd like to know. Now, why didn't you stay to live with your cousin when he inherited your home? What will you do when you've saved up your money? What are your dreams?"

She told him. She spoke of her annoying cousin and his spiteful wife as they dined on fresh turbot. She had a slice of beef and told him about the dancing academy she hoped to have one day, whether in London or at home. And then she paused over the braised pigeon to think of more to say.

"No marriage in your plans?" he asked.

She shook her head. "I won't marry unless I must."

His eyes widened and he put down his fork and knife.

"Not that kind of *must*," she said, laughing. "Your mind certainly runs in one direction. I mean *must*: as in feel that you'll never be truly happy unless you share your life with someone you've met. A forever sort of thing. I know it's a gamble. And one I may never take. But if I do, be sure I hoped for the best from the start."

"I hope for it for you too," he said, and set to his meal again.

They had an array of tiny cakes brought to their table. This impressed Jane, and made Simon smile as he watched her carefully select one for herself. At last, she sat back, with a satisfied sigh.

"This was wonderful!" she said.

"If I'd known how much you'd enjoy it, I'd have brought you here sooner."

"You couldn't have," she said. "You looked too disreputable. As I would, I suppose, if I went to one of your elegant restaurants—no! That's not a hint or a nudge. It's just true. Thank you for a good evening. But could you do me one favor?"

"Anything," he said, his hand on his heart.

"If there is a caricature of today's debacle tomorrow morning, will you have someone bring it to me before I leave for work? I'd like to be prepared. Mrs. Smythe, my regular Thursday client, doesn't travel in the same social circles, but she reads all the gossip. I had a lot of explaining to do last time. She asked if the female dance instructor might be me."

"I'd forgotten," he said. "Strange for me, but I did. You have other clients, of course."

"Of course," she said. "Lady Harwood is my most influential one, and I've promised her I'd go to no other Society lady while I was with her. My other clients aren't ever likely to walk down the same street as she does, so they don't matter. Working for them is all right."

"Is it?" he asked quizzically. "Take care, Jane. You're already sliding down a slippery slope. Did you ever tell the lady you have other clients of lesser degree?"

"Well," she said, in a troubled voice. "No, not actually."

"Your morals are showing, my girl," he said, with a devilish grin.

"I'll tell her first thing when I see her again," she declared.

"And she won't care a jot. You're right. I

just wanted to see you in one tiny moment of self-doubt."

She looked at him steadily. "Simon, you've no idea of how many of those I have."

He paused in taking out money to pay their bill. "I suppose I don't," he said.

They left the landlord bowing, bowled over by Simon's gratuity.

"An agent would never give that much," Simon whispered to Jane after they'd left the tavern. "Nor would a gentleman of means. A footman with a windfall would." They walked to the corner of the street and stopped. "We have to wait," he told her. "It would be foolish to have a coach waiting. But he should be here in a few minutes. Are you cold?"

"No," she said, lifting her face up to the skirling night breeze that had arisen. "I like the fresh air."

"This is about as fresh as it gets here in London," he said. "Do you miss the countryside?"

"Yes," she said simply. "But I couldn't have made my fortune there."

The notion that she thought her attic room and a few good dinners to be her fortune silenced him. It was good that he saw their coach rounding the corner. "In you go," he told her. "No one is watching. I'll take you home. I hope you feel like walking. This time I think I'll leave the coach several streets from your lodgings. I'll walk you to your door. It's late. And it's hardly likely anyone would object to a footman seeing a young woman to her door."

Simon read the list of names in the dancing light of the carriage lantern as the coach moved through the streets. He finally folded it and handed it back to Jane. "There's nothing new here," he said. "But it is interesting that he has my name down too."

"Wouldn't you put his on any list you made?" she asked.

He laughed. "You learn quickly."

She frowned. "I wish I hadn't. I know there are such things as traitors, but I never thought to meet up with any. Do they do it for a cause? Or is it just for the money?"

"They do it for neither, either, or both. Each traitor has a different tale, and they're all sordid. Betraying your country always is. I'm sorry to have brought you into it. But I can't really be that sorry, because otherwise we'd never have these meetings. I enjoy them, Jane, I really do."

"As do I," she said seriously. "But if you'd remember there's no future in it for either of us, I'd like them a deal more."

He took her hand. "It's hard to remember that when you're sitting beside me. Don't give up on me, please. The world is filled with unexpected bliss. Who knows where this will take us?"

"It might take us somewhere if you could ever trust in me," she said sadly. "But honestly, I don't think you ever will. I can't blame you."

"I can," he said, and bent his head to hers. He gave her a light kiss on the lips. She didn't pull away. "Oh, a mistake," he murmured, as he did. "You trusted me." And then he caught her in his arms, and kissed her again, his mouth warm, his tongue searching. This time she drew away for a second, and then threw her arms around his neck and kissed him back with all the ardor she possessed.

The coach stopped, and reluctantly, so did they.

"Here we are," he said. "Just as I ordered. A few streets from your new flat. Or should I have the driver go round London a few times first?"

"No," she said in a shaken voice. "That was a mistake. I mean it. If you do that again, I'll have to stop working for you. I can't . . ."

"I know, I know," he said, as he opened the coach door. "You're right, entirely. Apologies. Insincere ones," he added on a flashing smile, "but apologies anyway."

She took his hand and stepped down from the coach. They left it, and walked slowly, speaking of trivialities, in low voices so as not to disturb the dreaming night or their own bemused moods. When they reached the door to her new rooms, he bowed over her hand.

"Give my regards to Mrs. Smythe," he said. "I'll see you soon again. Jane?" he called back in a curious voice, "I hope I can discover all soon. And then we can go to dinner with no secrets or plans except in our hearts and minds. And then, perhaps, we can be done with them too."

She didn't know what to say.

He flashed her another smile, and turned away. She stood a moment, watching him walk down the street, and then across to the other side. He looked tall and regal, and she wished she knew what she should do. A life of sin with him looked better every time she saw him. The future faded when she looked into his eyes, and the present mattered more and more.

Then, like the coming of sudden night, a black

carriage, with no lanterns lit, drawn by four dark horses, came careening round the corner. It knocked him down, and ran him over, and the coach went plunging on its wild way until it vanished into the darkness again.

Chapter 19

J ane gasped, and then ran wildly across the street to the figure lying curled up there. Simon had his hands over his head, his knees bent. He didn't stir. She knelt beside him and put a hand on his forehead. It wasn't cold. But when she brought her hand back it was bloody. She rose to a knee and shouted for help. Then she knelt beside him again, touching him lightly. He was warm. He breathed. But she didn't know how broken he was. She was afraid to touch him, and yet she couldn't stop. "Help!" she shrieked, raising her head to the night sky.

Soon she was surrounded by people roused from their nearby houses. Women in their wrappers and men in their robes, maidservants and children; they clucked and speculated and stared down at Simon. The coachman that had taken them to the tavern was suddenly there, kneeling beside her. He turned his head to Jane.

"'e's been knocked for a loop, to be sure. But the blood is from a cut, and there ain't nothing broken that I can see. Best we take 'im 'ome, and double quick. Then we can send for a sawbones to be sure."

"A bad idea," a fat old gentleman in a dressing gown said, looking down at them. "Never transport any man who lays senseless unless you have a door to put him on, so his neck isn't broken any more than it already has been."

"'is neck ain't broke," the hackney driver said. "Trust me, Miss," he told Jane. "I been a few places in my day. I'll get 'im into the coach and you 'ang on to 'im, and we'll get 'im 'ome in a trice, safe as 'ouse's, you'll see."

Jane nodded. She didn't know what else to do.

"'ere!" the driver said, looking up at the spectators. "'oose going to 'elp me lift 'im? Meanwhile," he whispered to Jane, "you ask 'oo saw 'im being knocked down. And if they saw 'oo done it."

Four men bent beside Simon, and with many whispered cautions and criticisms, got him off the ground with their arms under his neck and torso, hips and legs. Then, slowly as though they were his pallbearers, they bore him to the coach.

Jane turned to the fascinated crowd. "Did anyone see this happen?" she asked. "Did anyone actually see anything?"

There was a moment of silence.

"We heard the commotion, dear," one elderly lady answered at last. "But I was in my bed."

"And I, in my kitchen," said another.

It turned out that half the crowd had been dozing, and the other half preparing to do so. The only person who had seen the disastrous event was Jane and, from afar, Simon's waiting coachman.

"'e's in," the coachman called to her from high on the driver's seat. "C'mon, Miss, get in. We got to move like lightning now."

She stepped toward the coach. The crowd drew back.

"Miss," a thin young man said, "you must hold his head steady, even if it means raising his neck up on you lap to make sure he doesn't move as the coach does, or he may come to ruin."

Simon lay stretched across the seat facing forward. His tall form was too long to fit on the seat, so they'd left his knees bent. Jane slid into the coach. As helpful spectators gently lifted Simon's shoulders, supporting his neck so it didn't bend, she carefully slipped beneath his prostrate form until his head lay on her lap. She cupped her hands around it, and held her breath.

"Thank you," she breathed, sitting upright.

They left her, and then, with a small jolt that made Simon's head jog and her breath stop, the coach began to move.

Jane looked down at him. His dark hair was scattered around his ashen face, making his complexion look even more pallid than it was, and trickles of dark red blood ran down his forehead. She could see they were from a cut on his scalp. She yearned to wipe them away but dared not move a muscle, lest she move his head. His eyes were closed, but not in pain. He was unconscious.

Jane prayed for a while. Then she reached some conclusions as they drove through the dark streets. One was that even if Simon's neck was broken, he wasn't dead, because she could feel his warmth and see his chest rise and fall. And the other was that she didn't know that she could feel so bereft, so frightened, and so very sorry that she'd ever met him. Because now, too late, she realized how much he'd come to mean to her.

He'd brought excitement, desire and laughter into her life. Now she could see that her world had been safe, but cold and lonely before they'd met. Maybe he'd meant no good for her. *But his bad would have been wonderful,* she thought wistfully, *if only just for a little while.* And if a woman had that little while, with no bad consequences, wouldn't her life be enriched by it? Now, frightened and angered by what had happened to him, she began to think that even a consequence wouldn't have been so disastrous. She wouldn't have accepted money for his time with her. But it would have been wonderful to know at last, how it felt to be loved, even if that love was only temporary.

Times were hard; there were many war widows. If she'd been left with a child she could have pretended to be one of them . . . far, far from London, of course. There was nothing that said a widow couldn't teach dance.

Seeing him now, all that alarming sensuality and vitality reduced to nothing, made her weep. She blamed herself. Not for his accident or the bad business he was in, but because she'd withheld herself from him.

"I'm sorry," she whispered, bending her head to him, taking his hand, and lightly, so lightly she scarcely felt his skin beneath her fingers, stroking his forehead with her other hand. "I didn't know half of what I thought I did. Please recover. Please be well."

Simon's household responded quickly and efficiently. He was carried out of the coach with care, and was taken up to his bedchamber immediately. Jane came with him. No one denied her. It hardly mattered. Nothing would have induced her to leave his side. She only left the room when a physician went into it. She stood outside his chamber to wait. When the doctor came out after what seemed a small eternity, she faced him squarely.

"He'll do," the physician told her. "I used salts to bring him back to his senses. I bled him a little to reduce the chance of fever. I cleaned up his head wound too. Scratches, merely. Well, one gash that took a stitch or two, but nothing vital broken so far as I can see, apart from some ribs. I've bound them. If he does worse in the night, send to me. Oh, and no alcohol for him, if you please. He's dizzy enough already. I left a powder for pain. If he falls asleep, wake him every so often to see if you can. I'll be back in the morning."

He looked at Jane's ashen face. "He should make it through the night, and the next forty years without trouble," he added. "Unless he runs into another carriage. Good evening." He clapped on his hat, and left.

Jane went straight back into the bedchamber. Simon was propped up on a pillow, in a dressing gown, a white bandage across his forehead. For the first time, she felt out of place, as though she might be trespassing. Accompanying an unconscious gentleman to his bed wasn't the same as seeing the vital, smiling man who looked at her now.

He held out his arms, welcoming her. "I'm here, I'm whole, and I'm sorry I frightened you," he said.

"You're sorry?" she asked. "I'm overjoyed to find you alive and well. How does your head feel?"

"Not as well as it will tomorrow. Come sit down and let's talk. Come perch here beside me. You certainly can't be afraid I'll attack you. I need company, and we need to talk. If you want, you may stroke my aching forehead, and hold my hand as tenderly as you did in the coach on the way here."

She was taking a chair but stopped at his words. "You were awake?"

"Now and then," he said with a flashing smile, patting the bed. "Come, sit here, please."

She smiled, shook her head, but dragged the chair closer and sat beside the bed. He held out a hand. She took it in hers, and asked, "How did you escape what looked like certain death?"

"My ears," he said, his thumb stroking the back of her hand. "I heard a coach coming, horses galloping too fast. I had one look and a quick decision to make. When something's aimed at you there are few choices. Whichever way I ran could have been wrong, because I didn't have time to see where it was bound, and the light was bad. I imagined it was coming straight at me. It could have veered wherever I did. So I dropped to the ground and curled up tight, hoping to escape the worst. I did."

"But you could have been run over by any of the horses or all of them. There were four horses, and the coach itself was heavy," she said. "Maybe they veered away from you at the last minute."

"I knew you were a clever lass," he said approvingly. "Just so. Whoever was after me wanted me to live to know it was at his mercy. That incident was meant to warn me away, not to kill me. It was done by a master, because delivering that kind of cautionary message is much more difficult than outright murder."

"Do you know who did it?" she asked eagerly.

He nodded, and then winced. "Don't send for the good physician. My head is fine if I don't wag it. Do I know? I think I do now. It will need exploration, but now that I have an idea the route becomes easier to trace. Someone has been passing on information about troops and munitions; someone in the service of Bonaparte. There are those who want their little emperor off the isle of Elba and on the English throne. I believe at last I know who they are. And I will stop them. At least, the one who's been using Lady Harwood's salon as his meeting place. And that's better than good for you, and not just because you're a British citizen, but because this game is getting too dangerous to go on. You shouldn't be in it. I'm glad you're not anymore."

"I'm not?" she asked. "Oh. I suppose not, of course, if you know who the villain is. Oh!" she said a little more quietly. "I expect you don't need me anymore then?"

"There's need and there's need," he said with a

wicked smile. "But you're out of the spying part of it. That means you give up your extra employment with me, and your lady, and the viscount, and whoever else asks. Whatever else happens in Lady Harwood's salon is no longer a concern of yours. Don't look so sad. There'll be less money, but a longer and healthier life, and that's a fair trade."

"It is," she said, forcing a smile. She was shocked, devastated, and determined not to show it. "What shall I tell them? I mean, when they ask me for a report on what I've seen or heard?"

"With luck, you won't have to tell them anything," he said. "Once I'm up and about, and I judge that will be by tomorrow, I'll call the game over as soon as I can. Then we can all go back to normal, or what passes for that with us. I'm battered, but I'm sound."

But she felt as though she was the one who'd been hit by a large, fast-moving carriage. Because if he'd solved the problem he'd come to her with, that meant she wouldn't see him again. There'd be no more reason for those stealthy dinners in out-of-the-way taverns. No chatting with ratcatchers and lamplighters in the streets. No going to bed wondering when she'd see him the next day. No more daydreams of what might happen when she did see him. None of that lovely, dreadful fluttering in her stomach at the expectation of seeing him standing at the door to Lady Harwood's ballroom. He'd leave her life as abruptly as he'd entered it. And he'd never know the vast emptiness he'd leave behind him. Nor would he ever know how much it hurt her. She'd see to that.

She'd give up her new lodgings, of course. She'd say good-bye to all of her employers. It was time for her to leave London. She gazed at him and tried to engrave each and every detail of him forever in her mind. His dressing gown, she noticed, was open at the neck. *Such a strong neck,* she thought. His chest was wide; she saw the white of his bandages and shivered. She forced her eyes back to his.

"So," she asked carefully, trying to sound nonchalant, "who is the villain?"

"I'm afraid that you'll never know," he said. "Nor do you need to know. This is more dangerous than I'd thought."

"Well, at least they'll be no more caricatures of me," she said, forcing laughter.

"I wouldn't bet on that," he said, eyeing her curiously. "Why are you suddenly pretending with me?"

She slipped her hand from his and touched her own forehead. "It's been a difficult night," she said. "To tell the truth I'm a bit dazed. I don't know exactly what I'm doing."

"There's something else," he said. He raised himself up higher on his pillows, and took back her hand in both of his. His expression, as he gazed at her, was full of sorrow. "You'd have already guessed it if your wits hadn't been so stirred up by the accident. You'd have figured it out on your own by morning. So I'll tell you now. I'm sorry, Miss Piggott is dead and gone now, and Miss Chatham is compromised. The fact is that your association with me will now be known. That is, it will be if it isn't already. All the nightly walks and talks and dinners will be common, and I do mean *common* knowledge. Gossip in London rides harder and faster than the horses that ran me down. You were seen with me tonight."

"I was seen with an injured footman!" she protested.

"Who was taken to Lord Granger's home by his servants," he said patiently. "Anyone watching the house, and there have been observers this past week and more, knows the footman was me. And they saw you clear. At night, at this late hour, together, here in my chambers. It sounds much cozier than it actually is," he added. "I think that's the greatest pity."

She took a deep breath. "That's all right," she said. "I've already decided to leave London. So it doesn't matter."

"Of course it matters!" he said. "You were the one going on about your reputation all the time. Why shouldn't it matter to you now that the worst has happened?"

"The worst," she said with pride, "hasn't happened. I told you I was leaving London. Do you think anyone anywhere else in England cares about an impecunious dancing instructress who supposedly dallied with a gentleman in London? I was Miss Chatham; I became Miss Piggott, and so I can be anyone I choose now."

"Gads!" he said, staring at her. "You make me feel terrible. Don't be an idiot. It's what you most feared. I ruined you in the eyes of Society, so I'll make it right. I'll marry you."

Her eyes opened wide. She stared at him and found her vision growing dark at the corners of her eyes. This had only happened to her during those rare times in her life when she'd found herself livid with rage. She swallowed hard, and tried to calm herself. She put a hand on her chest, and forced a smile.

"Such an impassioned proposal, my lord. I am overcome. How good, how generous, how kind. I'm honored, but no, of course not. No, thank you. You don't want to marry me. You don't even trust me. You don't want to marry anyone. It's not necessary."

"It's necessary to me," he said, and sitting upright, he pulled her into his arms.

It wasn't the kiss of an invalid. His arms held her close, his mouth was warm and searching, his temperature might have been high, but so was hers, so it didn't matter. What did was the absolute ecstasy of that kiss. She poured her soul into it. He took it and gave back such pleasure that she found herself, all unknowingly, somehow now beside him in his bed, rapt in his arms.

"Now say no," he chuckled against her neck, as his hands slipped beneath her gown, warming and chilling her all at once. "You will marry me, my dear Miss Chatham, and there's an end to it."

He kissed her before she could answer, and

rolled her over so that she looked down at him. With his hand on her breast and his lips on her neck, she couldn't breathe for a moment, much less answer coherently. But neither could he. Then she noticed he was breathing with difficulty, and it mightn't be passion that was hindering him. She came to her senses enough to realize she was lying across his bandaged chest.

She leapt back, horrified. "Are you all right?" she asked anxiously.

"No," he said. "Come back. I want more."

She took a deep breath and let it out. "No," she said sadly, raising herself on her hands. "You can't do that. Your ribs are cracked. And no to the idea of marriage too, my lord. Marriage is a beginning. We'd have no end to it that way." She sat back on her knees in the deep feather bed. "You're being honorable, and that, I'll never forget. But I'd never force a man to marry me. That's what this union would be. I'm not of your station in life, if I were, I might. But as for me? I'm filled with air dreams and fancies, my lord."

"And bright ideas and hot blood. Come back here, Jane," he said.

"You're not well yet. Otherwise I would. I vow I'd do just that." She gently touched the bandage on his forehead. "I'm not a physician, but love-making isn't the best treatment for a man who has just been run over by a coach and four."

"I feel as though I just was, again," he said, and dropped his head back on the pillow. "Lord, I'd do just about anything to make love to you now, properly."

"Improperly," she murmured.

"No, or yes, whichever way you choose," he said. "I'm well enough. The physician said I'd live through the night, but I wonder if I can if I didn't make love to you now."

She'd been so warm and willing that he was willing to try, and his battered body and rattled brain be damned. But even with his body and brain clamoring for fulfillment, he realized that she shouldn't be so willing.

"Why so willing now that I'm unable?" he asked suddenly. "I see. Is that it? Would you be so acquiescent if I really were able?"

She looked affronted, and then, infinitely sad. "You still don't trust me, do you?"

"I do," he said, his hand on his chest. "But only the other day you shrieked like a banshee at seeing me ready to make love, and now you're leaping into bed with me. I got confused. Pardon me."

She shook her head. "Perhaps I'm trying to grow up. Maybe I was just too relieved at seeing you so alive to worry about my foolish fears. It doesn't matter now. Yes, I would have been willing tonight. I remembered just in time. It was your ribs I was thinking of, not my heart. I'm honestly sorry we can't end this in pleasure. But I wanted to make love to you because this is the last time I'll see you. I'm leaving London, Simon."

"At least stay until I can make love. A jest!" he said. "Don't shoot."

She pulled herself upright and stood, adjusting her hair and her gown. "I wish I could stay. If I had a title, or social standing, or a large brother or two, I'd dare anything. But you know this world. I'm alone in it. If I'm 'ruined' in reputation or reality, the world becomes a savage one, and my life forever after a hardship."

"No reason for it. Marry me. I'm serious."

"Now, yes," she said softly. "With desire riding you, and honor goading you. But later? Oh, Simon, you don't love me. How can you? You don't even trust me."

"So I misread your sudden passion. It was a mistake. My head's still addled. How can I prove that I'm serious? I'll stand by you whatever happens. I have no family either, but I do have position, title, and money. So I can marry whomever I please, and if I please to marry you, there's no one who can say a word to stop me."

"Oh," she said, "I see. And if there were family, they would?"

"Who knows?" he said. "I was going to add that I wouldn't listen to any word said to me."

"You would," she said, "with time. Perhaps I'll come back in a year or so. That would be a good test, wouldn't it? Or maybe in months," she said, looking at him. "But just now you're not thinking right and I would be some sort of a monster to accept your proposal, and a murderess if I accepted your proposition," she added, smiling. "Take care, and be well," she said as she walked to the door. "I'll never forget you, Simon."

"Don't go," he said. "Not fair. I can't chase you now."

"Wait until you can, and you may be surprised to discover you don't want to," she said.

"At least come back tomorrow to say a proper good-bye."

Her smile was wide. "Oh, my lord, I can never do a proper thing with you, and that's a fact. Be well. Good-bye."

She heard him say, ". . . not fair," as she closed the door behind her.

Jane stood in the hallway a moment, wondering if she'd done the right thing, tearing her heart out this way. And then she thought of Lady Harwood and her salon, and all of Lord Granger's lofty friends. She knew she'd done right. He was filled with life, as was she, because he'd almost died. Even so, he hadn't trusted her reasons for kissing him. If he didn't trust her now, he never would, and that would be worse than never seeing him again. She needed time to heal as much as he did.

Jane went down the stair toward the front hall. She was so immersed in her thoughts she almost didn't see the gentleman coming up as she was descending. He stopped, and so did she. She stood a few steps above him, so at last they were face-to-face.

"Good evening Miss Chatham," Viscount Delancey said, bowing. "Or should I say 'good morning'?"

"I don't know," she said. "It's been too strange a night. I've lost track of time."

"It is two in the morning, Miss Chatham," he said. "And do not fear my censure. I don't suspect naughty doings. Indeed, I heard of the accident

346

that befell my friend and hastened here to see how he does."

"He's weary, and a bit befuddled," Jane said, "but very lucky. He has to stay still because of broken ribs, and he did take a fierce blow to the head, but the physician said he'd do."

"He's a tough fellow, I'm sure he will," the viscount said. His cold gray eyes looked softer in the glow of the gaslights on the stair wall. "I'm sure you were terrified. I heard you were with him when he was struck. In every way, as one can still see," he added, watching her.

She stiffened. "I stayed to see that he'd be all right. He is and I'm leaving. I'm also leaving London, my lord, so I'm sorry, but I can no longer work for Lady Harwood, or for you." She dug into her reticule, pulled out the much-folded list and handed it to him. "There's no need for me to have this anymore. I'm only sorry I couldn't discover who it was that tried to do such harm to Lord Granger. As for now, I'm going home and, then, away."

He took the list and turned it in his long fingers. But he didn't step back so she could leave. "So he tired of you already? I'm not surprised. But you shouldn't give up, my dear. What's a reputation in the occupation you ultimately choose? There could be another position for you," he said softly. "Much less tedious than trying to pound graceful movements into the limbs of ungainly little ducklings, or staying with a fickle fellow whose sentiments change with the wind. I could offer you gainful employment for merely staying on in London and pleasing me."

When she only stared at him, he added, "Yes, exactly. You could be for me what you have been for Lord Granger. I'm generous and not demanding, and a creature of habit. He will never stay with any female for very long, you know."

She straightened her back. "I know," she said. "I wish you did not. Thank you. But no, thank you. Good evening, my lord." She shouldered past him, and marched down the stairs.

She heard him chuckling as he went up them.

Chapter 20

"**A**live," Viscount Delancey said as he was shown into Simon's room, and stared at his old friend. "But evidently not so well. You look pained. And the delectable Miss Chatham just exited looking the same. So it must be that which causes your sour expression. Too bad. The word is that she was with you at the scene of the accident. Congratulations. I heard she was a selective miss. Perhaps that's why she just left." He smiled. "Jealousy speaks, pay it no mind. But affaires of the heart are often painful and just as often mended."

"Not this time," Simon said. "Or maybe not. I need to think."

"It looks like you need to sleep," the viscount said. "I'd heard you were not hurt badly. Still, I hastened to your bedside. And now this? What else is the matter?"

Simon looked up at him. "Oh, much is the matter, Proctor. Much. You may go, Mr. Morris," he told his valet.

"But your powders, my lord," the valet said. "You haven't drunk them, and the physician gave me distinct orders."

"Oh, very well," Simon said, taking the glass of cloudy water and draining it. He made a face. "Why do healing powders always taste like poisonous ones? Thank you, Morris. You may go with a clear conscience. There's nothing else anyone can do for me now. It's all up to me. No more visitors tonight, please. I'll see you in the morning."

The valet bowed, collected some toweling and bandages, and left.

"The scowling is also because I tried to get out of bed just now," Simon explained to his friend, waving him to a chair. "Not possible yet. That pains me more than the pain does. I can always take some more powders for that, but I want to move around. Still, I'll live. Thank you for coming to see me at this hour, Proctor. I suppose you had doubts. Don't worry. Your man did an excellent job. Missed my vitals by inches. Trust you to employ the best. And so, now what?"

"I beg your pardon," Proctor said, as he took a seat. "Whatever are you talking about?"

"Play time is over," Simon said wearily. "You sent a message to me tonight. I received it. Who else could send it to such a nicety? But it came too close, and it came too late. I've discovered all, my friend. I didn't want to believe it at first, and that almost killed me. My fault, I suppose, for still daring to trust. But why the devil *you* would be selling government secrets is more than I can guess. Did Richard bankrupt you? Are you a secret gamester? Your art collection getting out of hand? Or is it that a mistress discovered too much and is bleeding you? God, Proctor, I wish it had been anyone but you."

"Your brain's been addled by the accident," his friend said calmly.

"My brain was always addled," Simon said laughing. "But no more subterfuge, please. We've been friends too long for that. I wish I'd taken the time earlier tonight to tell you, but I was diverted by the diverting Miss Chatham. Proctor, I knew before you sent the coach to warn me off by mowing me down. Who else could give me just enough poison to sicken, but not kill me? Who else knew all the tricks I do? That list you gave Miss Chatham with the names of people to report to you about: who else knew which ones to watch as well as I did? I didn't want to believe it."

"You didn't want to believe that they were courting Lady Harwood? Simon, you suffered more injury to your brain than you know."

Simon moved his hand as though he were brushing away a fly. "You sent me to find out what was happening with your brother. I did it as a favor. But it didn't take long for me to see there was much more than lovesick advances being made at that house. Richard is enamored of the lady. But she, for reasons I fail to see, is similarly interested in him. There was no earthly reason for you to worry about the liaison. If the lady wanted him, it would be excellent for you as well as for Richard. You wouldn't have to worry about his follies anymore. As for the lady, the success of her salon was perfect for her too. That way she could see what slim pickings there were for her in the *ton*. She was ruled by her late husband and didn't like it much. Richard is comely enough, young, and of good breeding and temperament. She encouraged her salon to make sure she was making the right choice. There was nothing there to interest me or cause you to ask me to go there and see what was afoot."

"Don't you mean 'off foot'? Don't tell me you weren't interested in the way the lovely Miss Chatham kept falling on her bottom and showing her splendid legs every other day?" Proctor said sweetly.

Simon shrugged. "Poor girl. I don't think it was intentional. And I admit that was a lure. It made me a more frequent visitor. But I soon saw that Richard's courtship was nothing worth noting. I didn't know why you needed me there. At first I believed it might be an act of kindness on your part. Get that poor hermit Granger up and out of his house and into the social world. Then I remembered you don't do that sort of favor. Then why? After all, you were there too. That was a mystery worth solving, and a mistake on your part.

"Then I saw what else was going on right out in the open," Simon said. "There was treason. Traitors were swapping information like gamesters changing cards at a gambling hell. I still can't believe you were involved."

"Then don't," his friend said airily. "Are you forgetting Marlowe? He's a gamester and he works for the war office. Or Burlingham? He's with the army, that is, when he's sober enough to find his office. Or the Lady Harwood herself. She's looking for a husband. But is the one she wants French or English?"

"None of them," Simon said, with a suppressed yawn. "The men are fools, but have been investigated thoroughly and we both know it. No, others were in the market for secrets and the salon was as busy trading them as Billingsgate dealing in haddock on a Friday afternoon. Markham, Pierce, and old Sir Walters will not be coming to the salon by next week. I'm giving in their names. There's another. The ringleader. I saved the best, or worst, for last, because I wanted to speak to him first. As for the lady of the house? She knows what she wants and it's only a husband, after all. He's not French. And here you are, at this late hour, making sure your latest plan went as it was supposed to do. Good lord, Proctor, you know I know. It can't be anyone but you. Don't shame us both with foolish denials. But in God's green name, my friend, why?"

"Not for the money," the viscount said, smoothing his gloves.

Simon cocked his head to the side. "No?" His

eyes widened. "But then why . . . Not for the politics of it?"

The viscount's silence was his answer.

Simon tried to sit up, but sank back to his pillows. "You?" he asked. "You're allied with Bonaparte? *You?* But you're a nobleman who loves every privilege of class and regrets every one that's been lost to time. You know the name of your ancestors back to Adam. You inherited a castle and a manor, a hunting box, acreage, and more money than you can count. You'd give that all up for social equality? You'd share your bread with the starving masses? I can't see that. Your family gave out leftovers to the poor, after the feast, and at the back door. They owned serfs for centuries and would still if they could."

"True," Proctor said calmly. "But what a leader says and what he does are very different things. Bonaparte preaches equality, but made himself an emperor and his family kings, queens, and nobles. I do know my ancestors, and have always known I have some who were French. They owned quite a bit of *la belle France*: nearly half the south of it, at one time. I don't expect that much. But a title there, some ancestral lands, and the lands I already own here are quite enough for me. I'm not greedy."

Simon lay still. Then he shut his eyes. He opened them with difficulty. "I am a fool. It was *you* who informed on me in France, wasn't it? Not Martine."

"Yes and no. She readily played her part. She, after all, had no heart. I do. I didn't have you executed when I could have. I didn't have you maimed when I had the chance, then or now. And if I started the rumor that you had been grievously bereft of certain parts, at least you had a quiet time to recuperate from whatever had been done to you."

"Thank you," Simon said quietly. "But I begin to believe the tale of my supposed gelding might have been your intention at one time, except that there are some things even menials won't do, for fear of retribution. Never mind that. It would have been a more grievous mistake. I wouldn't have rested until I found out where the orders came from. And then I would have had to reciprocate. I think you knew that. And as for Miss Chatham? Is she in your employ too?"

"No, but I hope to remedy that soon and employ her, although not as an informant. She seems quite displeased with you and will need a new position soon. I have many in mind for her. At that, she was a bit of luck for me. A lively distraction, wasn't she?"

"Why did you call me in from retirement for this, Proctor?" Simon asked slowly, ignoring what he said about Jane. "What reason could you have for setting me on your trail?"

"Because you were the best, Simon. You were my bellwether. If you discovered me then I'd know I was running too close to the wind. When you came too close, I tried to move you away. You didn't go. You were very good at your job, Simon. Your leave of absence only made your mind clearer. Good for you, and for me too. Now I know I have to move my base of operations. By the by," he asked in a tighter voice, "are there Runners lurking behind your draperies now, ready to bear me away?"

"No," Simon said wearily. "But you already know that. We're old friends. I said I saved the worst for last. Now that I've told you, you can leave England. I'll give you a head start."

"I've more than that. And there's a limit to friendship, didn't you know that? Trust no one, not even yourself, that was our motto. Too bad you forgot. Now something else must be done as well. You're a patriot when all's said, Simon. And I've worked too long and too hard for it all to come to nothing now, especially now. Bonaparte is readying to leave his stony island and take the world, and carry his supporters to glory with him. So what am I to do with you?

"I thought to have you arrested again for my crimes," Proctor mused. "But this is England, not France, and you have friends in high places. Something like that might lead the curious too close to me. A pity, but there's no clapping people up in the Tower for years on scanty evidence anymore either. And I need a year, my friend. Next spring will bring changes that will change the world. Can I ask you to be quiet about this for a year? Would a high position or another title, new lands and a place in the future England tempt you?"

Simon's smile was tired.

"I thought not," Proctor said. "So, what's to do?"

They stared at each other. The night was still, the hour advanced; there was no noise in the room except for the sound of Simon's breathing. It seemed increasingly labored. Proctor rose to his feet, and sighed as he looked down at his friend.

"You were seen coming up here," Simon said quietly.

"So I was," Proctor said.

"So you can't shoot me and claim someone climbed in the window, did it, and climbed out again."

"Give me more credit than that," Proctor said.

"I've a pistol under my pillow," Simon said, wincing as he slowly tried to reach beneath his pillow.

"And if you shoot me, you will definitely be hanged for murder," his friend said. He quickly bent, deftly slid his hand under Simon's pillow, and extracted a pistol. He dropped it into his pocket. "This will be a souvenir of our years together. Come, Simon, we are not so crude."

Simon frowned, and shook his head to clear it again. "But we have to be *something* tonight, don't we? An' you're not leaving. So what's the game?"

"You took your powders, didn't you? Don't fret. They weren't poisoned. They were just increased in their efficacy. Your valet is innocent; he won't be able to tell anybody anything was amiss with your medicine. But the physician's assistant is terribly underpaid. Yes, that's why your eyelids feel so heavy. But your ribs were badly cracked, and though you were bandaged, you must have turned on your side and one or two ribs just happened to pierce your lungs in the night. It happens. It has to be, Simon. You were always the one burdened with morals. I sometimes wondered if you were really a nobleman, after all." His laughter was dry, almost a cough.

Then his pale face grew sad again. "I'll wait until you fall asleep, old friend. It won't hurt. And then I'll leave your room and tell your valet all is well. He will be devastated when he finds you in the morning. Don't struggle, Simon. You know that when it comes to this point the best thing to do is to accept it. I do like you and I will miss you, but I've worked too long and hard to let sentiment rule me now. Some dreams are too important to sacrifice for anything. Good night, old friend."

Simon fought a growing languor. He couldn't get up; he knew that. He couldn't so much as shout out now. But he willed himself to do something. Proctor had picked up another pillow and was standing above him, patiently waiting. Simon wished it were a bad dream brought on by the medicine, and knew that if he believed that, it would be the last thing he'd ever believe. He stared up at his impassive friend.

"Sorry," Proctor whispered. "I really am. Come,

make this easy on yourself. Close your eyes, Simon. It's time to sleep."

Simon saw Proctor raise the pillow, and forced himself to keep his eyes on how close it was coming. He couldn't roll away. All Proctor had to do was to put it over his face, and then lay down on top of him, or hold the pillow there and pound his chest a few times. And Simon knew that he would. Proctor had no choice. But neither did he.

"I'd put that down, at once, " a clear voice said.

Proctor spun around.

"I have a pistol, and I do know how to shoot it," Jane said. She stood in the doorway, a long nosed pistol gripped in both hands to steady it. It was pointed directly at the viscount's heart. "And Mr. Morris has gone to get his own pistol and wake the footman. But I won't hesitate to shoot you dead if you so much as move. Oh, I suppose you must. Drop the pillow please. And slowly take the pistol from your pocket and drop it as well. There will be no souvenirs tonight."

"If you shoot me you'll be hanged," Proctor said, nevertheless dropping the pillow.

"Maybe," she said. "But if I don't, Lord Granger will be dead. I don't want that. Please step back from his bed, if you please, my lord. I'm very nervous, and the pistol is a finely tempered one and is primed to respond to the lightest touch. The pistol now, if you please."

The viscount stepped back. He reached into his pocket and hesitated.

"Don't even think about it, my lord," Jane said. "I can fire before you get it aimed. There. Yes, that's right. Drop it now."

The viscount dropped the pistol and it hit the floor.

"Now, kick it away, and then move further away from it," she said.

The viscount did as she said and raised his hands. "Done. Now, I swear to go away, never to return?"

"That's not my decision to make," she said.

"S'mine," Simon said in a soft slurry voice. "Go 'way, Proctor. Give your word. Never return."

"My word on it," the viscount said.

"Your word is no good," Jane said angrily.

The viscount drew himself up. "I am a traitor and I'm certainly immoral, but my word as a gentleman is always good, young woman. That is why I never give it."

"Give it now, then," she said.

"I did. Oh, very well. I will leave England on the next tide and never return, except in triumph," he said proudly, "at the side of Bonaparte, the man who should be sitting on the throne of England."

"Then you'll never return," she said.

"I have no choice but to go, do I?" the viscount asked Simon bitterly. "She heard. Doubtless so did the damned valet. And you have the evidence."

"S'true," Simon breathed. "Go 'way."

"Did you hear him?" the viscount asked Jane. His voice was a little shrill, because she'd trained the pistol on his face now.

"I did," she said, nodding. "But I'm not sure your word is good enough for me."

"Let 'im go," Simon whispered. "Got th' evidence. Gave it to the right people. They'll snabble him up if he sets a toe 'n England again. An' for God's sake, gemme something to wake me up. I don' wanna sleep now."

"Oh, very well," Jane said truculently. She lowered the pistol, but still clutched it tight and kept it raised just enough to show she was alert.

The viscount quickly brushed past her as he strode to the door. But then he stopped. "What the devil were you doing here?" he snarled. "You were furious with him when you left."

"I was furious with myself," she said steadily. "I came back to tell him so. Go away, Proctor."

He left.

"Should he be allowed to go?" Simon's valet, appearing in the doorway, asked her.

"Your master said so," Jane said. "Can you bring hot coffee and buckets of cold water, and send for the physician?"

"I have already done so," Mr. Morris said, and disappeared again.

Jane went to Simon's bedside.

He opened one eye. "Nice pistol," he said.

"It's yours," she said, laying it down on the bed. "Morris told me it was in your desk drawer in your study."

He closed his eyes. "Come here," he whispered.

She climbed up on the bed beside him.

"Where did you learn to shoot?" he asked.

"Sshh. Rest. I learned in the countryside. But," she said, putting her lips to his ear. "I'm very bad at it."

She heard him chuckle.

"I finally have you where I want you," he whispered. "An' I can't do a damned thing."

"You do, you did," she said. "I'm here. I couldn't sleep. I couldn't rest. I didn't even get to my lodgings. I came running back here. I couldn't leave you hurting. Mr. Morris saw I couldn't be sent away. Besides, he heard some of what your friend said to you. Then I certainly couldn't leave. I need you, for however long you want me. The viscount was right. Some dreams are too important to sacrifice for anything. I'm strong, and if I have to be on my own again, I can do it. I just can't let life pass me by again. I need to be with you for however long it may be."

"Never," he whispered. "Always."

She smiled, although she wasn't sure just what he meant. It didn't matter. She was where she wanted to be.

Chapter 21

H e came up behind her and put his hands on her waist, and then moved them to cup her breasts. He kissed the side of her neck. Jane shivered.

"Afraid?" he asked, lifting his head and meeting her eyes in the looking glass. "Don't be. It doesn't have to be tonight. Wedding nights are a cliché, anyway. We can kiss and cuddle and whatnot, as we've done before. It can be any day or night now. When we actually really do make love I want you desperate for me."

"I am already," Jane said, turning in his arms to look directly into his eyes. "You who know everything, don't you know that?"

"No," Simon said, smiling. "Show me. But if you change your mind, just tell me. If you screech, we'll have to lie about rats again."

She chuckled. "No screeching, I promise."

His eyebrow went up. "Really? So blasé now? Been going to the museum and ogling young marble Greek and Roman lads, have you? Be warned, I don't come with a fig leaf."

"Just as well," she said, lowering her gaze, a faint flush appearing in her cheeks. "They look as though they'd be terribly uncomfortable."

"Something has changed, though," he said, cocking his head to the side.

"You've changed too," she said defensively.

"Indeed, and I'm delighted. How can a man mistrust a woman who saves his life?"

"At one time," she said seriously, "you could have."

"I'm so pleased that time is over. You may kill me at will."

She smiled. "But you trusted your friend Proctor," she said sadly.

He took her chin in his hand and looked at her steadily. "He was a fellow officer in the same cause as I was, or so I thought. That trust made me a poor spy. I couldn't leach out that last bit of belief in humanity that lingered in my soul. Thank God you came into my life. You gave it back to me." But he didn't lose his quizzical expression. "You keep dancing around it, and changing the subject, but something else has changed in you too. What could it be?"

She looked at the base of his neck where his dressing gown didn't close, and concentrated on the vein pulsing there. "It could be a book I found in Lady Harwood's library."

He laughed. "Lord! First I worried about frightening you, now I worry about disappointing you. One of those Persian books?"

"One illustrated by Mr. Rowlandson," she murmured, without raising her gaze. "A very naughty one. I became interested in his caricatures after he made that one of me, and when I saw the book had his illustrations in it, I took a look."

"Now I know I'll disappoint you," he said. "Don't blush. He's Prinny's favorite pornographic artist too."

"Simon," she said seriously, gazing up into his eyes, "I'm tired of looking at pictures, and I'm weary with wanting you."

He locked his hands around her waist, and gently kissed her forehead. Then he put a hand in her hair, and gently pulled it from its ties. He sighed with pleasure as it fell to her shoulders in silky streamers. "First, there were my damned ribs," he said, as he ran a hand through her hair, arranging it so that it made a curtain over her high breasts. "And then, all the mess to clean up: testimony and court appointments and so on. And then Proctor's disappearance to lie about, if only for Richard's sake, now that his brother has named him lord of the manor.

"And then, there was Richard's hasty marriage to Lady Harwood to help arrange," he went on. "That, at least, was a good thing. The boy is as loyal as his brother is not, and as certain of himself now as he is fertile, and the lady is thrilled with a younger husband. The delay wasn't my entire fault. You had to be conscientious and find another dance instructor for the lady, didn't you? And then more waiting until we could finally get this time together. I didn't want our first time together to be harried or hurried or in fear of discovery. I'm sorry. Let me show you how sorry."

He blew out the lamp on the dressing table, picked her up in his arms, and carried her to the bed. He only paused a moment at the table by the bed. And then after a second's hesitation, he smiled as he blew out the lamp there too.

"And since we waited so long, let's let it last a long time too," he added, as he lowered her to the bed, and followed her down. He helped her slide out of her filmy nightdress, and then looked down at the firm dancer's body that lay before him. "So lovely," he said, staring at how the moonlight that filtered in the high window showed her pink-tipped breasts rising and falling with her rapid breathing. "So silken," he said, as he ran a hand down her body. "So long desired," he added, as he raised himself and shucked off his robe, and then slipped beneath a coverlet.

She sat up. "What's this? Why are we sitting in darkness? Why are you hiding under the coverlets?"

He sat up as well, holding the coverlet to his chest, as modestly as a young girl might do. But he was grinning. "Amazing how much routing a villain, saving my life, and reading a naughty book has changed you, Jane. I'm shocked."

She laughed. "Amazing how much realizing what it is that matters in life changes a person, I agree. Now please stop acting as though I'm a timid creature who will faint at the sight of you."

"You may faint at will," he said as he threw back the covers. "But you may not screech."

She frankly stared at his slender muscular form, his broad chest, narrow waist, and the inescapable sight of his absolute readiness for her. "You are," she said, and paused, "very fit."

It took a while for him to stop laughing. She turned her back on him, and curled into a knot.

"Jane," he said, stroking her long cool hair and the shoulders they covered. "Jane," he said, as he gently turned her over and looked into her eyes. "First times are memorable, but such a bother. Let's pretend we've been doing this for as long as I've wanted to, at least. And remember that pornographic pictures and marble statues can only show a few sides of physical love. We can love, and we do, and we will, and we'll put them all to shame, if you're willing."

"Willing?" she asked, and threw her arms around him.

They kissed. Their hands sought each other, learned each other, praised each other, while their lips promised unheard, undreamed of pleasures. They turned again, and once more, because suddenly it seemed as though neither could get enough of the other, and it was vital for them to do so. She shuddered when he touched her where no one but he had before. She shuddered and gasped and clung to him as thrills of pleasure coursed through her when he moved his hand, his fingers, his lips, over her. When she recovered from that, she turned to him again and he shivered when she dared hold and caress him as she never had before.

When at last he rose above her on his elbows, and parted her again, she clung to him, and slowly, with infinite care and uncaring eagerness, he joined them together. He stopped then, raised his head and sucked in a deep breath. Then he looked into her eyes. "All right?" he asked.

"Very," she gasped. "Go on."

They moved together, straining toward a goal unknown to her as he withheld until he thought he'd die of the frustration and pleasure of it. And then when he could restrain himself no longer, he gasped, and surged into her. And she clung tight to him as though protecting him from the great waves that seemed to threaten to wash him away.

They lay still then, side by side, breathing slower, bodies cooling.

He spoke first. "Are you all right?" he asked.

"Better than that," she said. "Although I'm afraid there's some mess."

"I'll get cloths, and water," he said, rising from the bed. She lay still, her mind whirling, until he returned. He was as gentle with her as a nurse might have been, except that no nurse would then have enfolded her in his arms, twined his legs with hers, and held her close.

"Next time," he said. "There will be ecstasy for you in that too. In fact," he whispered in her ear, "they say more for you even than for me."

"Been reading naughty books?" she asked.

He laughed. "Oh, my dear lady wife," Simon said. "The waiting was worth it."

"Not really," she said, her arms going around his neck. "But think of the time we have to make up."

*Next month, don't miss these exciting new
love stories only from
Avon Books*

In Bed With the Devil by Lorraine Heath

An Avon Romantic Treasure

Lucian Langdon, Earl of Claybourne, is thought by many to be beyond redemption—a fact that makes him perfect for Lady Catherine Mabry. She needs a man of his reputation to take down her vicious uncle. But the more she gets to know Lucian, the more she realizes that what she asks of him will destroy the man she's come to love.

A Match Made in Hell by Terri Garey

An Avon Contemporary Romance

Nicki Styx is slowly adjusting to her new life as guidance counselor to the dead. Things are going well, until the devil himself makes an appearance—and it's Nicki he's got his eye on. And there's no escaping the devil, especially when he's after your soul.

Let the Night Begin by Kathryn Smith

An Avon Romance

Years ago, Reign turned his wife Olivia into a vampire—without her consent. Enraged, she left him, swearing never to return. But revenge proved too sweet to resist. When an enemy turns out to be more dangerous than either of them suspects, Olivia and Reign are forced to trust each other—and the love they once shared.

Lessons From a Courtesan by Jenna Petersen

An Avon Romance

Victoria and Justin Talbot were happy to part ways after their forced marriage. But to rescue a friend, Victoria must return to London, this time disguised as a courtesan. Her new "profession" enrages Justin—but seeing her again makes him realize that, despite their rocky beginning, their love was meant to be.

Visit www.AuthorTracker.com for exclusive
information on your favorite HarperCollins authors.

REL 0608

Available wherever books are sold or please call 1-800-331-3761 to order.

AVON

The End of an Error
MAMEVE MEDWED
978-0-06-133535-8

978-0-06-144589-7

Jacquelyn MITCHARD
978-0-06-137452-4

The Space BETWEEN BEFORE and AFTER
JEAN REYNOLDS PAGE
978-0-06-415218-5

THE DEPARTMENT of LOST & FOUND
ALLISON WINN SCOTCH
978-0-06-116142-1

THE BEST DAY OF Someone Else's LIFE
KERRY REICHS
978-0-06-143857-8